Tanith Lee, born in London, began writing at the age of nine, and was first published in her early twenties. Since then she has produced numerous novels of a fantastical nature and several radio plays, and has twice won the World Fantasy Award for her short stories. Also published by Headline are her novels *Heart-Beast* and *Elephantasm*, and her story collection *Nightshades*.

She lives in East Sussex with her husband, the writer John Kaiine, and a black-and-white cat.

'Restore's one's faith in fiction as the expression of imagination and original thought' – *Guardian*

'One of the most powerful and intelligent writers to work in fantasy' – *Publishers Weekly*

'Bizarre imagination and elegantly decadent atmosphere' – *Daily Mail*

'Unlike most fantasists who wish they could write magnificently, Tanith Lee can actually do it' – Orson Scott Card

Also by Tanith Lee

Heart-Beast
Elephantasm
Nightshades

Eva Fairdeath

Tanith Lee

First published in 1994
by HEADLINE BOOK PUBLISHING

First published in paperback in 1994
by HEADLINE BOOK PUBLISHING

A HEADLINE FEATURE paperback

10 9 8 7 6 5 4 3 2

ISBN 0 7472 4383 2

Typeset by Keyboard Services, Luton

Printed and bound in Great Britain by
Cox & Wyman Ltd, Reading, Berks

HEADLINE BOOK PUBLISHING
A division of Hodder Headline PLC
338 Euston Road
London NW1 3BH

Author's Foreword

If the past, as Hartley says, is another country, where things are differently done, then perhaps we were other people, there. It certainly seems to me that the Tanith Lee of fifteen years, the Tanith Lee of twenty-five, are not the same person as the forty-five-year-old woman who now looks back at them. And for this very reason they interest me, that girl, that young woman, who I was.

And, as with anyone who intrigues you, what they do is of interest too. Especially when they are creative. *They* were, both of them. Somehow the first one, through a deluge of school and homework, managed to produce plays and novellas, and finally, a little older, at the age of seventeen, a whole novel – set on a picturesque and very cruel parallel ancient Graeco-Cretan island. The later Lee of twenty-five, of course, had already written what would eventually become quite successful books, *The Birthgrave*, *Don't Bite the Sun*, and *The Storm Lord*. But about three years after, when she was at art college and her sole preoccupation should have been (presumably) art, there she was in the college library, writing yet another novel. Her excuse was that it sprang from things about her, incoherent things mostly, the temperature and mode of the time. But really she could not help herself. She was probably always meant to write, even if largely unpublished, as then. (It would be two more years before the three aforementioned books came out in the States, from the house of Daw.) In fact, in an even earlier incarnation, about six years old, someone had asked her what she wanted to be – how are children of this age supposed to know? Or is it only one more patronizing adult game? – and she had answered: 'An actress.' That then, what she *wanted* to be. But what she was, was a writer. Evidently. Demonstrably.

The novel in the library, scribbled long-hand (then as now) on a large lined pad, was unlike its three forerunners. Then again, she tended to write differing things, as she still does. A change is as good as, etc. This one was a sort of Gothic Science Fiction. It concerned a beautiful white-haired girl in a future world polluted to the point of anarchy and dissolution. The social fabric has broken down almost completely. The trees are dead, the sky is yellow, and no birds sing. The population, where it has clung on, lives in a primitive state that continues remnants of 'middle-class' plastic moral comfort with the hygienic standards of cavemen. Everything and everyone is tinged by madness. The beautiful heroine is decidedly half crazy. While the two heroes to whom she attaches herself, also in their own unlike ways, are in one case what might be termed nuts, and in the other certifiably insane.

The novel had its roots, as is often the case, in personal experience and observation of new things, and in the oblique perception of three particular people, not exactly those finally given rein in these pages. The characters, as I did and do always find, took on a vivid and often raucous life of their own. The impetus may have come from without, but the petrol on which they then ran was their own. They took hold of the book and moved it, as characters do, thank God, by their own volition, to its development, climaxes, and conclusion.

I have kept the novel by me through the years, even though it did not, then, find a publisher. It was not, I was told, the time for it. Or – it was not what my newly-found readers expected. Perhaps this was a fair directive caution. In any case, it has given me the chance, over those years, to re-read the novel, tighten it a little, tidy it a little. I stress the little. There is a reason why I have, seeing flaws that by now I could easily eradicate, still not laid rough hands on the work.

One hopes to improve, and I feel that I have moved forward, at least in some matters of style, from my twenty-five-year-old self, but even so, she produced a work that was faithful to her skill at that time, and, *at that time*, was as good as she could get it. I am never made ashamed by my literary mistakes – though sometimes amused or nostalgic-ally saddened by them. I really always do my best, and I think that deserves its own honour. I have tried to honour *Eva Fairdeath* by leaving it as much as possible as it was, even to the point of allowing repetitions of words, turns of phrase I would not now use, and some structural points that seem to me less neat than the scenarios I would today strive after. The 1970s ambience which inevitably overshadows the polluted future of the book, I have not attempted to disguise. All historicals show their own era – the often extraordinarily authentic *Ten Commandments* is a film unmistakably of the 1950s; the gorgeous *Cleopatra* of the gorgeous Elizabeth Taylor is '60s to its last lotus. Books cannot always escape the tint or taint of their written time, and certainly *Eva Fairdeath* has not done so. Nevertheless, since 1970 is itself now historical, maybe that is not too offensive. To try to expunge all trace of it would, I think, perhaps pull out some of the psychological underpinning of the book.

The advantages that struck me, when going over the work for the final time, in order to present it, at last, for publication, were in the freshness of its attack – that is, my twenty-five-year-old attack upon *it*. It is not that, with maturity, one becomes less effective, only that the initial impact becomes – not blunted – but *expected*. Usually when one has read numerous works by a particular author, one comes to guess, instinctively, how they may tackle a particular ethic, how they may respond to and build upon a certain set of concepts. This may increase pleasure, or promote irritation. Perhaps it only depends how well you like and understand the intention of that writer. In writing the works, too, one can be party to this factor of *growing accustomed*. The writer, when reading herself, begins intuitively to know how she will have reacted. How she will have deployed and destroyed. And this has nothing to do with inherent knowledge of the plot-line.

But in an early work, which this is, the impact is still very new. Possibly even it may be said to be experimental. And so, that alone may provide an element of interest.

In addition to this newness, for me, of my twenty-five-year-old novel, I found an amount of relevance in Eva's feminine psyche. Fallen, as perhaps women would be bound to in such a debased society, back into the rôle of object and adjunct, she manages to find two men who, at least, see worth in her, largely because she is spiritually linked to them, and physically resembles them both – but then she is partly drawn to them also for this reason. Her emotions are, it seems to me, true to her situation, and additionally redolent of a woman who is herself a fount of energy, and maybe healing, who has been suppressed and is only just learning, by accident as it were, how to break loose. Her fear of the male bond of friendship, which may naturally exclude her – Maupassant's masculine communing thought; since women and men are members of different races – is blatantly and unapologetically displayed. Men, of course, can feel the same way towards women. The expression 'hen party' must carry one of the greatest trails of affright in the language of the casual. In Eva there is no self-questioning and no sense of guilt or striving to resolve her feelings. She merely *experiences*, and acts. One line from the book I have always felt wholly relevant to her, moots that Eva wanted to kill someone, but did *not*. The *not* is the important word in this sentence, for Eva too is able swiftly to slay, like both her lovers, and perhaps with less of a qualm.

On the hem of this emotional basic, I liked the way the book had accepted certain moral limitations – the censor then was not so free – and written itself definitively about the 'adult' sexual themes, written without, I hope, lies, while remaining, shall I say, *discreet*.

Lastly, what startled me on current re-reading was the accurate predicting, from a basis of no knowledge and no vaguest idea that such a devastating pollution could ever come about. Now that we cower under the threats and spillages of such as Tchenobyl and a depleting ozone layer, with freak weather assaulting us almost every day, the kind of world Eva must struggle to survive in no longer seems centuries off. I have added nothing to my then-descriptions of storms, hurricanes and heat-waves. They stand as they were then 'invented' by me, in 1973. I had missed some things of course. I grimly wondered now, for example, where all the feral foxes had gone to? Mutated? Turned into dogs? I noted too that I had not scented the coming terror of AIDS, or the availability of skin cancer. But then, in Eva's world, maybe one has burned itself out with its victims, and the other become so everyday that no one mentions it.

Nevertheless, the novel is not a warning or a judgement, and is not meant to be, for that is not my job. I am a story-teller and that is that.

But, even so, I do believe in the pure value of optimism and hope. There is no need for us to end up on an earth like Eva's, and still time to prevent it. We have a chance. What shines for me out of this book is not its direness or violence or gravity, but the rays of human love and human ability, that are the best of all of us, in our past, and in our future, today, tomorrow, always.

Tanith Lee
1993

EVA FAIRDEATH

EVA

One

Night was coming. It was unstoppable. Eva, the white-haired girl from the marsh settlement, was running for her life down the derelict highway.

Uncountable years before, things with spinning wheels and ice-green eyes had roared and smoked either way up and down this road. Now it was wide open and empty of everything except the running girl and her hard bare soles. Eva, Belmort's daughter, the one who had grown up slight and pale out of the dark, dun, heavy men and women who toiled their hearts out by Foulmarsh. Her feet hit the road. She had been searching for berries, but had no luck; only stabthorn, briars and mildewed lichens. The day had gone by too fast as she dreamed her way through her hopeless task, sucking her torn fingers, thinking of other things, and picking the stings off her skirt and out of her hair. Then night loomed over the rim of the highway, pitch black, humming. Night sounds started up – clicks, throbs, whistles from the unimaginable distances of the dark. There was never quiet here. All day things whirred and screeched and dragged their slimy personalities in and out of the marsh, slavered and whickered in the matchstick woods. But night brought other sounds, sounds of hunting and death and unwholesome pleasure. Superstitious, like all the Belmorts, like all the marsh settlement, like all the settlements indeed from here to there (wherever that was, probably where the ruined land finally rolled off into some abyss too chaotic even for men to scrabble a living from), Eva felt a terror of the dark. It was bad to look up and realize the black face would be over her, one-eyed skull with its moon-monocle, long before she reached the wall-gate. Then, swiftly moving on the broken-up tar, she heard the new night sound behind her. It might have been one of those long-ago chariots of the highway – she thought of this, and her knees melted with panic. She began to run, blind save for the pink moon, the odd flicker of stars. Things tore her ankles; she stumbled and occasionally fell. The sound drew closer. If not a ghost thing, it was still certain to be bad. A dark wicked something conjured up by the presence of night.

Nearer and nearer the sound came. Now she could distinguish wheels. By day, she would have identified it already as the noise of a wagon or cart, pulled by an animal – shaggy horse or outsize dog. She had not seen many examples of such wealth. The settlement had none, yet some travelling men rode, their wares stored behind them, and their women and brats if they liked company. By night, her reasoning was snuffed out. She stopped running at last simply because she could run no longer.

She slunk off the road into six foot high brambles; she pulled the tangled shadows round her.

Then the vehicle came up over the crest of the road, swinging its lamp.

Her teeth clamped together, a perfect white line except for the absence of one lower left molar almost out of sight. Her tongue strayed to this absent fang as it always did in moments of perplexity or fear. (Possibly her tongue recalled the pain as old woman Belmort dragged with her pincers and Eva screamed in agony.) Her eyes, violet, a kind of stained glass, like the scraps still clinging in some windows, slitted against the lamplight.

It was only a wagon. The dray animal was only a horse. She could smell its dungy, raw smell. Almost level now. It came to her that the Belmorts had spoken of a god-speaker due to pass the settlement in the next few days. Perhaps here was the man? Their carts were usually more gaudy, strung round with counting beads and carved dolls of angels, piled up with the hand-written books only a handful could read.

Then the laugh came and caught her by the throat. Partly she had enjoyed the panic, and relief was even better. She barked like a vixen out of her cover and the horse broke its trot and shook its head, the lamp jolted and flung bat wings of light across the broad road. With her narrow hands she pushed the brambles aside and stepped out on the road. She took the horse's reins as if she were used to it. The horse nodded and quietened. She stared up over the lamp glare at the man-shape beyond.

'There's a village about three miles on. They'll give you good stuff for what you're selling.'

She had hoped he was a god-speaker when she said this. They always took their dignity along with their preaching, and did not like to be compared to traders. A voice said to her: 'What I'm selling is a man's death.'

7

She was not sure she had heard him right. She walked along the length of the horse towards him, trailing a hand on its fur.

'Are you a god-speaker?'

'No.'

'What was it you said about death?'

'You heard me.'

She found herself looking up into a couple of eyes so cold a blue they made her think instantly and consciously of all coldly-burning things – frost, phosphorus, glass. His jaw, like a cat's, narrowed out towards the chin. He was beautiful, every line of his face and body tense and elegant and fine. He was an oddity. His hair was short compared to that of the men in the settlement. She had never before seen a man or woman with white hair except when she looked into some cracked bit of mirror. He looked old to her, very old, yet there was nothing in his face to say this. It was behind the face, the oldness, in the backs of the arctic eyes.

Having reached him, she felt a need to speak, and nothing came either into her mind or mouth to say. He was indeed a figment of night, yet also a man.

'Get up,' he said.

He let down one hand to help her. She did not think him particularly strong; like her he had a kind of narrowness, brittleness. But his fingers and palm were like iron and she was up beside him, above the back of the horse.

The reins flicked. The horse began to move. Thin trees passed, pieces of stars hung out between their whip-like branches.

'Who is it you'll kill, then? A village man?'

'You'll see.'

She felt no horror or alarm. She did not analyse this. All her life had been hard work, starvation, cruelty, pain, frustration and stupidity. She sat by him, warming herself at his cold fire. She did not understand. She watched his face. Sometimes she had dreamed of men, not the squat dark men around her. The dreamed men had no faces, only the feel of silence and coolness.

'My father's name is Belmort. Is it my father you'll kill?'

'No.' He said nothing for a minute. Then: 'Did you want him dead?'

Eva grinned and shut off the grin. 'We all die by the marsh, sooner or later. Poisoned crops, bad weather, snake-bite, an animal – something.'

He said nothing.

'People die quickly. Old Woman Belmort is fifty. They say she's charmed. At thirty most of us will be dead.'

'Probably,' he said.

'I'm seventeen. I have ten years of life, or less. I'm thin and dried out already. And crazy, they say.' She chuckled. 'Where do you come from?'

'A place.'

She reached and touched the hair where it lay against the rough hide collar of his jacket. She felt the skin of his neck beneath the hair which was like a kind of coarse silk, and he flinched, though there was no expression on his face.

'Sometimes they say I'm a freak because I grow white,' she said.

'You are.'

'Then you are too.'

'Yes.'

9

After a while she said: 'My name is Eva, Eva Belmort.'

'Fairdeath,' he said.

She hesitated. 'What?'

'That's what your name means.'

She said, then, 'Why?'

He said nothing. The trees ran past. She lifted back her own white hair with her hands and began to sing in a hoarse, thin, but not unpleasing voice. Sitting with fear, she was no longer afraid. This was how he seemed to her. Terror, a white angel, bringing the tomb to Foulmarsh – she sat at his side like his priestess (Fairdeath) – the new and dreadful religion.

After a time the smell of the marsh – acrid and fumy – came blowing across the road. The highway rolled on beyond the trodden track leading to the village. The undergrowth was thick here, and the trees scaled over in a kind of enamelled leprosy. Vague stirs of firelight underlit the sky.

The wagon halted.

'Only a minute more,' she said, 'and we'll be there. Here's the track.'

'Get down,' he said.

'Aren't you coming with me?'

'No.'

'What about your man?' She hissed, to tantalize him with this titbit of death.

'Not yet. Perhaps tomorrow.'

'I may find him and warn him.'

'You may.'

She slid down from the box without assistance. He did not look at her, only waiting apparently for her to go.

She rubbed her cheek against the horse's furry one, and walked between two trees away from him. She heard the wheels and hooves start up behind her, moving off along the highway. Fear of the night again took hold of her. She ran again, towards the brick and stick village wall, smelling the marsh. The man was only a dream now; she thought she had imagined him.

At the gate a couple of toughs were making pretence of being sentries. They had got hold of a thick glass bottle of settlement-brewed beer. They swung round from it staring when she came up the track out of the dark. Flint levelled his rifle, menacing, as if he had killed anything more than a rat. Billy laughed and pushed the butt aside.

'No need for that.'

They lounged, making no move to open the gate. Billy drank from the bottle. Long ragged black hair fell greasily around his shoulders, and on his stained leather coat lining erupted through rents.

'Want to come in, do you?' he asked, wiping beer-froth off on his sleeve. 'Been a naughty girl, have you, staying out late? Who d'you think she was with, Flint, eh?'

Flint leaned his rifle on the wall. 'Who'd want her?'

'Don't know, ' Billy said, smiling generously, 'she's not bad for a crazy woman.'

Three months back he had raped her at the edge of the turnip field in the moist black mud. It had been raining and he hurt her; both these facts had caused her to bash his nose with a sharp stone conveniently lying near to hand. She had not broken the nose, but there had been a good deal of blood. Presumably that part of the tale was left untold as he

11

recounted her sexual virtues and demerits to the men later. Not, however, to Belmort. Belmort would have had Billy's hide, and a marriage probably too. Eva was his property.

Eva stood on the wrong side of the gate. She yawned. Billy leaned forward across the gate and caught a handful of her hair.

'What'll you give me if I let you in, Eva Belmort?'

She spat accurately in his eye.

Billy cursed.

A shrill voice called out of the huddle of brick shacks: 'What's all that noise out there?'

Eva recognized the tones of Billy and Flint's mother of whom they went in utmost terror.

'Nothing, Ma,' Flint yelled back. He thrust up the bars and swung the gate open rapidly, pulling Eva through. 'Get off home, you effing cow.'

As she stalked down the track she heard Billy shouting nastily after her: 'Crazy Eva, cracks in the head!' A cry she no longer found offensive or disturbing, having been intermittently subjected to it since childhood. As a skinny little brat with a mane of colourless hair she had stood sucking her thumb, her head half on one side. When the children grouped and beat her, she would weep piteously, going black and blue for days, planning little revenges on every individual tormentor. She singled them out and punished them one by one, in her own way. Libby Moss she told a story about a ghoul who would come and devour her, starting at the feet, while Libby listened wide-eyed. And night after night for a full month after, Eva learned the breadth of her imaginative powers by the frenzied screams issuing from the Moss shack. Libby's nightmares were so

bad the doctor from Burnwood had to be fetched in his
cart, and his complaints were almost as loud as the
screaming. He cost the Mosses two jars of beer and a pouch
of smoking weed, and did Libby little good, being half
drunk and half out of his mind from the smoking during
most of his stay. Other of Eva's vengeances had been more
instant – she had eased a couple of slats out of the wood
bridge some of the children built across a marsh pool, and
loosened the rope. No one drowned but there were
splinters and green slime: parents administered all the
beatings Eva could have hoped for. She was a devious child
of necessity. They came to fear her a little and left her
alone.

She ignored their labels of 'crazy' and 'dreamer'. Was
she crazy? She expected so, and did not mind it. Often
there would be tasks she could avoid because she was too
careless and stupid to be trusted with them.

She slouched down the earth street between the shacks.
Chimneys smoked, firelight showed lividly in the windows
where occasionally dirty glass was flimsily tacked up. Dogs
barked or whimpered on their chains. She passed Nibblet's
forge and the stone cross on its high leaning pedestal, the
relic of ancient forgotten observances. She thought vaguely
of how Billy had had her in the mud; and there had been
one or two before him she had gone with out of curiosity. It
had been uncomfortable, messy and disappointing. One
day Belmort would tie her to a man, if any man would have
her. She would live out her days cooking on his hearth,
having the messy disappointing thing done to her in his bed,
until she produced a baby and either died or nursed it up till
it was strong enough for him to beat along with his dog. But

then, probably no one would take her. Crazy Eva, cracks in the head. Only an invalid or a freak with scaly skin or warped legs would consent to wedlock with a mad woman. As there were settlements of men, so there were settlements of freaks, it was said, but in the wild places. She had seen a freak once, part of a traveller's show – he was greenish and hair grew on one side of his body and none on the other. Perhaps she would end her short life in a freak village.

She reached the Belmort shack. It had two low-ceilinged storeys, and a plywood porch which creaked. A religious amulet was nailed on the door. Inside the big room Old Woman was frying meat over the fire-bellied stove. Jom and Hazel, the kids, were playing a game on the floor. There had been two brothers, but Mac was in Burnwood now with his woman, and Saul was five years under the marsh. Eva's mother had moved in this room also, once, before Eva remembered. Belmort sat drinking leaf-tea, the big brown pot on the table beside him. He had a rifle across his knees, and the huge, scruffy, yellow-toothed dog was lying on his feet. He looked up and stared at Eva, then put the rifle against the table leg, and shoved the dog away.

'Where have you been, you damned girl?'

'Looking for berries.'

'He was for going out after you,' Old Woman Belmort snapped, unbending from her cooking. 'I've told you and told you be back before it gets dark. There're animals out there, and men or worse on the prowl. You've no sense.'

She was fifty years, but she looked seventy. Her skin was wrinkled, stretched too tight on a wire mesh of bones. She was Belmort's sister, but he slept with her when he felt the need. Fun was scarce, and looks and genealogy were considerations no longer.

Belmort still stared at Eva. She shifted her feet. She did not like her father, nor the way he pawed at her sometimes when he was drunk. She would be next, she guessed, now Old Woman was growing so ugly – would have been long since, except that some men still prized virginity in their daughters, and absurdly (and mistakenly) Belmort was one of them.

She sat down. The room stank of food, human dirtiness, the dog. Something came bright and icy into her mind. She remembered how clean he had smelled, the man in the wagon, when she reached towards him. She washed herself each day, carefully, but it was hard to be clean. Water went into the belly not the bath. Yet the Belmorts had a bath, an old cracked enamel with chrome taps still uselessly attached. Eva got up.

'Where you going now?' Old Woman rasped.

'I want to wash,' Eva said.

Old Woman made a sound of derision.

Belmort watched her out of the door, drinking his tea.

She drew two buckets from the pump. It was good, white water, a spring that ran down from Burnwood into the marsh. She lugged them into the back room and filled the bath and took the kettle from the stove to warm off the chill. Old Woman yelled at her angrily – the kettle had been for more tea – but it was too late. Eva crouched in the cold green bath sluicing her body and scrubbing with the hard unlovely soap, to the accompanying sounds of eating from the next room. Once Belmort came to the door, and leaned on it, looking at her, picking meat off a bone in one hand, fried bread in the other. Eva ignored him.

'Not so hard to find a man for you, I reckon,' he said at last, his mouth full.

'I don't want a man.'

He laughed. In the background Hazel and Jom began to squabble.

'You do, my girl. I can see that much from here.'

'Don't look then, if it bothers you. You won't find a man for me.'

'Billy'd have you.'

'He has.'

Belmort moved, his face altering. Her father had a violent streak Eva feared. She said quickly: 'Told me he'd have me, I mean,' which different connotation was untrue. 'But his ma wouldn't let him.'

'She's no bother,' said Belmort.

'I don't want Billy.'

Belmort's hand came down a moment on her bare shoulder.

'We'll see,' he said, as if promising her something she had said she wanted. When he went out she sluiced and sluiced his touch from her shoulder with the cold water.

Where she lay to sleep in the windowless back room, she could hear the bed creak upstairs, the muted piggy murmurs of Jom as he slept by the stove, and the dog out on the porch grinding its teeth on an old piece of bone. Dim light from the stove bled across the floor. She lay on her back. Through the stale smell of mattress and bedding she could pick out clear as a note of music the scent of water still white as starlight on her skin.

She thought of the man she had ridden with on the road. Had she imagined him? He was too unlike the rest to be real. She thought of him beside her, thought of moving her hand across his hair, neck and chest, and felt him cold as the water to her touch.

As a child she had imagined others to keep her company – a tall thin girl with flax hair, a boy who taught her how to shoot at things with a rifle that seemed made of silver with bullets of crystal. She called them Lydia and Saul. They had been more real for her than Belmort, Old Woman, Billy, Libby and Flint.

Her mind opened its doors and she slipped inside. Somewhere a beast howled in the black night. She did not hear it.

Two

The dream had been good. She could not remember what it was, only that she had not wanted to wake. A woman shouting and shouting had woken her.

She opened her eyes. It was morning, and cold. Hoar frost made a delicate pattern on the slice of front room window-glass she could see beyond the door. The stove, of course, was out.

In the street the woman shouted. Now a man was shouting too. The sound struck into Eva's belly; this altercation and alarm meant something bad, some cog out of place, some dangerous development, threatening safety. There had been cries like this when the East barns burned with the wheat in them, which spelled hunger; when one of the Crow boys had stabbed another and then run with the knife across the village to the marsh, which had spelled death and a man's body creaking in the wind from the spike of a tree.

She heard Jom stirring, then his anxious unbroken voice: 'Da! *Da!*'

'Be quiet, you,' Eva called. Jom did not like her, and the feeling was mutual. She got up, wrapped a blanket round her, and went across the front room, past sulky Jom to the

19

shack door. Hazel was on the bottom stair chewing a strand of hair.

'Get up to bed,' Eva snapped.

'Shan't. 'Sides, da's sent me out while he does things with Old Woman.'

'All right. Start the stove then.' Eva pulled open the door.

Outside the day was stiff with frost. Every movement – the snap of a wizened branch, dogs' feet between the shacks – seeming to crackle on smashed glass. The settlement appeared unruly, crooked, makeshift in the harsh light, cut out in black shapes, slanting every way like a colossal rubbish heap. Overhead the filthy beauty of the day sky, dandelion yellow, with the village smoke on it like a lavender gauze.

There was a group stock still by the pump, frozen perhaps. The shouting had stopped. As she watched a woman drew her bucket from under the spout and upended it on the street. It was a shock to see that precious liquid spilled. One day they had all known the stream would dry out. And it was not customary to waste anything. Then Eva saw the colour of the water running over the earth towards her. It was black.

The woman straightened and looked into Eva's face. It was Billy's ma. Her eyes were narrowed and unaccountably filled with a particular and definite hatred.

'The water's bad,' she said. She put her free hand on her hip, broad from carrying babies which had struggled up into being Billies and Flints. 'Ida Moss saw *you* at the pump last night.'

20

Eva shrank back. She was a coward. What were they accusing her of now?

'Come off it,' the man said. He was one of the Crow clan. 'What could *she* have done? It's turned foul underground. We'll have to dig a new place nearer the wall, that's all there is to it.'

'I don't trust her crazy ways,' Billy's ma snarled.

'You're talking like a fool.'

There were one or two others now, standing around in their doorways.

'I bet she did something, she's silly in the head,' said Libby Moss, Libby with black hair, gold earrings, and some village boy's impending brat lifting her belly.

'Not half as silly as you, you swollen-up tart,' Eva said loud enough to be heard, but she felt sick and immediately she slunk back into the shack. The bulk of her father surprised her thrusting past. He stood massive in the doorway, his trousers held together in one hand.

'You want trouble?' he roared.

'My Ben'll speak to you!' Billy's ma shouted back.

'He's welcome.' Belmort rocked back and forth with his own awful majesty, the porch creaking under, over and around him like a slowly capsizing ship. Jom and Hazel huddled by the stove with pasty-looking faces and big eyes. Outside the noises of abuse were loud.

Then Eva picked up another sound, beyond the din. Horse feet, wagon wheels. They were part of a dream. The hair rose on Eva's neck and scalp. A coolness came like an eraser over her mind. Without considering, forgetting even her enemies in the street, she twisted by her father, ran naked except for the blanket, out between the shacks. Luckily others had broken off to stare at the stranger, therefore no one molested her as she stood transfixed with disappointment, her hot violet eyes on the brightly painted wagon and two outriders. A scarlet canopy, much patched and repaired, a bell or two jangled softly, frayed tassels. It was an enormous, nightmarish dog in the shafts. The outriders – two thin and hunched-over boys about fifteen – straddled donkeys. A banner trailed from the hand of one boy, gold lettering on black, reading: JEZUBAL SAVES. The man in the wagon, presumably Jezubal, wore a black velvet coat, lace shirt and a gold chain round his neck from which dangled a tiny carved doll. He was fat, a thing not often seen. Obviously pickings were good in his trade where he came from. His black pits of eyes collided with Eva's, as she shrank from them, disgusted.

Billy was walking behind the wagon, cocky, having seen the visitor first, and let him in.

Eva turned and walked into the shack's back room. No one followed. There was a big group around the wagon. Already suspicion, anger, fear were dissipating before the new interest.

She pulled the curtain to, dividing this room from the front, but then a violent urge came to smash open the back of the shack and run out that way. She heard her father swearing at Jom beyond the curtain, and laughter from outside. She got on her mattress and crawled back among the chilled sheets, biting at one nail.

'He'll preach them soon,' she muttered to herself, 'then the pipes will go around, and they'll go half stupid, calling on god and getting drunk.'

It occurred to her her father might come looking for her.
'I'll go with Billy. Belmort won't find me then.'
It was a bad but necessary price to pay.

Jezubal and his boys had set up his box of tricks around the
leaning cross, using its upright to support the scarlet canopy
which had only two poles. On the terrace of the steps they
put out a brazier of coals and a big carved chair of black
wood. Sitting in it, if he wanted, Jezubal could see right
down the street, across the tumbling shacks, the compost
heaps and wooden lavatories, over the strips of fields to the
final erupted boil of the marsh. A fog hung over the marsh
today, and clickings and chirrupings came out of it,
monotonous and hellish.

Eva's father had come to the doorway, buttoning his
shirt.

'Get up, you lazy cow.'

'I've got my pain. I'll be sick if I do.'

He scowled at her. It must have occurred to him she
always had a bad period when she did not want to move
herself, and most likely it was not true, for like many
women now, she had seldom bled. But he seemed disposed
to be lenient.

'Please yourself.'

This could be a bad sign. He would know where
to find her later, if she stayed here, when he came
from the meeting, reeling with weed-smoke, beer and
religion.

She heard them all out – Belmort, Old Woman, Jom and
Hazel whining, and the shack door slammed. Through the
timber and the brick she could hear the sounds as the

streets filled, and the noise of gathering at the cross steps. She knew how it would go. First their fear – how god had punished them for their sins and the sins of their forebears with the rotten land on which nothing would grow, the dying trees, the poisoned waterways, the encroaching wilderness. After that, hope. The god-speaker's own particular brand of salvation to which they would all respond, as they responded every time. The pipes of smoking weed would pass. Perhaps Jezubal's dull-eyed boys would swing old church censers of the stuff. There would be shouting and frenzy and visions. A few, overcome, might tumble over in fits. Joyous in rebirth, certain they had bribed god with a new observance, they would bring out beer and wine, and buy raw alcohol from the preacher himself. They would give him food, knives, bullets and harness from the forge. They would take in exchange hand-written texts of salvation, carved god-keep-you dolls with magic religious properties, amulets and charms of all shapes and sizes. There would be dancing – perhaps the preacher had an old violin in tow? – or the Mosses' untuned piano would be bowled out on the street and bashed in unharmonious and primitive rhythms. It would last through the sallow day, ending in fires, fornication and theft – all of which god would overlook because it had been done in his name.

Eva had been personally saved when she was three, five and ten. Why she had been singled out, she could not remember. Probably her pallor, or perhaps some sign of hysteria misinterpreted as ecstasy. She remembered a thin woman forcing her head into a plastic bucket of water. Eva emerged shrieking with terror, and to muffle her protests, the congregation had been called on to praise god. At ten, a man had pinned a tin heart on her dress, feeling surreptitiously one of her tiny promises of breasts as he did so.

A general shout came from up the street.

Eva flung off the covers, got up, stood naked and cold in the dark room. Then in a kind of terror she ran to get her dress, fumbling with its buttons. Yesterday she had gone barefoot, today she pulled on leggings and shoes for the freezing weather seemed to be eating her up with teeth of fire. This was how it was – one day mild and muggy, the next iced over. She pulled a jumper over the dress, and took one of Old Woman's shawls from the peg. A bitter panic and despair had come on her so that she shook and trembled, leaning at the stove to get warm. There was no escape, she knew it. She would go out and be one with the crowd. She would go to Billy and after today Belmort would angrily see the god-speaker join the two of them. Billy she might perhaps handle. He fancied her, and was scared of her too. Not that he would want to marry but Belmort would see to that. Billy would beat her often, but that was nothing new. She could handle him. Tears started out of her eyes. She could not remember why she was crying. It seemed some favourite thing had been lost, something loved, like the day she found the bird frozen stiff by the pump and tried to warm it and her father took it and threw its corpse into the rubbish tip. But what had been lost? Nothing. It was one thing or the other, and she must choose.

She went out into the cruel day, forgetting to shut the shack door. She scuffed at stones, and sidled away from the foul pump. The smell of the marsh was strong. She coughed and wiped her eyes. She could hear Jezubal's voice but oddly not the words.

Reaching the edge of the crowd, she looked about for Billy. She saw him lounging against the tethering post, not far from the terrifying dray dog which seemed asleep on its feet. Billy held a pipe to his mouth, smoking with half-shut eyes.

Jezubal was standing on the terrace, his hands raised, his black eyes wide.

'God *hears*!' he cried, but she heard *him* as if through cotton wool. 'Call on him and he *listens*!' Then the eyes came down and found her. She saw the look in them. Another feeler of breasts with a tin heart.

Eva put a narrow hand on Billy's broad shoulder and fiddled with a bit of escaped lining. He turned and looked at her as if peering down a long tunnel, grinning.

'Keep yer spit to yerself,' he remarked lazily.

Eva smiled. She took his free hand and drew it round her body by its bulky cumbersome arm. The god-speaker looked away. His preaching had not faltered.

'Pass the pipe, Billy,' she said. A couple of tears leaked out of her eyes again and down into the two corners of her carved smile.

'Don't cry, Eva,' Billy said, cuddling her. ' I forgives you.'

He slid the pipe clumsily into her mouth. She drew on it hard. He took out the pipe and put his lips and tongue just as clumsily in its place.

'Knew you'd come round to it, Eva,' he said, congratulatory.

'Call on god!' cried a dim voice far away.

The crowd roared.

Eva felt a thread of ice sew itself along her spine as if a cold trickle of water had fallen on her from one of the overhanging roofs. She turned, still leaning on Billy, to see if it had. The crowd was all blurred over, but just beyond the crowd, the street seemed strangely clear and vivid. A man was standing at the end of the street, black as ink against the topaz sky.

Fascinated, Eva stared and stared, leaning out on the leash of Billy's arm. She watched the man walk down the street. There was a gun slung across his back. As she watched he reached the Moss shack and vanished behind it.

'On your land shall come up thorns and briars, god said. Thorns and briars and blight and rottenness all your generations. There shall be wailing and lamenting if you do not call on me!'

'I love god!' screamed Libby Moss. 'Oh, how I love god! I love him but he won't have me.' She began to weep, obviously confused.

Watching, Eva saw the man reappear on the roof of the Moss shack. He kneeled on one knee, elegantly. She had seen a prince kneeling like this before a princess in a mildewed, pasted-together book. Could Jezubal see him? The man unslung the gun.

'Mine is the way, says god!' Jezubal cried.

There was a sharp crack in the air.

Eva gazed at Jezubal curiously; he looked surprised. Instead of two black eyes, he now had three, and the third one was in the centre of his forehead.

He fell backwards abruptly, relinquishing himself with a crash, taking the brazier with him. One of the outriding boys started to scream; even the shaft dog looked up. The crowd milled in confusion. Heads turned every way.

'There goes the bastard!' shouted an excited male voice.

A new kind of roaring took hold of the street.

'Well, I'll be,' said Billy.

Eva pushed away from him. As the crowd surged forward, she surged with it, but she seemed to be running through marsh mud; she had to get free. The crowd milled around a corner, spasmed, tried to turn back on itself.

'That way!'

Eva stumbled back into a doorway, and the crowd raced past.

Where? Where? She turned to run between the shacks. A chicken coop squawked at her, filling her mind with yellow chicken-demons. The marsh wall was where he had come from, climbing up slimy bricks, through briars and sludge. But it was easy now, the air electric to her running body. He pulled her as if by a strong rope, the kind of rope the men would have out by now for his neck she had touched.

Running, tendrils of fog enveloped her, she upturned a bucket, ran into stinging weeds, slammed against brickwork, began to climb. She did not know where the crowd was, though she heard its murderous row like a far-off storm. She tore her nails and fell over the other side into darkness. She could not see properly.

But the horse made a sound somewhere ahead. She heard it kick its hooves to be off, no wagon now to slow it, only the man with the rifle on its back. She rushed headlong after the sound. In its first moment of speed her reaching hands slid frantically on its mist-slippery shanks. With a cry of despair she scrabbled and lost all except the streaming mass of tail. She clutched and held to it, and the horse plunged and struggled to be free, neighing in pain and fear, but still galloping.

Eva fell. Mud suffocating her. Tree roots stabbed her body, dead branches caught her hair so that for a moment she experienced a similar agony to the one she inflicted on the horse. It was flying, surely it was in the air. She had no breath or energy to scream. All her concentration, her strength, was centred on her grip. She would not let go. Would never let go. She thought she would die.

Soon she was only a pair of hands knotted into strings of fire, in a world composed of whirling motion and searing, endlessly variegated pain.

She struggled and fought to keep her hold. As one finger came adrift she forced it back among the flaming wires. Her wrists seemed broken. But she was weak now and eventually all her grip had been ripped open and her hands hung like dead flowers in the marsh. She realized then that the rushing speed had stopped and that her hands had not been shaken loose but prized away.

She thought she could not see him in the mist, but she had forgotten to open her eyes. Expressionlessly he said: 'Why come on after me? I don't want you.'

She gritted her teeth.

'You've got me,' she said, 'and no time to argue.'

Almost at once there was another sense of movement, up, and down into a new interior darkness. She heard the horse in the shafts, felt the rattle and shake and bump of passage. She curled against a soft thing, her eyes still shut, and slept immediately, insanely content in the moving wagon of the stranger who sold death.

EVA AND
STEEL

Three

Eva woke up wanting to vomit. On the heels of this urgent need came the urgent need not to dirty this wagon which was his, for she remembered at once where she was. She leaned on a strut holding up the canvas top, and bit her tongue. After a moment or so the ghastly sickness abated totally.

They were still moving. A greyish light filtered in which might have been dusk or dawn.

She examined her arms which were scratched and bruised and filthy with mud. There was mud everywhere – in her hair, down her dress and jumper, all over her face she supposed. There was no means to clean herself, and no mirror to see in. She sat back on her heels, her tongue lying over where the missing tooth had been. She felt excited, and then something clutched at her insides and she imagined for a moment it was Jezubal's wagon she was in, having exchanged one misery for another, similar though more exotic. Yet none of this was Jezubal's.

She had lain on a folded blanket of dark blue stuff, against a roll of other blankets. In the far corner stood a bolted-down stove and a store of coals and logs in two or three small crates. Among the struts various things were pegged secure and still – cook-pots, bowls, leather bottles in which a liquid softly slopped which was either water or liquor, or both, a rifle on hooks with a butt of some yellow-white bone, inlaid with silver – a thing that amazed her, reminding her of make-believe Saul. Were there crystal bullets to go with this ornamental death? A wooden chest, nailed down like the stove, prompted her to pull open drawers. She found a few folded clean clothes, smelling of their cleanness, packets of dried food and musty books, printed not written by hand, which took up most of the chest – and the space behind it. Eva puzzled over the books, keeping one hand irresistibly in the clothes drawer. Finally she needed to believe he was still there on the box seat, not Jezubal or Billy or any other phantom. She crawled to the flap and pulled it open, and found his straight dark back mere inches in front of her face.

It was dawn. Dawn noises had started up and the sky was gold in the distance beyond a spider's web of branches. She had slept through the evening and the night; he had driven through it presumably. The light made his hair shine like a cap of pale metal on his skull. She wondered if he still had a face, for he was a kind of night-demon to her, and, though she had watched him silhouetted on the shack roof, and had run after him so fast and hard, she had not actually *seen* him since the night on the highway. She did not want to touch him with her mud-caked fingers. The rifle still hung across his back, a twin to the gun in the wagon.

An initial imperative question formed itself.

'Why did you kill him?'

At first she thought he would not answer. Then he said: 'It doesn't matter to you.'

She looked over his shoulder at the horse's back and its long tail she had pulled and struggled to keep a hold on. She felt dispirited.

'I'm dirty. The marsh mud's all over me.'

'You shouldn't have come then, should you?'

'You shouldn't have taken me,' she said with ridiculous accusation.

'If I'd left you, as you understand perfectly, your tribe would have connected you with me and beaten you to pulp. Or worse.'

'They wanted *you* for the rope.'

'No doubt. But anyone would have done. Particularly an albino mutant.'

Eva narrowed her eyes.

'Where are we going?' she asked.

'When we pass the next settlement you can get off there.'

'I won't.'

'I'll throw you off, then,' he said noncommittally.

'Don't forget I know you're a murderer,' Eva spat at his turned, faceless head.

They were going down a kind of half-track, bumping. It was very silent now, between the permanently leafless spines of trees. He said nothing. She recognized her threat as superfluous.

'I wish a bird would sing,' she said, a statement quite alienated from all her life, for she had never heard one.

A line of something came into her head. She whispered like a kind of curse: 'The sedge is withered from the lake, and no birds sing.'

She began to cry and rock herself. He drove in silence. They seemed to be in the vaults of a colossal black skeleton through which sauterne light streamed like smoke or gas. Great black bones arched up, supporting a roof of thinner and more delicate bones. Eva wept and the bones ran together down the sky like the black water out of the pump.

They came to water about half an hour later, and it broke up the silence with its sound.

The wagon rumbled into a dip. The trees ran up the sides of it, but the bottom was flat with a carpet of greyish mauve moss. Out of the moss thrust flanks of chalky rocks and boulders with faces eaten out by weather. A fall dropped down from above into a basin choked with strange wild-flowers.

'You can clean the mud off here,' he said. It was the first time he had spoken to her for the whole of the half hour, though she had ceased crying long since.

Eva stared at the fall suspiciously.

'The water's yellow.'

'It won't hurt you to bathe in it. Don't drink it.'

He leaned back into the wagon, produced a cake of soap and a large coarse cloth for her to dry herself on. She finally saw his face, going past her. He seemed unaware of his effect on her. She tried to dislike him. Taking the soap and towel she jumped down from the wagon without thanks and ran towards the tawny water. She stripped perversely behind a boulder, knowing he was not looking at her.

Stepping out, the fall caught her with a blow of pressure not cold, for this day was much milder than yesterday. Her feet slipped on glossy pods and waxen flower bells in the basin; the soap frothed and produced bubbles which lingered round her body in a swarm. She soaped her hair, and soaped and soaped it.

Somewhere overhead a twig snapped like a bone.

As she rinsed her hair she stared back at the wagon. He was busy with things – feeding the horse, bringing a blanket and a packet of food out from the interior. A small fire worked between stones. She shouted at him with a long, wordless, animal howl, and he looked up at her, standing quite still with one hand on the horse's neck. The horse did not trouble, its face buried in its feeding bag.

Eva laughed. She caught a handful of water off the fall and put it in her mouth. He took no notice, only turning away, going back into the wagon. The water tasted bitter and flat and she spat it back among the flowers and bubbles underfoot.

She rinsed out her clothes under the fall, and carried them dripping with her to where the small fire was, setting them out to steam over the upjutting rocks. She towelled herself and her hair by the flames.

He came out of the wagon. She felt him looking at her now, and this was disturbing, she discovered, almost unpleasant. She turned her back to him and said: 'I drank the yellow water.'

'Then you'll be sick,' he said.

She began to tremble, trying to hold herself rigid at the same time. His shadow fell across the ground in front of her. She became aware that he was a good deal taller than she, which had not occurred to her when they were seated in the wagon. His hand passed her arm, holding something blue. She saw it was a shirt he was offering her, still standing behind her. She took it, and he walked away at once. She put on the shirt, weak and angry, not wanting to look round.

Finally she sat by the fire, not looking at him, with the blanket he had put out wrapped round her. She stared at the moss, counting its starlike colonies. She lost track of time, until he put a bowl into her hands with soup in it. When she looked at him again the rifle lay dissected on his knees and he was cleaning it, a clip of bullets waiting in the grass, which were not crystal after all.

Eva banged down the bowl on a piece of stone.

'Jezubal saves,' Eva said harshly, staring at him hard.

He did not look up.

'Not any more,' he said.

He had strange hands, the fingers very long but squared off across the tops. They moved on the rifle.

Eva felt bewildered and distressed. Uncertain of what she would do, she slipped out of the blanket, got up, and walked away from the fire, up the slope towards the trees. He did not say anything to her. She did not look back. She still had no thought of what she was doing. She had always tended to wander off known tracks; as a child she had been lost a million times.

In the trees lay unknown things – armoured beasts and dark pools with poisonous vapours. Would he let her go to be asphyxiated, crunched to splinters in red fanged mouths, starved in the hollow of some charcoal tree? Yes, Eva decided, understanding herself at the last instant, the wagon already several trunks and thickets behind. Yes, he would.

Well, then.

Scared, she walked on, whispering a snatch of song against the enfolding doom-drone of silence.

Suddenly shadows fluttered, separated and reformed in front of her. Out of nowhere and nothing came a Shape. Eva stopped still. It was not a beast, it walked upright and had arms. It had a face. Eva moaned. Its eyes and mouth were sunk back into a papery dough, its nostrils amalgamated in a single blowhole, quivering. It wore hide leggings and a fur jacket. It made a sound and lumbered forwards, groping, half blind, but nevertheless intent.

Eva began to back away, but her stiff legs would scarcely move her. The clearing must be behind her – surely she had not come so far from it? She dared not turn and see. She wanted to scream but the scream was somewhere in the pit of her lungs struggling like a live thing in a trap. If only something could release the scream he would hear and come – surely he would run up here with the rifle? But perhaps not. Perhaps—

She backed abruptly into something solid – a tree? But it was warm, bone and flesh. Her knees gave way but there were two hands on her shoulders holding her up. She managed to scream now, though he was here and did not need to be called. He shook her and the screams became broken up into an insane warbling.

'Be quiet,' he said.

Eva stopped screaming. She realized he did not have the rifle and that they were not running away but standing still in the path of the myopic, determined monstrosity now bearing down like some great pile of something tumbling over. A yard away its ghastly progress came to an end. It stood peering at her from round black eyes which had no white. The stasis lasted less than ten seconds. Then it swung about, huge, clumsy, yet curiously silent, lurching off into the trees, into the shadows which repatterned themselves to absorb it.

Eva said, chattily, 'I saw a freak in a traveller's show once. There were dogs jumping through hoops, and puppets, and a freak.'

He had let go of her, was standing a little way off, and she had not noticed.

'Eva,' he said, 'he's not a sideshow. Give him your pity nicely, but remember he'll outlive you. If you bear children – which is improbable because very likely you're barren – he'll outlive those. Even with your white hair, Eva, you're almost the last of your kind.'

'Then you are too,' she said.

'Yes, of course.'

He turned to walk back down to the clearing and the fire, but hesitated until she caught up with him.

'You came after me,' she said.

'Yes.'

He looked at her, and she looked away for his eyes seemed to shine now into the core of her mind, her sex and her soul with a coldness that was no longer cold.

When they reached the fire he said: 'I prefer to drive these roads by night, so I'll sleep now, if you've no objection.'

'What if I have?'

'You haven't,' he said.

He swung into the wagon and did not come out.

She sat by the fire, feeding it sticks, listening to the snapping as the sticks were eaten. Once something shrilled in the woods, but that was all. She wondered if the mutant would reappear, and was not afraid at the prospect, but no one came except one whip-thin snake, trickling itself like a tear across the clearing. After a while she forgot the fire and it went out. The lack of sound and activity oppressed her, even the fall seemed muted, and the horse was out of the shafts and lying asleep in the moss. She went to it and stroked its face but it did not wake. It might have been dead except for its breathing. She had never seen a horse lying down to sleep before. She got up on the box seat of the wagon and slipped between the canvas lips into the dark.

He was lying on his back, also completely still. Unlike the horse he did not seem to breathe at all. Eva remembered stories of undead, the soulless who slept in dark places by day, shielded from the sun, emerging at night to dispossess their victims of will, life and every drop of blood. She kneeled by him, intently. He really might have been dead. He had told her she could wake him, but could she? Could anything human wake him? He looked cold to the touch, a kind of marble, but beautiful, beautiful. She leaned forward to catch even the faintest whisper of his breathing, and could hear nothing. She put her finger to his cheek, and it was indefinitely warm. Her finger slid of its own accord across the smooth plane of the cheek to the coarser plane of the jaw, to his long, firmly-shut mouth. His eyes opened in one fluid movement, and he made no sound. She could not believe in him; she had never seen anyone wake like this, so serenely, instantly, totally.

'What is it?' he asked her softly.

'I thought you were dead.'

'Not yet.'

She had leaned so close, it was a very little distance for her to make up to reach his mouth with hers, but at the last instant, in a kind of fright, her lips slid aside and fastened instead against the angle of his jaw and neck, and then she could not seem to let go of him. He did not respond to her or encourage her and finally he thrust her off.

She sat against a wooden strut, a cook-pan digging in her back, hugging her knees.

'Why not?' she said. 'I'm not a virgin if that bothers you.'

'No?' he said, with a gentle, slightly insulting emphasis.

'Three times is all,' she flared. 'And one time of those was rape.'

'Really.'

She was not sure if she were angry or shamed. She picked the cook-pan off the wall and slung it at him. He caught it neatly and laid it aside.

She pushed back her hair and said, 'You're impotent.'

'If you like.'

It amazed her. Once someone had called one of the Crow boys impotent and he had knocked most of their teeth down their throat. She could imagine Belmort's reaction to such a taunt, or Billy's, or any man's.

With dignity, forgetting where she was, she stood, and cracked her head against an upper strut, sending several items clattering down. The shock triggered a fresh outcry.

'I'm ugly,' she said.' You don't want me because I'm ugly.'

'You're clutter,' he said, 'that's why I don't want you.'

She angled herself to get out of the wagon and he said: 'And it doesn't bother you that I killed a man?'

'No.'

'And like your virginity, Eva, he wasn't the first. There are more I intend to kill.'

'I don't care!' she shouted furiously.

She took hold of the canvas flaps, and was impaled immediately by a man's voice shouting also, but down from above, hoarse, slurred and menacing.

'Come out, come out you bastard!'

For one instant the noise seemed totally unrelated to that piece of life she was living in. Then she knew it – Flint bellowing from the woods. And still more crazily, from beyond the fall, Billy yelling: 'Come on, you murdering rat! There are four of us! And let the girl out first!'

He was already at the closed opening, behind her.

'Who are they, do you know?'

'Men from the village – Billy and his brother—'

'Come out!' Billy shouted. 'There are four of us I tell you!'

'It's not true,' Eva hissed. 'Only the two of them. They'd say that to try and scare you.'

More than anything it astonished her how silently they had followed, those loud clods with their stumbling feet.

A shot barked across the clearing, but very wide.

Outside the horse suddenly neighed and plunged. Simultaneously the wagon rocked and tilted under the impact. A sudden unexpected glare burst open the vaulted ceiling, struts snapping, the canvas turning black and golden in it, curling and splitting while the wagon filled with smoke.

Billy's laugh sounded raucously. Flint must have thrown some burning thing down on them.

'Out,' the murderer said.

He thrust her. She fell down on the moss against the wheel. Next moment he was crouched beside her. He had attempted to save nothing from the fire.

Another shot whined by and split a branch beyond the rocks. There was a soft explosion in the wagon – probably the box of coals – and white-hot needles showered on Eva's back. She jumped up coughing and screaming, and ran headlong out of the smoke waving her arms.

'Billy!' she wailed, rushing towards the fall.

She wondered in a confused way if the murderer would shoot her in the back, but then, he would be glad to see her go.

'Come on, Evie, I've got you covered!' Billy called triumphantly.

Her eyes were watering so much she could hardly see. She slithered into the basin of wild-flowers, and fell directly against Billy's chest.

'Did the bugger hurt you? Murdering sod,' Billy mumbled anxiously. He leaned his rifle on a rock while he steadied her. 'Knew we'd catch him up with that horrible dog – can't half run it can't. And ran off as soon as we let it go. Where'd he get you, Eva?'

'In the marsh,' Eva said.

'Some of 'em said you'd taken off with him on purpose, but I knew better,' Billy avowed.

Eva widened her eyes over Billy's shoulder, and screamed again.

Billy flung round, slithered and fell on the wet flower pods.

'What – what—' he pleaded in alarm.

She caught the rifle up and swung it at his head with all

her strength. It was the second time she had hit him. This
blow sounded final. Billy gave a grunt and flopped under
the fall, while Eva, skidding in the wet, fell on top of him,
the rifle flying out of her hands. She struggled up again,
thinking the water soaking her was blood, and ran back
towards the wagon.

The smoke came in gusts and between them she could
make him out by the wheel which was now on fire. The
horse was nowhere to be seen.

'Eva!'

Her head jerked up, and she spotted Flint lying flat a
little way along above the fall, staring at her, startled out of
caution.

'Get down, you silly bitch!'

'Billy's dead!' she shrieked at him.

Flint froze like something enchanted into stone.

'You,' he said.

She saw him lifting out of his trance, saw the black eyes of
the gun turning to fix her with their empty yet purposeful
glare. Yet the shot sounded too close and too quickly. She
staggered, touching at herself in a frenzy, to feel where she
had been hit.

In the middle of this she saw Flint, a great black bird, fly
up from the leafless thicket above the water's mouth and
plummet over and down without a single movement of his
outspread wings.

He came out of the smoke, marked black from it, the rifle
smoking in his hands as if it had caught alight. She felt
bewildered; for a moment she did not know him. Behind
him the wheel burst in a spangled shower, and the wagon
fell dismally sideways in a last bloom of flame.

Four

Eva did not know where they were going in this trackless land. But they had moved fast – for it was probable, was it not, that Ben would come looking for his boys, perhaps not alone, following the trail of Jezubal's dog.

From the wagon there had been nothing to salvage. Food, blankets, water, ammunition, books, even the second rifle with its ivory panels, all had vanished in the conflagration. Only her clothes had survived on the steaming rocks, black with smoke. And the horse, neighing in terror, had fled. All losses were presumably acceptable. *He* did not mention them. For two days, as they walked through the woodland into incredibly ever-increasing silence, he mentioned nothing at all. She no longer attempted to breach his reticence, but she found a name for him. The outer quiet got into her ears and deafened them, into her mind and emptied it of almost all thought, into her mouth and around her tongue so that it seemed she might never speak again, but for the name. And perhaps oddly, he answered to it. She called him Steel.

The ground was soggy, wound round from dead tree to dead tree with a cat's-cradle of creeper. Stabthorn had grown up in the husks of trunks and burst out on the branches above like a fantastic miraculous leafing. Everything was damp. Moisture clouded in the air. Yet there was no water anywhere to drink, and dank foggy thirst settled on Eva. On the third day the thirst and the silence and his name were one thing.

She began to blame him, her eyes fixed on his back. If she fell down would Steel stop? Would Steel even notice?

Then, in the soup-thick, ruby-red dusk, she realized he had stopped ahead of her in the distance, and was lifting aside a creeper, and uprooting thorns, reminding her vaguely of a large, thin, black and white dog trying to bury something. Soon he called to her however, amazing her at his powers of speech, and pointed down into a rocky hole, and showed her something. Water in a channel.

It had an iron tang. She thought it might poison her after all, and perhaps this was part of some obscure plan of his to get rid of her. At last he pulled her roughly away and drank too, leaning down to drink like a cat, swiftly but sparingly. She sat on her heels dazedly, watching. He fascinated her. She had trudged, scrambled, woven and stumbled and swayed fascinated behind him for two days.

'Where we going,' she managed to whisper, '*Steel?*'

'A small settlement. Not far now.'

'I don't want to leave the water,' she said, 'I don't want to.'

She lay down and went to sleep in the fern (convinced that he would be gone when she woke), with a fatalistic miserable defiance.

But in fact she woke to find that he was lifting her up on

to the back of something warm and muscular and animate. She cried out and clutched wildly at it, and found it was the horse.

Steel was leading it by its bridle, walking, the horse walking unembarrassedly behind as if they had never been parted. She began to concentrate on holding on. There was moonlight, and stars scattered across the sky, and the world still silent.

He had said before that soon there would be a settlement and he would leave her there. She did not believe it because the thought absurdly terrified her, while at the same time seeming inevitable. She should never have gone into the wagon when he slept and embraced him with such obvious intention. Why she had, mystified her. There was nothing to the act of lust that she had ever found worth repetition.

She stared about her at the dark, the dead branches, the emerald moon; at last, saturated with the vestiges of damned night, she stared at him.

'You won't leave me,' she said to herself, and to him. She was a witch and could get what she wanted by mere impulse. 'Never,' she said. He did not turn or seem to hear. But she imagined her words soaking into his skull, seeping into his brain and body.

Somewhere in the dark, they slept. Later, as the black was draining from the sky, they rode out of the night and the dead woods together, and below lay a great cauldron which seethed and glittered like a tip of splintered glass drenched in petrol and set ablaze. The sun spat down into it, and back spat fires of every colour and shade of colour. A blizzard, it pierced into Eva's eyes. She put her hands over them.

Incredibly, Steel did not turn aside. The jolting ride continued down into the blizzard-light.

Soon she put down her hands. The way was all twisting rock, but the surface of the rock was oddly bright, as if under crystal. They emerged abruptly on a black rim of shore, the cauldron boiling out from it.

'Prisms,' Eva said.

He led the horse along the rim, and Eva gazed at the oily glitter pulsing on its pebbles, spreading in an octagonal patchwork quilt to its rainbow ends. He did not look at it at all. But then, he was a travelling man. He had seen these things before. She pushed up her hair with her hands, defiant, searched her mind for a strange book word, and said with a weird, stilted grace: 'Steel is indifferent to beauty and walks blasé by.'

After a moment he laughed; it was a pleasing sound. Eva laughed too, parroting him.

'It's not particularly beautiful, Eva. It used to be water,' he said.

A large, darkly crystal rock suddenly melted itself up from their path and leaped away among the other rocks – a black armoured toad-thing with thick-lensed eyes.

'Metamorphosis,' Eva said. 'Rock into toad.'

The horse kicked a little with its feet, disliking armoured reptiles disguised as landscape.

Eva turned her head and saw an irregular outline tacked on to the outline of the shore a mile or so ahead. Woolly wisps of smoke clambered up from it to form a bronze chord on the white hard sky. The settlement.

He will leave me here.

She kept her eyes fixed on the settlement as if it were someone she hated. It, not they, came nearer and nearer. There was a high wall, and haphazard dwellings crowded inside like animals in a pen. A cindery path crackled up from the prism-place to the gate, which was in fact some ancient wooden door. It had that impenetrable look of defensively-closed places. Perhaps it would not be opened when they came to it.

But when they were still several yards away the shut wooden mouth creaked, and was pulled wide as if by magic. No one came out, and beyond the wall the earth street ran deserted between its leaning sheds and tin-roof houses. Eva experienced an awful conviction that she had somehow reversed herself in time and geography and was about to re-enter Foulmarsh.

'I won't,' she said.

'What won't you, Eva?' Steel asked her, not turning. 'You talk to yourself all the time. But then, the horse likes it.'

The horse's hooves split bits and pieces on the path. The door was a yard and a half away, obscenely yawning and open. A man came suddenly round and out of the door. He stood across the entrance, and Eva thought this must be Belmort. She had an abrupt, bright vision of Belmort levelling a gun at Steel, and the gun speaking its last word, silencing all others, and Eva shrieked. But it was the first thud of a hammer falling somewhere in the sky, and the man in the entrance was not Belmort. Not, in fact, any kind of man at all.

'Shut up,' Steel said to her calmly.

The apparition might have been carved from some kind

of white rock or plaster, and then animated, his skin was so thick and smooth and colourless. He had neither nose nor mouth – a small slit did apparently for both. His eyes were creased in raised lids top and bottom, like a lizard's, and he was hairless. Out of his face-slit came a thin whistling note.

Out of the gate now, shouldering past, came a second man in a chequered shirt and black trousers, and a fur coat reaching to his calves. He had hair in plenty, this one; only his eyes were strange, colourless and round.

'Back so soon?' he said to Steel as they came level. 'Get another one done then?'

'Yes.'

'And your wagon?'

'Some trouble in the woods,' Steel said noncommittally.

'And the trouble is up behind you now,' said the man gazing, grinning, at Eva. 'My name is Willowby,' he said to her, as if she had asked him. 'This is a mutant settlement. I too am a mutant. Does it bother you?'

Eva looked at Steel but his face was expressionless, his eyes intent on the man called Willowby. She looked up at the sky instead.

Willowby laughed.

'I see you learn his non-speaking jargon, this man on whose fine strong horse you sit your little backside. Well, if you're looking for shelter, what payment, with your wagon gone?'

'You can have the fine strong horse you mentioned,' Steel said.

'Horse? Did I mention a horse? Well, did I?' Turning to the alabaster mutant he struck him on the arm. The mutant whistled, eyes flickering nervously. 'Whitey says I never

52

mentioned a horse. However. If you like. I hate to turn away a traveller.'

Willowby strolled ahead through the open gate, and Steel followed, leading the horse. A bald woman was sitting outside a shack, paring pale, scale-skinned carrots, while a bald child sat between her knees playing with a piece of bone. When it stared up at them the woman cuffed it. No one else was in sight. At the far end of the street a small fire was burning, and beyond the fire a leather canopy stood lopsidedly on poles.

'Lunch time,' Willowby murmured. 'Come and partake thereof. Your skinny girl looks as if she could do with some food in her. And other things.'

'Where's Derry?' Steel said.

'Oh, it was Derry you wanted. Well, I'm sorry to disappoint you. But while you've been doing your work, Derry unfortunately found work of his own. Derry had charge of a lot of things, but Derry was a moronic freak. This place needs a man to look after it. Mutated I may be, but I have my wits about me. Eh, Whitey?'

Whitey, walking stolidly after the horse, whistled.

'See what it is to govern a democracy? Wonderful thing, the popular assent of the people.' Willowby spat. 'How long are you staying?'

'I'll trade the horse for any dried food you can spare. Not longer than that.'

Eva's thoughts turned inwards into an abrupt horror.

Willowby, sauntering down the street, clothed in his furs and his dark feudal mastery. How many extra packets of food would Steel get in trade for a woman as well as a horse?

They reached the fire, skirted it, and came to the leather awning, the entrance to a kind of large, ungainly tent. Animal skins were hung up patchily inside, smelling. Brocaded curtain stuff and thick nylon rugs from the ancient boxes of forgotten homes lent spills of uncomplementary colour. Willowby walked inside and sat himself in a large armchair. A pile of books lay beside it, of a pasted together variety, some open, all revealing female nakedness in varying stages.

Eva slid from the horse. She felt weak and miserable, and as if in answer to her mood the arched sky overhead seemed to be darkening and bruising, and green flames edged the fire.

'Whitey,' Willowby said, 'go tell your woman to bring the food out. Tell her I have guests. Come in and sit,' he added to Steel.

Steel left the horse to stand by the fire, flicking its ears, its long head bowed as if in an enervation similar to Eva's. She kissed its face in mawkish despair.

'You, too, blondie. You can come and sit by me.'

Eva looked at Steel but he had sat down on one of the tent's rug heaps. Eva marched into the tent and sat herself on the arm of Willowby's chair. As she did so she caught sight of one of the naked ladies – oddly elongated, yellow-haired, apparently absurdly standing in a shell. She leaned across Willowby to look at it, fascinated by its perverse beauty and the quality of the skin which looked like a kind of marble under water.

'Like art, do you?' Willowby inquired. 'That's a reproduction of a Bottikelli. They're all reproductions. I like to

54

get a look at a normal woman from time to time, even a paper one.'

Eva sat up again, and his hand went round her waist. She would not look at his egg-white eyes.

'Don't mind, do you?' Willowby inquired of Steel. 'Host's privilege. Yes, I like my Bottikelli there. I should say you're a bit like her.'

'If I stay,' Eva said in a dull voice, 'will you let me keep the horse?'

Willowby's mouth opened slightly. Then he shut it and used it to smile with.

'What do you want a horse for? You won't have time for a horse.'

As his hand moved up her side Eva kept her eyes on the tent-opening. The sky was cabbage-colour now, and the fire was yellow. Between the two a crouched-over woman shape was wheeling a bumping tea trolley of eroded chrome. Things jumped and rattled as the squeaking wheels hit unevenness, and gravy slopped.

'Enter, slave,' Willowby said. 'No caviare?' The woman grunted. 'And for the *guests*, slave.'

The woman crept about in the dark, handing a bowl to Steel first, then to Eva. Eva began to eat, very neatly, her back rod-straight. When Steel rode away, she would let this creature have her. Then she would take the horse and escape into the outer wild. She would fly for several days and nights at the end of which one of the many forms of death the wild had to offer would overtake her. Or better than this, she would hang herself from a fancy tassel in the tent, and let them all, Steel included, find her. If he had already gone she would leave a small note pinned to her dress that, on pain of her haunting, she was somehow to be packaged and crated and sent after him. She saw him open the cask and see her there, mostly skeleton, only one whole, accusing thin hand lying limp as a bell-flower on her breast. Unlike Willowby's hand which was there now, far from limp, or flowerlike.

Eva looked at Steel and looked away. He was watching Willowby.

A pink flare blanched the world. The fire was purple and the sky magenta. With a sound of cymbals and ice gongs several tons of hailstones cascaded into the street. Tin roofs tintinnabulated, the leather awning shuddered uneasily, the fire sizzled and spat. The horse shook its head and danced briefly. Where the stones lit they struck flame in skidding trails. Steel got up and went out, took the horse by its bridle and led it away behind the tent, presumably to shelter.

Willowby reached for a slice of bread.

'How did you pick up with that one?' he inquired.

'On a road,' Eva said. She thought she might begin to cry.

'He kills men,' Willowby said slyly. 'Know that, did you? The Angel of Death. Not that he speaks much about it, but there you are.'

'Why?' Eva said.

'Why? Why not, you might say. A sort of hobby, probably. His kind used to put up shelves in days gone by.'

'*You* kill men,' Eva hazarded. 'You killed Derry.'

'Oh, smart little bit, aren't you? Derry fell down a rock fall and banged his head. You'll do all right here. You're a proper woman, I can see that. You be nice to me and you'll do very well, thank you. These cretins here, I've got them in line. A hierarchy, you might say, has been established. Wonder how you'd look standing on a shell like that Bottikelli lady?'

'She'd fall down and break her neck,' Steel said from the awning. 'The same as Derry did when you pushed him off the rocks.'

Behind him the sky was now black and the fire lemon with silver steam. His hair was dark from moisture, and he was very slightly smiling.

Was this how his invisible face had looked when he shot Jezubal? Would he now shoot Willowby? To promote the situation, Eva leaned on Willowby and said: 'He didn't break his neck, he banged his head.'

'I heard,' Steel answered.

Willowby grinned.

'Well, and so what, pray?' He tried to push Eva off. She clung to him like a leech.

'Nice Willowby,' Eva crooned, stroking his hair. 'Didn't you say I'd do well if I stayed with you?'

'Damn you, get off me. Whitey!' Willowby roared out. 'Whitey! Whitey!'

Only the black sky replied with a snag of broken-egg-shell light.

Eva felt Steel lift her aside, and looked away squeamishly, but there was no sound of a shot. She looked up and saw Willowby crumpling over the side of his chair, mouth open and eyes shut.

'You didn't kill him,' she said in surprise.

Steel tore down a length of curtaining and dropped into it

57

the slices of bread and a package of dried meat from the trolley.

'The bottle has water in it. Put the stopper in and bring it.'

She did as he told her; as she turned he caught her arm. In the flickering of the coloured sky she could only just make out his face.

'I didn't intend to leave you here,' he said, 'even in Derry's time. It was another place I had in mind.'

'You would have let him have me,' she said.

'Would I?'

Lightning lit the naked woman in the book, then blotted her out.

A shadow stood in the awning mouth.

'He's all yours,' Steel said.

Whitey's hairless face worked briefly, then he came past them with long powerful strides. Steel turned her away from the dark out into the luminous storm-light.

The horse waited under the overhang of a barn roof, eating out of a stolen food bag. The hail raged around them, stinging and burning. Steel lifted Eva on to the horse and swung up behind her. A movement began which confused her – the blazing violence in the air, the running horse, his body behind hers and his arms snaked around her to take the reins, and all the changing colours of the sky.

She did not know why they had ridden away so fast. Surely there would be no pursuit? The lake and the settlement were gone. High rubbery fern brushed her knees.

Some time ago the hail had given way to a curtain of rain which in turn gave way to a drizzle that seemed gently to be washing down the jade green clouds on top of them. Everything dripped and rippled with water. The horse's fur ran like a furry river. Every hair on her head, every inch of clothing lay like liquid on her skin, too much part of the rain to be anything but strangely pleasant. She could see no horizon.

'Who was Derry?' she asked, leaning back on him in the rain.

'No one.'

'Yes. Someone.'

He did not answer.

As she leaned on him in the liquid greenness, the horse moving slowly beneath them, it seemed quite predictable and usual that he should begin to stroke her wet hair, and when his mouth came to her neck it seemed only a warmer and more purposeful rain. She felt it unutterably soothing, this embrace of human and element, but she said: 'Why now? Why do you want me now?'

'Be quiet,' he said.

'Tell me, why now?' she reiterated stubbornly, sleepily, as he slid from the horse and pulled her slipping after him into the wash of the tall and glittering fern.

'Why not now?' he said, and stopped her interrogation with his mouth.

She might never have been with any man, this was so different. And yet he did not really seem to be a man, at least not separated from herself nor she from him, and beyond this oneness, both of them one with the waterworld that moved and swam its eddying currents through the veins of their bodies. She seemed to be sinking backwards into a fathomless and primaeval sea, as she drowned in him and drowned him with her. A scuttled galleon, a mermaid. She did not want to survive beyond it.

She opened her eyes and saw him looking at her through the shimmering rain. She observed him lazily, thoughtfully, the water falling soft into her eyes.

'You have a lovely face,' he said, as if telling her of someone else.

'Will you leave me here now?' she asked.

'No.'

'At the next settlement?'

'No.'

'I love you, Steel,' she said drowsily, 'I love you, love you. You're all part of the rain.'

She felt him leaving her and did not like it. He stood up.

'Where are we going?' she asked him.

'That way.'

'That way,' she echoed dreamily.

He put her on the horse and began to lead it. She touched the parcel of bread and meat and it collapsed soggily. She looked about her at the world through half-shuttered eyes. Presently she leaned forward to one of the horse's ears.

'That way,' she told it.

Five

In the South lay hills.

They were tall and many-shaped, black as pitch, empty.

In the night she would sit and stare at him for hours as he slept. She would kiss his face without waking him, crooning to him, obsessed, as various skies flickered and faded.

She was running through the dark. The dark twittered and pulsed and occasionally screamed. She did not know where she was running, or from what, but she was afraid. She clutched at the brambles and spear leaves, and stumbled against a wall. She stared upwards and upwards. There was no way over. The wall towered into the black-ink sky. No door for her to crawl through. No escape.

Eva turned and stared back the way she had come, looking now, and only now, to see what it was she had run from, what it was from which she could no longer get away.

Over all the surface of the noisy, unharmonious night lay a uniform blackness except for one distant travelling bright speck. It spun towards her. She thought it was the moon fallen through space with the sole purpose of destroying Eva Belmort. Then she made out a face mouthing and grimacing, with three black eyes.

She woke. It was dawn, the sky a swirling, dreary orange.

'Jezubal,' she said. She turned and snarled into his ear as he lay asleep: 'Your dream, not mine.' And in a sudden dislike she raked his hand with her claws and spat at him: 'Why did you kill that man?'

As she had seen before he came awake at once, without a shock. He turned on his side and looked at her.

'Which man?'

'Jezubal!' she screamed. 'Why? Why?'

'Forget Jezubal.'

'I dreamed of him. His face ran after me.'

Steel smiled. Eva slapped him across the mouth.

'Now I'll dream of him again and again. One night he'll catch me.'

He turned once more on to his back. He looked up at the sky.

'Murder is a woman in labour,' he said. 'One killing gives birth to another. Once begun, it can't be stopped.'

Eva beat her fists on the ground.

'Was it because he was a god-speaker?' she shouted at him.

'No.'

'Then why? Then *why*?'

'Eva, be quiet,' he said. He shut his eyes.

She stared at his face which in the murky yet glaring light seemed suddenly old. The cheeks had fallen in, the eyes were sockets. It was a skull.

She could not bear this pain; she had never seen such indications of torture and despair. From him more than from any other it was terrifying. It frightened her much more than the dream.

'I won't ask. I didn't ask. I won't ever ask again.'

She scrabbled for his hand in the dust. She licked at the scratches she had made on it, trying to heal them with her tongue. He pulled the hand away and sat up.

A freezing flame scattered itself abruptly over her bowed shoulders. It had begun to snow.

The lemon flakes fell, and they were moving through the bitter-tasting storm. The cold seemed to eat the marrow from her soul, while devourers ate upwards from her feet into her guts. She shut her eyes and cried with cold on the horse's back. She cried and cried, and her tears froze on her face and she thought her face had become a mask of glass shattering and reforming with each convulsion.

Through the snow loomed a wall. She thought of the dream and wept more violently. They passed through the wall by ruined gates of incredible lattice work, buckling under yellow fringes. The fog enveloped her.

An awful pain began in her feet, moments or years later.

'Don't!' she screamed.

Someone was lifting her down and her whole glass body was cracking, splintering. Soon she would lie in a million smashed fragments on the ground.

A woman's voice said: 'For Chrissake, lovey. He's downstairs.'

'Where, where...' Eva thrust off the blankets among which she seemed to be lying. A thin strong female hand arrested her struggles.

'Down below, I said. Quite safe. They're not murdering him, you know.'

Eva lay back, her eyes darting. She made out now a long

room with low rafters, a tiny window covered over by board. A stove gave heat, knitting every shadow together with dull highlights into one amorphous, shifting, red togetherness. Out of that the woman's fox mask, pale, slant-eyed, smiled, smiled at her with a slovenly kindness and amusement the stove lit wrongly into a hint of grinning malice.

'Where am I?'

'Just an old house. We live here, me and my friend Suzanne. Been here about a month. With the men.' The Fox smiled and pushed at her shiny hair. 'Take a lot of looking after, they do. But it's better then field-work, isn't it?'

'Is it?'

'You should know. Your brother is he?'

'No.'

Eva made a move to get up; the Fox said: 'Me and Suzanne brought you straight up here to the warm. You were crying with the cold. That snow. It comes on so sudden.'

Eva felt giddy and leaned on the wall.

'What's he doing downstairs?'

'Doesn't he tell you, then?' The Fox now definitely looked malicious. She put her paws on her hips and swaggered. 'Like to keep you in the dark, don't they?' she said, receiving Eva into the despised sisterhood. She perambulated lazily about the room. 'He's selling your horse. To get you a ride on the train.'

Eva combed her hair with her fingers. Reaching a side table, the Fox picked up a plastic comb and tossed it to her. Eva looked at it. She thought of the horse being sold, and tears ran out of her eyes. She had liked the horse. She had equated herself with the horse.

'There, there,' the Fox said rather angrily. She came and combed Eva's hair roughly so that Eva snatched away. .

'He's punishing me,' Eva muttered. 'He'll always punish me.'

'Do you think Jack would let him on the train without a fare of some kind?'

'A train,' Eva said. She did not know what a train was. She went to the boarded-up window and knocked some of the flimsy boarding flying so she could look out. The Fox let out a yell.

'You little cow – just leave that alone!'

Eva resolutely stared out, half-cringing before the expected blow which never arrived. She heard the fox-woman curse, and swing about, then the sound of her shoes – sharp from high heels – going down some stairway beyond the door. Outside the window lay crusts of snow and a branchless, dead tree. Bisected by this, the black hills, untouched by the local storm, were close at hand now.

Abruptly Eva turned and ran from the room, down a passage. Turning a corner she saw a huge firelit room below. Echoes not voices came from it. A stairway plunged down to its once-polished floor. Near the bottom she missed her footing and fell several steps in silent confusion. The floor received her body, inert with surprise, and resorting to an ancient memory of itself, spun her across a yard or so of its length to bring her up against the leg of an ornate table. The leg was half rotten, the table-top responded to her arrival with an earthquake. Jugs of liquor clanked and slopped, cards skidded over her in a dog-eared bird-fluttery shower, men cursed colourfully. Eva lay on her back and stared at them all in frightened disdain – about six men in rough jackets, dark beards and one a dirty ginger, their faces turned down to her, scowling. Someone laughed. A big ginger hand hauled her up. She glimpsed the Fox and Suzanne at a fireplace like a picture of bar-girls she had once seen in another book. Suzanne was streakily henna-ed from some traveller's store, and the lids of her eyes were astonishingly green.

'Whoops-a-daisy,' commented Suzanne.

The ginger hand let Eva go. The room being empty of Steel, she stalked across it between two fireplaces. Through a big-arched doorway into a sort of hall with a black and white chessboard floor. A door hung half open; beyond it she saw a high-walled yard. She went to the door and stared out at a post-snow world of frozen things, all similar under their lemon icing, only here and there a black moving shape beneath the low sky. The clouds had done their worst and then clotted. Eva shivered and stared. Silhouetted, Steel stood talking to a stocky little man. Another man examined the hooves and teeth of the horse. It kept very still, its head bowed. Eva bowed her head.

'She's sound enough,' a voice said. 'Going over the Slag? Oiltown is it you're after? Right. We run there tonight. Phil, give this little lady some nosh and put her with the others. Better than a bicycle, innit?'

Eva leaned on the doorpost and cried. She was vaguely aware of the horse being led away somewhere. Steel and the other man were coming back across the yard. Crying, Eva walked out into the snow and deliberately past them.

'There goes your girl,' the man said to Steel. 'If you want

the lats, love, it's the wooden lean-to round the corner.'

Steel said nothing.

Eva looked down and saw the pansy-dark bruises of hoof-pocks. She followed them. After a moment or so she came across blunt-nosed Phil edging the horse into a box, one of a line of twenty down the two sides of the L-shaped courtyard.

'Your feller went back with Jacko,' Phil said.

Eva stared at him with hate in her eyes.

'Well, it ain't my fault, girlie, whatever it is.'

Eva thrust by him and into the box beside the horse. There was clean, faintly aromatic straw on the ground and clean water in a pan, some horse-food in another. Eva stroked the horse's face. Its large luminous eyes were running a little with the cold as if it also wept.

Phil gawped at them a moment, then elaborately shrugged, turned and went off, whistling untunefully. Presently the horse lay down to sleep and Eva lay down beside it.

Perhaps an hour passed. The muddied sky burst with raspberry rifts. Eva dozed, frozen and distraught, her head on the horse's flank.

'Eva, come out,' Steel's voice said eventually over the box-door.

'No,' she said.

But he came in and picked her up rustling out of the straw, and she was too stiff with cold to struggle. At the side door of the looming tumble-down mansion house he put her on her feet and she walked ahead of him till she reached one of the fires. The Fox and Suzanne were drinking and laughing with their men. Suzanne detached herself at once and came over bringing a mug of drink which she held out to Steel invitingly.

Steel accepted the mug, drank, and handed it back to her. She smiled into his eyes, ignoring Eva ostentatiously.

'Come play cards,' the ginger man called out.

Steel turned and walked to the table. He sat down.

Eva had seen card games before. They made no sense to her, she could not keep her mind on them. Once Belmort had tried to teach her, but she had been sullen and stupid and he cuffed her repeatedly on the head.

'We're playing for coin,' she heard Jack say. 'What you going to put down? How about the girlie?'

There was some laughter.

'You'll need coin in Oiltown,' said Jack grinning. 'I doubt if you'll need a doxie.'

'Try this,' Steel said. He unslung the rifle from his back and held it out across the table. It was faintly bewildering to Eva to watch him do this. It had seemed a part of him, another arm, or perhaps a tentacle direct from his brain.

'Not bad,' the ginger man said.

'Ivory,' said Jacko. 'You got bullets to go with it?'

'Yes,' Steel said. 'Not that you'll need them.'

Jacko chuckled.

'There's a brave spirit for the table, then. Deal away, Phil.'

Eva wandered along the table length watching the play with the cards. On their faded faces glared coloured symbols without meaning. Their backs and fronts were stained with burns from home-rolled fags, rings of leaf-tea and beer, ancient and unremembered food. She put her hands on the dark cloth of Steel's shoulders and stood in that way a moment, letting the Fox and Suzanne see her, letting them know her slender rights, which even in their slenderness were more than theirs, to his attractive body and tormented soul. After a moment she took away her hands and walked upstairs to the room with the stove.

Beyond the board she had broken the sky was going to early twilight, changing the colour of the snow.

The stove burnt low. Above the table from which had come the plastic comb was hung an oval mirror, a little chipped around the outside, otherwise intact. Eva went to it and stared inwards. Something out of a legend or ghost story stared back at her, with cotton flock hair. The large eyes were indigo, almost entirely pupil. Muffled laughter and cursing sounded in spasms from the room below.

A fragile moon lanterned the snow when they emerged from the house. Soon it lay behind them, something from an old romance concerning highway-men, one side gutted by an equally old and now meaningless fire. Wooden shacks and lean-tos peopled the ruinous park. Horses neighed from the stable court and Eva shut her ears. It was bitterly cold, but she had acquired a shapeless coat and a pair of boots and carried her shoes in a stitched canvas bag. These articles had been thrust on her by a grumbling Suzanne – part of Steel's luck apparently at the card table. He had cleaned them out of money, and the ivory animal of death hung still across his back.

They came down a bank to a long wooden pier, over it a wooden awning. A board swung lankly, memorial to a name the elements had long since scrubbed off. Two or three small groups waited on the pier, stamping their feet, carrying things. To the right, under the bank, a black yawning tunnel.

When the noise first came, Eva thought she imagined it. Once she realized she did not, a variety of terrors took hold of her. At the height of the noise and her fear bursts of black steam erupted from the tunnel. Eva clutched at Steel.

No one else appeared dismayed as the tunnel gave birth to a black and shining monster, its single tall nostril belching smoke, two glaring eyes set above its whirring feet. Screeching and thudding internally it came to a halt. A smell of heat, oil and unimaginable fumes blew into Eva's face. She allowed Steel to propel her up the pier.

'Is it alive?' she whispered, not looking at it.

'No.'

Behind the black shining body hung a kind of brief tail. Doors – there was no mistaking them for anything else – were being opened. People were fearlessly clambering inside the belly. Eva shuddered and laughed at this lunacy.

'Up you come, girlie.'

Eva looked up and saw the ginger man standing in the monster's brain, lit up hellishly by some flame inside. Steel lifted her, she found steps under her feet, the ginger man took her hands and waltzed her up beside him. A furnace roared. The ginger man slammed a door on it.

'Not afraid, are you? Only an old train. Old pleasure train in a museum she used to be, part of Lord Buggerall's estate up there. Now we run her on the tracks to Oiltown.' He smiled at her and patted her shoulder. 'Ought to know better than to scare the child,' he reprimanded Steel, who had joined them. 'Ring the bell?'

Eva reached up and rang it; it had a brazen sound. The

ginger man began a series of complicated actions. Abruptly the train lurched and Eva screamed. Next moment a great rolling movement possessed the giant. It sidled and rocked and roared and squeaked. It charged forward, ponderously, and the bank of trees, the wooden pier, the heap of the mansion drew away. Eva clung to the side and stared down, then up into the black, moon-licked hills ahead. Fear left her suddenly and surprisingly. She became one with the noise and motion, and was excited by it.

'Odd country between here and the town,' said the ginger man at his levers. 'That's why we run her at night.'

Hot, sparkling snow and smoke wind blew back her hair as she stood in the brain of the dragon.

Soon she forgot who she was, who she was with. She was a dragon-thought. Phil came and made them a thick, sweet, hot drink with the help of the furnace. The ginger man, strangely paternal and fond, stroked her hair. Steel sat immobile, his eyes half shut. But she rode the night, divorced from all of them. It was perhaps one of the best pieces of her life.

Eva and a black serpent rattling down the empty tracks between the empty hills. The serpent disgorging its cherry-coloured steam, glaring its white-hot eyes, a thing of fire and pitch, of sound and smell, a great, bursting, anachronistic noise in the deadly silent night. She caught its madness, and lit by its coal-consuming belly, she swung the raucous bell, and the ginger man laughed and cursed her good-naturedly. Once she thought she saw figures running down from the slag-black heights, shouting, waving. But they were only ghosts, weird people, or stranded washing . . .

The train thundered on across the fields of night.

Towards dawn she slumped exhausted beside Steel. She fell into a vampire sleep.

The slowing of great lungs, the creaking of robot joints, woke her. There was no longer snow, nor emptiness, nor movement. A nightmare landscape rose above the tracks, a muddy pathway leading up to clusters of skeleton trees, behind those, gaping, deserted, tall blocks of buildings. A little smoke rose in the distance, token of life. An aura of dilapidation and distress hung in the air.

They left the train. As they walked away up the mud, she looked back at it again and again. It grew gradually smaller and fainter as distance and mist and brambles intervened. No longer a dragon but a toy. The ginger man had vanished. A few other passengers straggled up the scarp. If this was Oiltown she did not like it. And she felt she had lost her soul on the train, as bygone travellers had lost their umbrellas.

Six

A mass of streets, cracked tar reminiscent of the old highway at Foulmarsh, overlooked by the tall towers with glass knocked out and walls knocked down. Waste ground and rubbish dumps lay between. They were alone now, the other passengers having slunk off in various directions, walking a broad street of giant nettles and ruins. An old kettle lay rusting into cheerful colour in the choked-up gutter. Steel unslung the rifle, carrying it lightly. A shadow flickered around a brick wall. The rifle swung a little way and the shadow vanished.

There was a smell – not of the rottenness or sickness which traders always spoke of as clinging to the towns – but of ghost things, a *past*. Eva stayed close to Steel.

A dead tree creaked and fell over abruptly on her left. She thought of Jom and how she had pulled him clear of just such a tree, and distaste overtook her.

'Why did we come here?' she demanded.

'I have to meet someone here,' he said.

Two huge rats came bounding out of a tenement, across the road, twittering hilariously, and flew into an identical tenement on the other side.

There was a newish stone and earth wall up ahead at the end of the wide street. Presumably it marked the lived-in quarter of Oiltown.

'Will you buy me a dress?' Eva asked, anxious to be bribed for her disappointed bewilderment, and for the loss of the horse.

'If you want one.'

'A silk dress? From a shop? With money?'

'Yes, and yes, and yes,'

A piece of white stuff lay in the nettles, with lettering on it.

'Glowkestor Aive,' Eva deciphered. A trader had taught her to read a little long ago, but her method was imperfect.

'Gloster,' Steel said.

Eva yawned.

'And high-heeled shoes,' she murmured.

The wall was very high, and colourless moss grew down it. Curlicues of barbed wire marked broken patches. Just inside a hole without barbed wire sat a man asleep in a blanket, sentry or possible tramp, and a dog on a chain fixed to a post. The dog growled, but the man failed to wake.

What must have been a park at one time laid out a ragged carpet of blight-burnt grass, a dry fountain in a cess-pit of a pool, uprooted flower beds grown wild with weeds, a wrecked greenhouse whose floral inhabitants had long since succumbed to the outraged elements. Beyond that, a road flanked by trees and wasteground, beyond these an area of compact building, still apparently intact. Here it was that the rising smoke had its origin.

The sense of desolation ended with the park. Living took place beyond the blank concrete backs of the walls now confronting them. The rusty fire-escapes, the eyeless windows were merely a mask on the probably snarling and eager face behind them. And noises rose with the smoke. Clatter, rattle, hum and whirr of known and unknown expressions of being.

They crossed the road and made down a narrow alley between the concrete. Emerging, the amazing sprawl of Oiltown lay before them, in all its glory.

A backdrop of ochre fog, revealing fragments of dwellings and smoke, pushed up a foreground of huge levels of concrete; ramparts, steps, rusted iron and immobile escalators where thorns clawed the wind. The levels craned up and up into angles, swirled round each other, and disappeared, it was like a stage set, a colossal castle. And it was in use. A cart was grinding down the nearest level loaded up with a heap of red and white vegetables and drawn by a couple of very small not-quite-horses missing ears and tails, a man walking behind. On other levels, other, to Eva, theatrical actions were in progress. Dogs yelped and ran, and small boys hollered, a pail of slops was emptied into a drain which apparently managed to deal with them, a girl was setting up a wooden stall and fixing a stove while the wind tormented her hair.

Eva flinched. Nearby, a great expanse of shiny dark had ignited with white lightning. She stared into a full plate-glass window, whole and gleaming, saw piles of skins and multi-coloured cloth lit up as if by the static flame of fifty lamps. She turned and turned as other windows followed suit, revealing pottery jars, an elaborate scene of sea-shells and drapery, glass bottles and tins, wax-faced women who stood incredibly still in red and green dresses. She stumbled on stairs, looking everywhere but at her feet. One of the wax women, this time real, appeared on the street and went past them. The heels of her shoes were three and a half inches high, and silver toenails poked through. She wore black and a scarlet belt, and bright earrings that might have been either diamonds or glass. She eyed Steel with painted eyes and left a smell of scent.

There was a man with one arm managing to sweep along interesting filth and coloured scraps of paper. Eva inspected the pile with her toe as Steel handed the man a medium sized copper coin.

'Who pays you?'

'That's Jallow, mate, does that. He's the boss around Oiltown.'

'Where do I find him?'

'Up King's Walk, that level there, turn left at the corner, over the bridge – can't miss it, tobacconist's sign underneath. Biggest ash-emporium this side of nowhere. Probably see a fellow on the door. Take you up.'

King's Walk was separate from but tenuously linked to the Levels by a scatter of small shops – one obviously a whore-house. A painted sign was nailed on the bridge: JALLOW it said. Below, a narrow river ran black and viscous, but neither bad-smelling nor choked with rubbish. Weeds encroached on either bank. Some sort of bird was walking at the edge, flightless and scaled.

Wasteland converted into fields of blowing weed and seed-tobacco and wooden sheds marked Jallow's hold, a glass-fronted shop of three storeys. The windows were lined with red velvet and displayed ancient dummy cigarette cartons, ornate pipes.

'Stay here,' Steel said.

He left her in the doorway and went in. A bell tinkled rather incongruously at his entry. Through the red velvet and cartons, she made him out talking to a man, then the man taking him through and up shadowy stairs.

Eva lost interest in the doorway. She went to the bridge top and looked over. After a while steps sounded behind her, and a male voice said: 'Jallow keeps the river clean.'

Eva did not turn. 'Why?' she asked promptly.

The man laughed.

'Why? Because There'd be sickness and god-knows-what coming off of it if he didn't.'

The man leaned beside her now. He was good-looking in the traditional dark and stocky way, about twenty not looking thirty – but they lasted longer in the towns, it was well known.

'Come on the train, did you? Enjoy it?' Eva looked sideways at him, and moved away along the bridge. The man followed. 'Your brother, he's an odd one. Walks straight in and asks to see the boss. No cap in hand, mind you.' He paused, following Eva. 'Jallow keeps the streets clear of muck, too,' he said. 'And see them,' pointing to the shops and brothel, 'Jallow runs them an' all. The Levels, too. I'm Jallow's man. You're nothing in Oiltown unless you're Jallow's man.'

'What does that make me then?' Eva snapped.

The man laughed. 'Oh, witty too, eh?'

Eva leaned on the bridge. The man's attention was

irritating but nevertheless made her alert and self-aware. She hoped Steel would come out and find him pestering her.

'Do you want something?' she asked.

'Wouldn't mind. Depends what you're giving away.'

'Why don't you try that place? I'm sure they've got what you need.'

'Oh, you're nasty as well, are you?' The man produced a home-rolled from his pocket, lit it with a flint, drew, and offered it to Eva. It had the sweet scent of weed tobacco. She took it but did not draw. 'Well, make up your bloody little mind, then. Expensive that stuff is.'

Eva flipped the cigarette over the bridge. Her courtier was speechless momentarily. Then reserves of invective burst their dykes. He grabbed her shoulder. While he was shouting at her, a lacy curtain was pulled aside upstairs in the whore-house, and pale, veneer-rouged faces stared down. A door shut farther up, and Steel came down the street. At first it seemed to Eva he would simply walk past them, but as he was going by, he somehow disengaged the hand from Eva's shoulder, and gave the man a casual shove that sent him staggering against the bridge.

'Look here, you sod,' the man yelled, but they were halfway down the bridge and he gave no pursuit. Perhaps Jallow did not allow brawling on duty.

Steel said nothing.

They came off the bridge and past the entrance to the Levels, making on down to the fog which got thinner as they went into it.

This was the living room of Oiltown. A maze of roads and lanes leading into dumps of derelict machinery, sheds and woodpiles, abrupt clusters of houses and apartment blocks still in good repair, around which mutated and manumissioned gardens careered in mad abandon. Coloured cloth hung in the windows and chimneys puffed. Gigantic survivals of dandelions, sunflowers, roses and their deviants stood in ominous ranks, flapping their paper leaves.

'Are you going to work for Jallow?' Eva asked.

'Yes.'

Someone had scratched JALLOW on a wall.

'Where are we going?'

'I get the use of a hovel with the job.'

A waste of more-or-less dead grass, dotted with rusting metal, tumbling away behind to an overgrown railway line. On the horizon stood up a solitary thin house with a pointed roof and narrow mostly-boarded-up windows. The sort of dwelling Eva as a child had seen witches living in in the paste-books. A petrified tree stood a few yards to the right of it, covered with glossy black creeper, leaning importunately sideways.

The door was sound. On the inside of it were three solid bolts. A passage with two fair-sized rooms lurking on one side of it led ultimately to a kitchen at the back. Stairs led up to a couple more rooms, a cupboard posing as a room, and the remains of a bathroom. Obviously the house had been in recent use, and, under the auspices of Jallow, presumably, was in astonishing order. There were oilcloth and tatty rugs on the floors, fireplaces uncovered from their ancient bricking-up for present day usage, coloured sackcloth at the one upstairs window still with cracked glass in it. Chairs and shelved closets abounded. There was a

double mattress in each of the two upstairs rooms, one on a
brass bedstead, but no blankets. There was a stove in the
kitchen which, however, needed attention and cleaning
out. A sink unit still stood, impotent, but the fittings in the
bathroom had been massacred, all save the white enamelled
bath.

A bolster ambushed Eva in a cupboard.

The rifle had vanished from Steel's back. She did not know
where he had hidden it. He went out, telling her to bolt the
door. She forgot. When she heard him come back she
wandered down from the upper regions of the house. He
had brought food back with him, a heap of blankets,
various odds and ends.

He fixed the stove.

'There's a bucket there,' he said. 'Go and get some
water.'

'Where from?'

'There's a pump at the back of the house.'

She obeyed dreamily. When the stove was going, she
heated water in a large iron pan, slopped it upstairs and into
the bath. When the bath was at fairly high tide and still
warm, she undressed and lay in it for half an hour, and then
fell asleep in it.

She woke up standing in cold water because Steel
was drying her. She leaned over him and kissed him
lasciviously, while the drying motions continued. Presently
he carried her into the other room.

An early red twilight fell across the shadows, polishing
the brass bedstead, as she traced the line of his jaw with her
tongue, delicately.

'Why did you have me after the lake village?'

'Inevitability caught me up.'

Disliking him yet enraptured by his flesh, combining dual needs, she bit his neck.

'You never wanted me before?'

'Yes.'

Surprised, she looked in his face, but he and she were both submerged by the crimson sun-doom of the glass window.

'Not in the wagon,' she said.

'Yes,' he said.

She put her head on his shoulder; she said: 'You hate to want me.'

There was silence. The window darkened slowly.

'Don't analyse me, Eva,' he eventually said.

The word brought on a curious mind picture. She seemed to be probing inside his skull, dissecting the bright metal plates and electric coilings of his brain with a needle sharp as pain. Her tongue slid to her missing tooth. She fell uncertainly asleep.

In the morning, unthinking, unremembering, she was disturbed when he left her. He was going to be the field-guard of Jallow up river, and he took the rifle. After her initial displeasure, she luxuriated among the blankets and soft blue sheets, dozing and eating apples, moving only once or twice to fetch further provisions, or to visit the latrine outside in the cold-cracked yard. Late in the afternoon a frenzy of action took hold of her. She fled to bathe and comb herself. Downstairs, she rummaged in cartons, peeled small potatoes, fried eggs. She astonished herself. It never occurred to her that he would not arrive at the exact moment that the meal was ready. He did. She was proud of her efforts.

'You see, I'm not a slut,' she said.

She scoured and washed the dishes at the pump while he laid a fire in the grate of one of the rooms. They sat before it into the dark, watching the flames change colour. He had somehow acquired a book in the Levels, and read to her out of it. Sometimes the fabulous words lost her, but she listened in a fascinated dream. His voice hypnotised her; she was happy.

So the first day went very well.

The second day, intimations reached her that days spent alone like this would be dismal for her. She had always been enclosed by people, had not liked it, but had grown accustomed. With him she had been neither alone nor crowded. Now he was absent, she felt bewildered, devitalized. Only the moments preceding his return had any meaning for her. And gradually, as the days passed, she could not recognize even these. He would come back and find her still asleep, or half-drowned in the bath with her white hair dripping on the floor, or wandering lost from room to room. It did not seem to trouble him. Yet, as she withdrew further and further into her own abysmal world, yearning to be pulled out of it again, he withdrew also into his, and seemed to suffer no pangs. Now his remoteness hurt her. She questioned him endlessly and got no answers. She sensed him waiting and demanded: 'Who are you waiting for?'

He would not say.

Frustrated and tortured, it was an indication of her

worship of him, her misunderstanding, her blindness, that it never occurred to her she might also be torturing him.

On the sixth day she woke up in the bed at noon, and saw a large woman leaning on the brass rail at its foot.

Eva was terrified. He had told her to bolt the door. She never did.

'What do you want?' she screamed at the woman, intention nastily paramount, identity superfluous.

'I've been cleaning up below. Didn't hear me, eh? Jallow sent me; he knows what you young girls are, and he likes his property kept nice, does Jallow.'

'What do you want in here?'

'Same thing. Needn't trouble you, though. Stay put. I've seen enough girls in bed in my time. Used to do the Establishment reception on King's Walk. And one or two other tart-shops around Oiltown.'

She was a well-lined, tough, swaggering, masculine creature, with a mass of frizzed black hair. She wore scarlet trousers and a male shirt, carried a dustpan and brushes, rags and polish, and grinned at Eva lecherously.

'Don't worry, duckie,' she said, aiming a swipe at the rug with a brush. 'My intentions are strictly honourable. I've had a word with your feller. My name's Angela, if you're asking. You can call me Angel.'

She wet-ragged the lino, beat the rug to a pulp, polished the brass bedstead, skinned the window alive, accompanying herself alternately with raucous song and incredible oaths.

Angel remained two explosive hours in all. Having scoured the bath and left it for dead, she brought Eva a mug of leaf-tea.

'Get lonely don't you?' she said. 'Never mind. Your feller gets his first pay tonight. Bring you something back, I expect. Staying long? Heard he only contracted for fourteen days.'

'I don't know,' Eva said bitterly. 'He never tells me anything.'

'Rubbish,' said Angel briskly, dismissing all whining with an anecdote concerning the brothel, at which she laughed uproariously and which Eva did not understand. 'Well, I'm off now. Live in Chancery Road if you need anything, anybody'll tell you where. Mind you get up and get that man of yours some food.' She clattered down the stairs and was gone.

Listlessly, in the dusk Eva rose to obey her. Injunction was purpose, of a kind.

And when Steel came back, he handed her, as Angel had predicted, a package. His working for Jallow now turned out advantageous for Eva. She found herself the proud possessor of a town dress, a kind of silky stuff, though not actually silk, black as if crows had dyed it. When she put it on she startled herself. She strutted before him, and he smiled, but his eyes were blank as blue slate. He had never seemed more distant.

In the second week Angel came and forced her out of bed to aid in the cleaning. Used to being bullied, Eva obeyed, and achieved, inevitably, little. Angel also took her walking through the smoky streets, and up and down the tumbled terraces of a derelict park. From the summit of the park Eva could see a distant ruin and rambling, grass-grown place of stones.

'Graveyard,' said Angel. 'Jallow still likes proper burial observed. Got my plot all bought up. Reckon they'll pop an angel on the top of it?'

Angel lived with a short, mousy ex-prostitute called Pat. They passed Pat on the street and Pat glared insipidly.

'Evil-minded cow,' Angel remarked, linking arms (Pat paled) with Eva.

When they reached the house a man was crouched on the ground by the door. He was little and thin, with a small puckered face.

'What the hell do you want?' Angel trumpeted at him. 'This isn't the whore-store, matey. See a girl on her own and they all come sniffing.'

'Blond man,' the croucher said sadly, his eyes watering at Angel's impact. 'I'm looking for a blond man. Very white hair. They told me I'd find him here.'

Some indefinable presage caught hold of Eva.

She hissed at Angel: 'He's here to make trouble.'

'Oh, is he?' Angel moved for the man and hauled him up by the scruff. 'Listen, Mr Trouble-maker, I'd take yourself off if I was you. Jallow doesn't like rats running round his town after his fellers.'

She put the man down and he cringed, looked piteously at Eva, and went off into the turgid dusk.

Eva ran at once into the house, slammed the door, and, for the first time, bolted it, leaving Angel slightly surprised outside.

When Steel returned she stared at him from the upper window before she would let him in. Then she rebolted the door. She made a great clatter with plates, a great splash of pump water. The fire seemed impossibly quiet and she poked it repeatedly into huge bursts of sparks and noise. She made him read to her, but all the while she was listening for another sound. When a sudden downpour of rain hit the house and spilled through cracks and crannies on to the floor, and fizzed malevolently in the grate, relief surged over her and made her tremble.

But the storm was brief. In the tinkling, trickling aftermath, a few soft blows came like muffled paws against the door.

Steel got up.

'No!' Eva cried out.

He turned and looked at her.

'It – could be anyone—' she whispered.

'It could be.' He walked across the room and out. In the passage she caught him, struggling to hold him back from his destiny. He put her aside, unbolted the door, and let in, dripping and shivering, the little man.

Steel led him to the fire, where he stood steaming. He produced a tiny flask from within his jacket and sipped from it, then offered it to Steel. Steel shook his head. The little man glanced nervously at Eva, and away.

She would have killed him if she could, before he could speak, but her hands were empty. She almost ran to fetch the potato knife, but already it was too late.

'I found one for you,' the little man said, his mournful eyes on his wet boots.

'Where?'

'A place farther south. I got a map.'

Steel took the damp paper and put it away without looking at it.

In turn he drew a folded envelope – of the kind still haunting the reclaimed stationers of Oiltown – from inside his belt, and handed it to the man.

The man looked near to weeping through his steam.

He moved, retracing his puddles across the room, past Eva, along the passage.

'Goodbye,' he said politely.

He opened the door, and went out, closing it behind him.

Steel stood with his back to her, facing the fire.

'How long before you go?' she asked dully.

'I finish with Jallow in three days. One day after that to collect stores together. I've already got a wagon put by.'

'What will I live on when you've gone? Do I have to work in the brothel?'

'I left some money with Angel,' he said, as if he were not really listening.

'It won't be enough.'

'It's enough.'

It came to her dimly that he must have played them at cards here too, to have amassed this extra wealth. Or stolen. Or owned it before. She knew nothing about him.

'But when it's gone? What then?'

'I'll be back by then.'

'You may not *come* back.' Panic seized her at her own words. She flew to him and clutched at his arms and began to wail, staring up into his blind and expressionless face. 'You may die – they may kill you! Don't leave me!' she shrieked. She clung to him, trying to dwarf him, imprison him by her flesh and her terror.

Abruptly he came alive. He held her off with a sudden terrible violence. The iron pressure of his hands holding her away from him squeezed all the blood out of her wrists. His face was white, all dead, frozen paleness, the skin pulled back on the skull bones, his mouth like a long scratch made in snow, his eyes seeing her now with an appalling, recognizing hatred.

'I do as I please.' She did not know who was shouting at her because she had never heard Steel shout. She looked round wildly for the newcomer, and he shook her almost stupid. 'I do what I want, Eva. I leave in four days. When I've finished, I'll come back.' He thrust her away and walked out into the passage and up the stairs.

She crouched by the fire, weeping in dazed horror.

She did not dare to go near him. She curled by the embers on the rug. When she woke the light pierced in pencil lines through the slits in the boarded-up window. There was no movement in the house.

She thought he had already left her, but he came back that night. She lay in the bed and would not go down. Whenever she heard him move below, her pulses stirred half in fear half in hope. He did not come up. At daybreak he was gone. The next day was the same. The third day she lay in a stupor of despair. She had not bothered to eat though she had drunk a little water. She was very cold and miserable, and had some vague plan of starving herself, or simply dying off the cuff.

When he came up the stairs she shut her eyes and would not open them. He stood in the doorway and said: 'I brought you something to eat.'

'I don't want it.'

He came and sat down beside her on the bed and she

turned from him scornfully, aware of a triumph over him, aware too that he would still abandon her.

'Eva,' he said.

'Why bother? I shall probably starve anyway, when you've gone. Or someone will break in.'

'Jallow's law exists here,' he said, 'and Angel will look after you. Eat this soup.'

'No.'

He put down the bowl.

'I'll be gone tomorrow.'

She opened her eyes then, and stared at him in sick fright.

'You said the day after.'

'I've got all I need together already.'

'Take me with you,' she said, her eyes swimming with tears so that she could hardly see him even though she had opened them.

'No.'

'You won't come back.'

He took her face between his hands.

'Yes.'

'If they don't kill you, you'll leave me anyway. You don't want me. You're always telling me even when you don't say it.'

'I'll come back. I have to come back to you.'

But she pushed from his grasp, and he left her.

Later it was dark. She sat up and pulled a blanket round her. As she got out of bed, she put her foot into the bowl of cold soup.

He was sitting by the unlit grate in the lamplight, cleaning the ivory killing beast with slow, meticulous care.

She leaned at the door watching him. After a time, without turning, he said: 'Come and sit down.'

She did as he said, flopped limply in a chair, staring at his hands on the rifle. It was freezing but she fell asleep.

She woke in the dawn. The house was silent, empty. There were blankets tucked around her, and something had been put into her hand. A pair of crow-black, high-heeled shoes, the kind of shoes the elegant women of Oiltown wore on their clicking feet.

She held them to her and sobbed.

When Angel came into the house half an hour later, Eva was still curled in the chair, clinging to the shoes and sobbing.

Seven

Angel saved her life in small ways. She saved it by coming into the house and creating noise, by dragging Eva up and frequently out. She pulled her hither and thither, drummed into her instructions on the use of Steel's money on the Levels, in the market and around the kitchen gardens and hen coops of the back doubles. She polished, broomed and bellowed, cracked eggs, snapped celery, de-bowelled onions, and tore cabbages limb from limb. She hammered up shelves and harried Eva into buying useful purchases to fill them. Eva periodically came out of her dull and desolate dream to catch herself in the act of washing, scrubbing, peeling, or simply being herded from place to place like a tragic sheep. Angel reminded her of Steel's imminent return. (Angel had also taken to calling him by this name, catching it from Eva.) Why else would he have left rent on the house so she could live in it? Eva had to be ready, had to get things comfortable to welcome him home.

'Damn him!' Eva cried. 'I don't want him back.' And wept.

Night was worst. Angel offered her a mattress in Chancery Road, with no strings attached, despite what that soppy mare of a Pat might say. But Eva would not go. The house, for all its imprisonment and isolated silence, had become a security, a memory of Steel's lost presence. Yet alone, she had refound her horror of the dark. She would huddle beneath the sheets afraid even to cry, for fear some night-demon would hear and guess her proximity. She began to leave candles burning by the bed. Angel abhorred the practice.

'You'll wake up one morning burned alive,' she said.

Eva, naturally, took no notice of this miraculous possibility.

But after two weeks, Eva emerged back into herself. She began to look around. It occurred to her she had – at least for the present – a secure tenancy, money, Angel's faintly criminal support, and the freedom of Oiltown. She became bright, taut, eager and alert. When Angel spoke of Steel she became bitter and malignant.

'He left me. That's up to him. He may come back. He may not. If he does, *I* may not be here.'

She learned to paint her eyes and darken her lashes, and walked out on her own. One day flouncing by the generator-run electric glory of the Level shop windows, she met Jallow's man from the Ash Emporium whose weed-fag she had thrown over the bridge. This, however, did not seem to stand in the way of his affection. His name was Johnny.

'All on your own, I hear,' he said. 'Tell you what. I'll take you out tonight.'

Inside the window something caught Eva's eye.

'I might let you. Buy me that and I will.'

Johnny stared at her, then laughed.

'Big deal. And what do I get out of it?'

Eva looked at him with large eyes, and began to walk on. He got her arm, pulled her into the shop and bought her the dress. It was indigo velveteen, and cost him several handfuls of silver coin.

She wore it in the evening when they sat in the Jallow Arms, eating rather burnt food and drinking quantities of resurrected wine.

Eva, getting tight, enjoyed her rôle of User of Men. She had picked up a few of her ideas from Angel's uncensored talk; mostly she was taking obscure revenge on Steel. But later, as Johnny mauled her on the way back to the house she began to foresee not only her distaste, but compelled fulfilment of her side of the bargain. Drink had made him trusting. At the door Eva whispered: 'Just a minute,' slipped inside and suddenly slammed it before he realized what was afoot. It was difficult to bolt it under his onslaught. Even the pail of water she tipped on him from above did not dispel his furious presence. She cowered in her bolt-hole until at last the abuse and blows died away across the wasteland. No doubt he would have broken down the barrier except for his respect for Jallow's property.

Contrasuggestively she cried all through her candle-bright night for Steel.

In the morning Angel came.

'Someone's written a message on your door,' she remarked.

She went to erase it with a knife, and returned, scowling.

'Nice dress over that chair.'

'Isn't it?' said Eva nervously.

'Act like a tart and you'll get treated like a tart,' Angel

said. 'And you'd make a bloody-awful rotten tart. I'll go and see the feller before he does you in. Who is it?'

Eva told her. Angel looked disgusted. Presumably she performed her task with vigour and suitable threats, however, for there were no further repercussions.

Once Johnny passed Eva on the street and said something under his breath. That was all.

For a long while after this incident Angel seemed determined never to let Eva out of her sight. She arrived even more unspeakably early, ran Eva off her feet, and dumped her back in the house at night, exhausted. Simply in retaliation, Eva made herself more and more glamorous, smiled at men on the Levels, swung her hips and generally misbehaved. Nevertheless, if a proposition seemed likely, she would take Angel's arm. Johnny's violence had scared her thoroughly.

It was in the market that she saw Steel.

Angel was trying to educate her buying instincts at a vegetable stall, and Eva was staring moodily in all directions but the right one, when something white snagged the corner of her eye. She turned and saw a male figure moving between the stalls with a cap of ice-white hair on his head. Shocked, she clutched at Angel.

'Steel! It's Steel!'

Angel scanned the crowd.

'No.'

'I saw him. There!' cried Eva.

Angel looked.

'Not tall enough,' she observed. 'Just because he's white doesn't make him Steel.'

But Eva was not convinced. She dreamed of Steel in similar situations – herself pushing frantically through a crowd after him, while he – unseeing or uncaring – moved steadily away. So she thrust forward after the streak of whiteness, losing it occasionally, but determined, with panic, dread and elation, to catch up.

She caught up.

She came out suddenly into a less crowded avenue between mounds of fruit, and saw him, standing about three yards away from her. It was not Steel. Even with his back turned, she could no longer doubt it. He was a lot shorter than Steel, thin and straight, and his hair – which was Steel's hair – grew down on to his shoulders and separated there into glistening white-metal strands. He idled among the stalls, and she followed him in a kind of anger at his deception. After a moment he turned and retraced his steps. She got a glimpse of his face then, and saw furiously that he had a look of Steel there too – though perhaps only she could spot it, having studied Steel's every look and angle with all the dedication of obsession. He looked placid and casual, his hands hooked in his belt. As he passed a stall, he abruptly, gracefully, slid a fruit from its place into his jacket. She barely noticed it. She really only saw it in retrospect. Admiring now, Eva continued to watch. He absorbed fruit, candy bars and rolls, willy-nilly, as he passed the busy stalls. Then his eyes slipped level with her face. Without any hesitation he strolled up to her.

'Go on then, love. Just muck it up, won't you?'

He was precisely her own height. It was ridiculous. Neither half an inch shorter nor half an inch taller. She stared straight into a pair of long, wide eyes, the irises strongly marked, yet a clear almost invisible blue, like pale aquamarines.

'I mean,' he said. 'I do want them all to *know* I'm nicking their stuff.'

Totally at a loss, feeling in some curious way that she was looking in a mirror, Eva felt Angel arrive at her elbow.

'Might have guessed it'd be you,' said Angel, observing the thief with terrifying contempt as she literally belittled him. 'Go on, bugger off.'

'And your charming self,' he said, bowing elegantly.

Angel spun Eva around and walked them both away.

Eva glanced back but he was already out of sight.

'Let him get on with it,' Angel said.

'Who is he?'

'Nothing,' said Angel.

They reached King's Walk and stepped off the Levels, Angel holding the full vegetable bag. Eva saw nothing for half a mile. Walking down the back roads, between the ranks of monstrous fifteen foot sunflowers, he appeared at her side almost out of nothing and fell into their pace of walking as if this meeting were prearranged. He was eating an apple.

'Didn't I tell you?' growled Angel.

'Ignore me,' he said. He put something into Eva's hand before she realized, and strolled off between two houses where weeds and briars covered his retreat.

Eva opened her hand and saw a gold pendant shaped like a leaf, on a thin gold chain.

'You can't wear it, of course,' snarled Angel. 'He's stolen it somewhere or other. Probably Sam's place.'

Eva fastened the pendant round her neck.

In a dark, boarded-up doorway farther up the street, someone whistled.

Angel hurried her as if they were pursued by devils.

The day after, Pat became ill, and Angel was tired-eyed and bothered.

'Shan't be in tomorrow. Got to wait in for that idiot of a doctor. Mind you don't get into mischief.'

A sense of freedom and slight madness settled on Eva. Angel was a rock in the storm, but a day without Angel's wardership seemed bright with possibility. In the end, though, she wasted it, lying in bed, staring through the pages of two books she had chosen for herself with a kind of illusory Steel at her side. But somehow none of the words made sense without his voice to speak them. She made little progress, and felt like a closed room with no one to open its doors and windows. In the dark chill she lit the stove and crouched by it on a rug, eating raw carrot and a half-cooked potato. Loneliness came and sat beside her. Reverting to her childhood, she tried to conjure up Lydia, but certain adult evaluations got in the way of fantasy. She took the lamp and hurried between close-pressing darkness, upstairs. She lifted the gold leaf and chain off a shelf and dangled them before her eyes. Angel had told her never to wear them on the Levels for fear one of Sam's boys should see it and report the theft as Eva's. She wondered for the first time why he had given it to her.

The next morning she woke late and Angel had not come.

It was steamily hot, the seasons changing as always now abruptly and impetuously from day to day instead of subtly, thoughtfully, month by month, as in the past. Eva stared from the window. The petrified tree stood like a sentinel guarding the house. Beyond, the wasteland wavered with moist haze, the lines of houses and distant levels absorbed into the overall glare of the mustard-yellow sky.

Soon she was out, unchallenged by the tree, tottering slightly on stones in her still-not-quite-certain high heels.

She idled among the neons, stared in at dresses and costume jewelry, ate an egg-roll on the street, and drank red, sour wine at a cafe, occasionally whistled at or joggled, her mind locked all the time in a weird stimulated expectancy. What stimulated her, what she expected, she neither knew nor guessed at. Whatever it was, however, it did not materialize. As the copper sun sank pulling slabs of orange sky down after it, Eva's brightness dimmed. Her feet hurt from clopping about like a horse and from standing still to be admired in various poses. She tore off her shoes and walked barefoot through Oiltown Levels. By the Jallow Arms she paused. Gaudy light spilled out, and Eva peered in.

He was standing at the bar counter drinking a dark fluid from a tumbler. A girl leaned lightly on him, a good head taller than he was. She was vividly pretty, plucked, powdered, perfumed, curled and painted. She swayed over and kissed him.

Eva turned away and leaned on the wall feeling faintly shocked at seeing him, Steel's manifestation, twined with a towering doll. A sharp small pain took place in her metaphorical heart.

What am I doing here? What am I waiting for? He'll never come back.

'What you charging, love?' inquired a pleased male voice.

'Drop off,' snarled Eva.

She turned and ran from the Levels, down the bridge, through the back roads to the house, where she bolted the door with bitterness and took spite to bed with her.

For a day and a half she languished in the house in the heat mostly in the bath. Finally she picked her way across the rusted iron dumps, skirted the creeper-choked basin of the railway tracks, and came to Chancery Road. Angel's house, once a semi-detached, was by now detached completely.

A dressing-gowned Pat, apparently in part recovered from her ailment, spotted Eva through the large front window between stalactites of glass.

'What you want?' Pat squealed menacingly. 'Angel ain't here. Gone to get my medicine.'

'Are you better?' Eva asked with sycophantic politeness.

'I was till I seen your rotten little face. Clear off! Coming round here with your soppy daft ways.'

Eva squinted through the glass, judged Pat too weak to attack, and said something formless but vile.

Going back up the road past amok hedges, Eva stared at clump after clump of black tubular thistles and finally at an only partly rusty scythe being swung through their juicy trunks. On the end of the scythe straightened up a pale hero, panting slightly but still managing to mutter something, and then whistle some snatch of tune. His long hair lay in sweat-stranded white streaks on his forehead, like indiscriminate swipes of paint. A torn blue shirt flapped round him without buttons, revealing a hard, thin, smooth male chest. A knife was sheathed in his belt, she could see the metal grip. His eyes, glazed by toil, heat and boredom, did not register Eva. She went closer and saw a girl coiled up on an empty water barrel around the hedge, staring in apparent fascination at his back, in the act of giggling at what he had said. Eva stopped in her tracks, feeling invisible. She was in clear view yet neither of them saw her.

He let go the scythe and moved across the brown turf to lean by the barrel. It was a different girl, but she swayed and kissed him similarly. Behind them trembled a rickety house with its door open.

'I rolled you a fag,' said the girl, extending her offering.

He kissed her hand, eliciting further giggling, and lit up.

Eva looked the girl up and down, assessing her as a pallid barrier between herself and a filled evening. Jealousy took hold of her because this idiot held his attention. No thought of Johnny deterred her, she felt neither out of her depth nor trespassing as she picked through the felled thistles, crossed the turf, took the fag delicately from his fingers, and drew on it.

The girl looked non-plussed – unlike the tall doll, this one was probably smaller than Eva.

'I hope I'm not interrupting,' Eva said, handing him back the cigarette.

He looked momentarily uncertain. His curious eyes flicked from Eva to the girl on the barrel, and back.

'No,' he said finally, 'I'm just knocking off, anyhow.'

He looked up at the girl.

'Can your mum let me have the money now?' he asked

her gently. She slid off the barrel and marched in through the open door and then out again, her lip trembling. Apparently aware of his responsibility, he looked both apologetic and ruthless as he kissed her cheek, pocketed three copper coins and one small shiny grey one, and turned out on to the road with Eva.

For several minutes he did not speak to her nor she to him. She felt vaguely uneasy that they might collide with a disapproving Angel hurrying home with Pat's medicine. Late afternoon mulled everything apricot and then burned it. Turning out of Chancery Road into a litter of side streets, he sloughed the tattered shirt by a pump and doused himself and it with the lukewarm water, thereafter carrying the shirt in one hand, his skin incredible in the swooning light. She wondered if he had done this deliberately to entice her, for there was something peculiarly attractive about his body.

'Why did you give me that gold chain?' she demanded.

'Thought you'd look nice in it,' he said promptly.

'But you stole it.'

'Possibly.'

'And if I wear it, Sam's boys will think it was me.'

'That is the kind of metaphysical problem that will prove the downfall of this age,' he remarked.

Eva fell silent.

'Besides,' he said, 'I didn't, actually. I don't in fact give nicked goods to girls for the very reason you just brought up. Who said I did?'

'Angel.'

'Oh, well, that lesbian tyrannosaurus-lady has had her knife in me for months. Some obscure matter of her Pat once giving me a meal when I flaked out over their garden fence. Quite genuine it was, but Angel begs to differ.'

He took coins from his pockets and appeared to be calculating.

'Have to be the Swan, I'm afraid. I'm not up to the Jallow Arms,' he said. 'Eva,' he added, as if tasting her name on his tongue.

'How do you know I'm called Eva?'

'I asked around.'

'Why?' she cried.

He lowered his eyes, grinned, looked at her and said: 'Because I fancied you. Why d'you think?'

Besieged by his personality in the grubby street, Eva stared at her newly-painted toenails.

'I came here with a man,' she said.

'The usual huge jealous brute with a shotgun and axe, I presume?'

Eva foundered on this brief derision.

'He had to go away, but he's coming back,' she muttered, and saw him look at her with a flicker of pity for her naivety she was meant to see.

She narrowed her eyes and started to walk away but he caught her up in an instant and took her arm.

'That's between you and him. Come with me if you want to, don't if you don't. I'm well-behaved and harmless, but it's up to you entirely.'

Already the first traces of brassy sunset. She thought of the empty house. She thought of Steel, who seemed now so far off from her, she could never be near him again.

'All right,' she said, uneasily.

He let go of her arm and they walked as before, separate,

himself softly whistling the snatch of melancholy tune through all the sky-drowned dereliction.

The Swan was small, dark and dingy, full of people, noise and drink fumes. It depressed her to begin with. She said to herself: *Why am I here? How did I get here?*

She was not certain what she drank, but after a time there was a decided lift in her outlook.

'This is a rotten place,' he said then. 'Humble apologies. I suppose your smashing feller took you somewhere better.' He sounded only faintly sarcastic, mostly miserable.

Eva felt a curious twinge of compassion but, also sensing victory, murmured: 'You were in the Jallow Arms yesterday.'

'True,' he said. 'Consider it a mistake well paid for.'

Altogether he said very little, apparently intimidated either by the place or her company. He rose first, and outside the sky was clear, and neoned with marigolds passing for stars and a copper-pot moon. They walked along the Levels among amorous couples and an old woman searching for fag-ends.

'This must have been very boring,' he said.

'Oh no,' chirruped Eva.

He glanced at her and smiled.

'You're tight, and it colours your perceptions. Wait till tomorrow.'

She noticed he was shivering in the cold and had an impulse to protect him from it with one or both of her arms. Oddly she resisted the impulse.

There was another long gap in conversation. As they turned off the bridge, he added: 'You make me uneasy.

That's the reason I can't talk to you, if you're wondering at all.'

'Why?'

He shook his head at her. They went through the back streets.

'Because you're extraordinary,' he said at last, 'that's why.'

'Really? And how many others?' asked Eva, snapping to attention.

'No, no. Just you. It's not a line.'

They reached the house.

Under the moonlight he looked forlorn, drained, outcast. She longed to embrace him without scruple, lead him inside, and people the house with his strangely satisfying presence. But she did not. She opened the door and stood in front of it, as if barring the way.

'Well, I'd better go,' he said.

'Yes. You better had.'

So he went, walking away up the wasteland, his shoulders bowed against the cold, or some defeat which stemmed from, yet ultimately had absolutely nothing to do with, her.

She refused to watch him out of sight. But she forgot to bolt the door.

EVA AND
SAIL

Eight

In the night the weather turned itself like a feather before the wind. In the morning a lemon rind of snow had sealed its fate on Oiltown.

Eva would not get up, she was so cold, but sometime during the day she managed to lug the stove upstairs and lit it there. The snowlight depressed her, reminding her of the sold horse, and Steel – Steel drinking from Suzanne's mug, walking in the yard, Steel at the card table, Steel waiting for the dragon-train.

She had been with another Steel the night before, she remembered.

She found, when she thought of Steel, she could hardly recall his face at all, and saw instead this other one washed over by the sunset, dark from the murky Swan, gold-bleached under the stars.

And yet, the few hours she had spent with him had lost their impetus – the snow seemed softly to have wrenched away any possible meaning in them. They were an episode, already historical, with no possibility of growth or extension. She did not even know where he had gone to in the maze of Oiltown. As with Steel, she might have dreamed him.

Days dragged by.

Angel came with a bag of groceries. She made leaf-tea, not smiling, though Pat was apparently better. Finally she glared at Eva and said: 'I hear you were out on the Levels with that Sail.'

'Who?' Eva asked. In a way, constantly aware of him as if of something abstract, she had forgotten that he was an animate personality. It was the first time she had heard his name. He had not told her.

'Sail,' growled Angel. 'Like on a ship. That pint-sized thief you've taken up with. One day Jallow'll catch him round the stalls and have the hide off him.'

'I didn't know his name,' said Eva.

'And what else didn't you know? Do you think your feller's going to like it when he comes back and finds you with *that*? He lays half the bleeding silly cows in Oiltown.'

'He hasn't laid me,' said Eva primly.

'Then keep it that way.'

Later, bundled by Angel in coat and boots, and accompanied by Angel, Eva trudged and slipped through the streets to get wood for the fire and stove. Black huddled shapes moved similarly all round them. Eva looked in every direction without even realizing she did so. Returning with a sense of disappointment she did not really understand why.

Incarcerated, Eva grew soured, and her thoughts evil.

She felt at certain times fifty years old or more, wizened and dried out as she had felt in Foulmarsh. Once a young woman passed over the wasteland with a tiny child in tow of indeterminate sex. It was done up in yellow woolly things, its minute feet and hands like little woolly paws. An irrational desire possessed Eva to produce personally a replica, small, woolly, squeaky-voiced. She imagined it lumbering lightly through the house and asking questions. She had never liked children much; the snotty-nosed, dirty, squealing brats of the settlement were a symbol of her own infantile victimization. Now, a maternal instinct quickened painfully as toothache. Instantly after, she remembered Steel in the dead woods, saying, casual: 'Very likely you're barren—' thereby denying her, at one blow, the oldest and most unique magic of her sex. She picked up and flung across the room certain breakable objects. She cursed him with a filthy and primitive intent. He had left her. And left her with nothing. It no longer mattered what became of him, only what he had done to her.

He had been gone five weeks and five days in all. But time had stretched itself thin and far. It might have been a year.

She found a poem loose in the back of one of her books, several pages of it, some torn, some with great chunks missing – as if a previous reader, possessed by literary frenzy, had tried to eat it. It was a kind of fairy tale – a woman shut up by a spell, finally breaking free to follow some man with an unpronounceable name. What became of her Eva never knew, for the last part had been lost (or eaten entire). Yet when she broke free of her prison, the mirror also cracked from side to side, though this time it was a mirror of brittle ice underfoot.

She walked on the Levels in her shapeless coat, conscious of being stripped by it of all glamour. She looked in doorways and down alleyways. She was alarmed at herself, nevertheless intent. Finally she came to the market. Hot dogs were in the process of creation in a miracle of blue steam. Rime sparkled over Jallow's generator-run hothouse tomatoes and among the hanged corpses of chickens.

She came to a tea stall, and he was sitting on a bench with his hands round a tea mug, and with yet another woman leaning up against him, though this one was a crone. Eva's heart jumped as if she had been frightened out of her wits by a ghoul in a cellar, though she had been expecting him with every step, turn of her head. He had not seen her but the crone saw her and grinned, displaying a pure darkness only despoiled stubbornly in places by a tooth or two. She nudged at Sail.

'One of your girl friends wants you, darlin'.'

'You're my girl friend, Annie,' said Sail. He looked up. His face was white with the cold but seemed to whiten further and his eyes flinched. Eva felt encouraged, then wondered if she had imagined it.

'Hallo, Eva,' he said. He coughed and looked away. The crone put up a claw-like mitt and stroked his hair.

'He's not well,' she shouted confidentially to Eva. 'Ought to take more care of hisself, he did. He's a good boy to old Annie, ain't you, sweetheart? Can't get no work now, I can't, with me legs an' all. Brings me things, he does. Nicks 'em off of bloody Jallow and gives 'em to me.' She cackled joyfully.

'That's it, Annie, for chrissake let everyone know,' he said.

Annie patted him soothingly.

110

'Come and sit down, lovey,' said Annie to Eva. 'Cheer 'im up a bit. If I was a bit younger we wouldn't be out here now, would we?'

Eva sat down next to him on his other side. This close, he looked like death, indeed as if he might be dying. An agonized pity cracked open Eva's heart, allowing all remembrance to trickle out, all new emotion to slink in. Annie had slid an arm around him and he was leaning against her now, perfectly relaxed and with his eyes shut.

'It's this cold weather,' Annie said to Eva over his head. 'I tell him he's got to find somewhere decent to shack up permanent. That's how I lost my Sandy. With his chest.'

'It's not my chest, you silly cow,' said Sail faintly though affectionately. Annie cackled.

'What is it then?' Eva asked, trembling slightly, her eyes burning from nervousness or tears, she was not sure which.

'Oh, for god's sake,' he muttered. 'Now you've made her think I've got plague or something. She'll never stay now.'

'Oh,' said Annie vaguely, 'this is the special one, is it? The one with the run-off feller.'

'He hasn't!' Eva cried, farcically furious. But he, lying there in the hag's arms like a wounded prince from a myth, said softly, eyes still shut: 'She's got a beautiful face, Annie, and she's unconsciously, guiltlessly cruel. Like an animal or an element. You're a sort of gorgon, Eva. If I look at you perhaps I'll turn into stone.' Two green-blue glints appeared between his lids as he squinted at her. 'No,' he murmured, 'I'm not sick, Eva. Simply trying to engage your sympathy.'

Annie clicked her tongue.

Eva reached out in a kind of slow motion, took the mug

of cold tea out of his hands, and put it down on the bench. His hands immediately fastened round one of hers instead. She stared at the phenomenon as if somehow she had been caught in a painless but inexorable trap.

'It's this cold weather,' repeated Annie. 'My Sandy could never take the snow, with his poor chest.'

This time Sail said nothing. His mouth and around his eyes were blue.

A spasm of fear went over Eva. She thought of the house, but an instant vision of an invading Angel with the flaming sword of her disapproval smacked this notion flat.

'What shall we do?' Eva implored in frightened horror.

Annie shook her head. Then shook him gently.

'Come on, duckie, there's a love.'

Sail opened his eyes.

Eva, in a surge of unbearable, irresistible grief and longing, allowed both her arms to wind around him, and held on to him fiercely. He turned at once and laid his head against her shoulder, deserting Annie with an impulse both traitorous and pathetic. Annie did not seem to mind. She nodded at Eva as if redesignating a responsibility to its proper owner. But a kind of burning relief was searing through Eva that she could finally touch him. She found her fingers sliding all at once through his hair, her mouth against its whiteness, at which the ghosts of two other women rose up, but she pushed them down and smothered them. She rested his head on her breast and rocked him as if he were a child.

'Used to be a juggler, before,' Annie said conversationally.

'Who, who did?' Eva whispered out of the well of her orgasmic sorrow.

'Sail,' Annie said. There was a lapse of silence then lasting possibly minutes or hours, after which Annie said: 'That Johnny's bin staring at us for too long, I reckon. Jallow don't like us – me and him. I think we'd better shift usselves.'

Eva looked up from the velvet lined pit and saw Johnny's malicious eyes on her.

'Sail!' she hissed urgently. To her surprise he stirred almost at once, sat up, and stared at Johnny in return. Johnny spat, and began to shoulder between the stalls towards them.

Sail got to his feet, unbalanced slightly, righted himself. Eva glanced at Annie's side of the bench, but Annie had suddenly, magically, vanished into thin air like the toothless wicked fairy she resembled. 'Come on,' said Sail. He still held her hand, and somehow he slipped them sideways, as a unit, through the crowd and out of the crowd, and off the Levels, Johnny lost behind them.

Eva pulled her hand away.

'You got better quickly.'

'Your kindness cured me, my lady,' he said with incongruous flourish.

There were dark patches under his eyes, and he walked uncertainly, but Eva tossed this visual proof aside, convinced she had been tricked.

At a street corner he leaned against a wall and coughed violently.

'You liar!'

He leaned on the wall and looked at her.

'Did I imagine your kind arms? It didn't feel like Annie.'

'I won't go with you!' Eva suddenly screamed. 'If I did, Steel'd never have me back.'

'How would he know? Geiger counter?'

Confused by unknown words, Eva caught herself chewing a piece of her hair as Hazel had done in Foulmarsh.

'Where will you go?' she asked him limply.

'There's a ruined church I hole up in. Next to the graveyard. It'll be nice and handy.'

She edged around and began to walk away.

'Eva,' he said tightly, 'I want you, Eva.'

'Make do,' she said, 'with all the others.'

She stumbled on an icy stone and turned her ankle. She did not stop or even hobble, determined to go on.

Fog had come down, and the world was full of sudden ghosts.

She dreamed she was running through the dark. Even as she dreamed it, she knew she had dreamed it before. The dark twittered and pulsed and occasionally screamed. As she clawed through the brambles and fell against the impenetrable wall, she strove and struggled to wake. But instead of waking, she turned and saw Jezubal's face spinning towards her. She could not open her eyes until she had experienced the full gamut of terror.

She lay on her back in the bed, remembered how she had known she would dream of this again and again, how she had said that one night Jezubal would catch her. What would happen when he did? Blind panic throttled her at the thought. Surely the face had come closer this time?

She sat up in a flicker of candle stumps, and shrieked for Steel, as if the empty house could conjure him up for her if only she could impress her need upon it. But there was no magic left in the world, and she, who had tried to chain him to her in the moon-greened woods with some spell of night, had lost him, and was not a witch.

She dozed fitfully after the dream, unwilling to be either asleep or awake.

Dawn turned the window into a sheet of stained glass, and brought a sound that circled around and around the house, neither settling nor fading, persistent as breathing. It spiked a fresh dream into her head. She thought a great bird was wheeling mournfully through the rooms, having got down the chimney. But finally she woke again, and it was a man whistling under the windows, melodic, eerie, insubstantial. She lay still, tense and knotting her hands, until at last the visitation of music went away over the wasteground, leaving silence congealing in its wake.

Nine

Unable to unknot either her hands or her mind now, Eva slid from the bed. She ran, in a blanket, out into the back yard. Then, in an outrage of uncaution, she stripped naked by the pump and sluiced her body with the icy water. The snow had melted with the night. The day promised steaming mud and a sluggish, almost primaeval warmth.

As she pulled on her black dress in the bedroom, she heard Angel rattling at the door and shouting. The door was locked, which was rare enough. Reaching it, Eva hesitated to unlock it. Angel had become suddenly neither friendly nor reliable. But as the woman cast herself against the timbers once again, Eva, reminded of some kind of battering ram, unbolted.

Angel thrust by her into the house, and slammed the door behind her. She glared down into Eva's face, and she was terrifying, like Retribution.

'You took your time,' Angel said, 'but it's not surprising. I know what's been going on.'

Eva's eyelids fluttered. She blinked her eyes to clear them.

'What do you mean?'

'What do I mean? I mean you've been with that thieving lout again – that Sail.'

'I only—'

'And last night, *I mean*, he was here. Don't deny it. I saw him slinking off by the railway tracks, coming from this place. You bloody little tart,' Angel finished, with a sort of satisfaction.

The injustice left Eva momentarily numbed. Then she laughed. It was irresistibly funny, so bizarre an irony she could never, never stand it. But Angel slapped her heavy-handed across the face. Eva fell back against the stairs and lay there, treads sticking hard in her spine.

'You can laugh about it, but I'll tell you this, you'll get no more of your Steel's money off of me to keep the two of you. I'm not spending his coin on that runt, nor on you while you hang round with him, you slut.'

Eva shook herself. Tears of anger and pain jabbed her eyes.

'You've no right – no right! He left it for me—'

'Oh, yes, so he did. And you won't get a penny-piece till you come to your senses, my girl. And another small thing – you bring your fancy boy here again and I'll stop the rent going to Jallow.'

'I never brought him here!' Eva screamed, hammering her fist on the stairs.

'You think I'm blind? I *saw* him. Whistling, too. You stupid bitch.' Angel swung about, opened the door and looked back at her stonily. 'You've got my final word. Either drop him, or out you go. Go to *him* if you like, and let's see him keep you off of the bloody market till Jallow catches him. A nice mess you'll be in then.'

Eva sat speechless. The door shut, and she slumped against the banisters. The marrow seemed to have deserted her bones.

And then the thought came to her that *he* had done this to her. All of this lunatic mistake had been his fault. She longed to shriek at him, to vent on him the poison Angel had voided on her.

At once she was up. She ran to fetch the golden leaf and chain, searched frenziedly, throwing things about the room, finally discovering it already around her neck – to her added fury. Then she ran out of the house in her old Foulmarsh shoes, mud leaping up at her like a pack of eager black dogs, her hair in an uncombed froth, her eyes unpainted, all one molten lava rush towards him in a search for vengeance.

Also because, abruptly, there seemed nowhere else for her to go.

It took her an hour to reach the overgrown graveyard. She had never been there before, only seen it in the distance, and she lost herself several times among the dead ends of Oiltown. She was no longer angry now; anger had seeped out of her, bit by bit. Neither was she calm. Still sick from Angel's blast of malignant energy, she walked with a forlorn, unfaltering, strengthless speed, which ate up distance and ate her up with it. The world was a bad dream in which someone had locked her. Once she rested against a fossilized street light, and said to Angel: 'I *didn't*!' And then to Steel: 'Well you left me, didn't you?'

Eventually, when it seemed she had been walking for

ever in strange circles of forgotten intention, she came to a broken wall with a rotted lych-gate still precariously set in it, and beyond, rolling sweeps of blond grass from which protruded dead yews with writhing branches. Here and there was an open wound of earth, the moss already crawling over it as if anxious to absorb the death beneath. Grey oblongs of stone marched in lines between the trees, leaning in all directions, and sometimes on each other. A fallen angel lay beside the gate with broken wings and damp-eaten eyes. She seemed to be clutching a clump of thistles which had grown through her fingers.

A dark greenish melancholia seemed drawn upwards from the ground by the heat. Eva felt stifled. She shrank from the angel, and thought she might find a skull in the rank grass, or bones some scavenging dog had dug for.

The church, a tilted, age-shattered hulk, was joined to the landscape by a procession of elms. Eva moved down it, burned and cooled in stripes. She was no longer very sure why she was here. She read epitaphs on lopsided slabs; they became a deathly sing-song in her mind. Loving memory, who has been taken away, to meet at last in heaven . . .

A shriek of laughter cut the tongues from the tomb-voices.

Eva shivered and stood still, while the shattered air fell in fragments about her feet. Between two fungus-papered trunks she saw a man sitting on a grave, and a small girl of about ten, rocking with abandoned mirth beside him. It was ludicrous and hateful to Eva that she should have seen him now, every time but one, with a female companion, and that these companions should range from hag through woman to child. Even as she watched, the girl reached up and kissed his cheek. And then slipped down and began to run towards her. Eva cringed back behind a tree and the child, still grinning and pleased, ran by her unaware in the direction of the gate.

Eva stared out again. He seemed to be looking at her as he sat on the grave, but she could not be sure. Then he got up and turned and walked away out of sight behind the church.

She snatched the chain off her neck and held it crushed in one hand. Her feet broke through tight cordons of weeds. She came to the deserted grave and went by it, after him.

A vista of tall marble lay behind the church. She could not see him at all.

She skirted the church cold-spined, wandered down among the slabs, came to a slab with a knight lying on it – but the knight was no longer there. Her head jerked up; she saw the carved figure stretched instead across another, more distant, slab.

Eva stood very still, her body throbbing with the uneven pulse of the day. She took in a jagged breath and ran down the lanes of coloured stone, round a plot or two, and reached the knight, and found that he was gone.

This time she flung her head right back, and saw the yellow sky wheeling over the pinnacles of the grave-city. She sensed a game of sorts, and the game terrified her. Her legs weakened and she bit her tongue with unreasonable fear.

'Sail!' she screamed.

The sky took her scream and opened it like an umbrella.

'I'm here,' he said.

She turned so fast she almost fell over herself still standing rooted to the spot.

The knight was lying behind her, but the dank breeze lifted strands of his hair and smoke coiled from the corner of his mouth.

Eva held her breath. She would not look at him, nor he seemingly at her. She could just catch the infinitesimal sweet fumes of what he drew into his lungs.

'Why come whistling round the house?' she panted.

'Why not? You drew me. You're a magnet. I serenaded you like a troubadour. Or a randy cat. Whichever your ladyship prefers. I could see you,' he said dreamily, 'listening, lying on Jallow's brass bedstead. I could hear your heart drumming in the ground. I can hear it now.'

He sat up and gazed at her with wide, drug-darkened, sun-splintered eyes. She flung the gold chain at him. He caught it one-handed, not looking, then stared down at his hand to see what he had caught.

'Angel saw you!' Eva shouted, gripping a stone to steady herself. 'I shall starve because Angel saw. He left money with her – all of it. She says she won't give me a penny, that she'll stop the rent on the house—'

'Wait,' he said. He paused, looking in her face. Then he said: 'But there must have been a condition.'

'If I never saw you again—' she began, and broke off.

He looked down, half smiling.

'Do you know what you just said?'

Eva shut her eyes to shut him out, but his image persisted inside her lids. So she opened her eyes and walked across the grass and sat down on the grave beside him.

'Then it's done,' she said. 'Already.'

He passed the cigarette to her but she threw it in the grass and killed it with her heel.

'Eva,' he said, 'I'm delighted that you're destitute of his money. I'm delighted that you'll have nothing left of his to lean on or enjoy.' He slipped his arm lightly, casually, about her. She hung her head in anticipation of her shame. Then turned and pressed her lips against his cheekbone. He locked his fingers behind her head, and kissed her politely, reservedly, twice. The third time he took her mouth from her, possessed it, ravaged it. He seemed so familiar to her, so known. She experienced a glorious sinking despair rather than any pleasure. He drew away from her and sighed, and she felt him trembling.

'I take it,' he said, almost inaudibly, 'we have an understanding.'

Again she hung her head.

'Oh, yes, but not here.'

'No. Not here. Not a grave. It would be too trite.' He rose and she rose with him. In her Foulmarsh shoes she had made him a present of an inch or two, and was now shorter than he. He did not touch her, but she followed him, and found that they were going in at a ruined door of the church. Inside, silence thrust like wool in her ears. Tall pillars in pale velvet gloves of age soared up to pierce the practically intact ceiling. Windows with fragments of glass sent flights of wine and indigo butterflies skeining over the floor. Beyond the altar the great openings had lost their glass totally leaving a lacework of lovely skeletal limbs and flower-shaped lattices.

The church overpowered her, and the use to which they would presently put it held all the horror – not of sacrilege –

but of very old things disturbed. She could imagine formless shapes made of dust and unremembered prayer, rising up from behind pillars and out of the dark places, staring at Sail and at her from the transparent webs of their eyes.

They crossed before the altar. He opened a narrow door. Beyond it part of the roof had collapsed into the waiting nettles. Another door stood ajar on a small room. They went in. She had a feverish glimpse of incongruous things – a mattress on the floor, a small cupboard, an oil lamp, a piece of curtain hanging up on one wall shivering with draughts. With the door pulled shut night tried to manifest itself in the room. He lit the lamp which flared up wings of pink glare, illuminating a rat seated on the cupboard washing its paws. Sail opened the door again and the rat glanced at him inquiringly.

'Fuck off,' Sail said.

The rat skittled down and rattled out. Sail slammed the door after it, and the room shook. He leaned on the door and flicked a little plaster listlessly from the wall. He looked depressed.

'Gracious, isn't it? Just the place to bring a lady.' He grinned sourly. 'Not Jallow's man, you see. I live by lopping weeds and trimming the grass off graves, and what I don't earn, I thieve.'

Eva looked away.

'Annie said you were a juggler.'

'Oh, Annie did, did she? Well, that was a year ago. I came here with travellers – and a girl who told fortunes.' He slid a handful of small stones from a scatter by the door and spun them in an arc between his hands, not looking at what he was doing. 'She taught me to throw things and catch them, and how to nick things if the show didn't pay so well.'

Eva hissed: 'Why didn't you stay with her if she made you so clever?'

'She was like you,' he said nastily. 'Basically hard as nails. She wanted someone else and thought I was it which I wasn't.'

He caught all the stones in one hand and set them down. Then pulled away the curtain to show a finger-thin window in the wall. In the window sat the picture of a young white-faced woman with yellow hair and a blue veil, holding a child in her lap. Eva thought she recognized in her a totem of the god-speakers. Sail tapped on the glass.

'Can you read?' he asked.

'Yes.'

She saw words scratched on the window frame. Haltingly she made out a rhyme of indefinite yet somehow frightful meaning.

> *Unsilent night, unholy night,*
> *All is not calm, nothing is bright.*
> *Round the swollen whore and her bastard brat*
> *Spring the dungheaps of our careless crap.*
> *We shall sleep no more in peace,*
> *We shall sleep no more in peace.*

And while meaning nothing, it sickened and appalled her – she sensed the putrid hate, the crude blasphemy, the despair. She stared at him.

'No, I didn't write it. It was here to welcome me when I moved in. It's the curse on the room, and it gets shut out with the peroxided lady and the draught. I used to call her the Fair Death.'

He let go the curtain.

'Why did you show it me?' she asked, beginning to tremble uncontrollably.

'To see if it got to you the way it does me.'

She kicked off her shoes and went and lay on the mattress on her side, with her back to him. She felt nothing for him now except nervousness; she could not imagine why she was here with him nor what she could possibly have felt when she held to him before. She shook so hard, she believed she would probably shake herself to pieces, and she wanted it only to be a swift passionless transaction, swiftly and passionlessly over.

He came and sat beside her, his back against the wall. He did not touch her. He said: 'I understand. You've changed your mind. Go if you want.'

She turned and looked up into his face, which might truly have been Steel's then, for it was blank and blind and shut.

'After all,' he said, 'I'm always around. You can come back any time you want me. I'll be only too pleased.'

The knife stabbed into all the old wounds of her emotional body, one by one. She took his face in her shaking hands, and a vast wheel began to turn inside her, and the great tide of exalted misery overcame her as on the grave.

It was neither swift nor passionless, it was irresistible and prolonged, and agonized. She cried out because she could not bear the turbulent ascent and shattering fall; her own womb seemed to swallow her. She had forgotten him even when she clung to him, but the sea cast her up for dead, and she remembered then. And bright as the stained glass window she saw a picture of Steel lying on his back in a street with a bullet like a black wasp hived home in his brain. At once, in a frenzied egomania, she thought this sad little act of betrayal on a worn mattress in the midst of the dilapidated necropolis had killed him. At the moment of fulfilled lust he had died. She *knew* it, and began immediately to cry.

'Eva,' Sail said, half-laughing at her, distressed. His arms tightened around her. 'Eva, don't cry. Eva, Eva, don't.'

'He'll die now,' she sobbed and the pain of it almost tore her in half.

'Darling Eva, he's tough. He skinned Jallow's gang at cards, and he shot a rabid wild cat when it jumped him in the fields. Didn't he ever tell you? You see, I know more about him than you.'

'No,' she wept. 'No.'

'And he left you,' he said, holding her even more tightly. 'He went away. I wouldn't leave you, Eva. I wouldn't ever want to. I'm here now. I love you, Eva.'

'And all the rest,' she wailed.

'You are all the rest,' he said urgently. 'Every woman I've ever known squeezed and crammed into your body.' He put down his face on to her tear-wet hair. 'Ah, shut up crying. You'll make me cry in a minute.'

But she could not stop. She continued in great shuddering gasps. It was luxury to weep and be comforted. It was wonderful to clasp flesh and bone and skin in her arms, and to feel other arms clasp her as she did so, with no holding back, no antipathy, no sense of blame.

She woke up to find herself being kissed and kissing in return on pure habitual reflex. The curtain was drawn back a little from the madonna window, and her whole image was flooded with a turquoise storm of twilight.

'Time to go home,' he said to Eva, looking in her eyes.

But Eva curled again to sleep, ignoring the words. He lifted her up a little way so that she grumbled at him.

'Home,' he said.

Eva opened her eyes again. The words were stupid to her. They had spent the whole day here, in sex sudden and violent, or tortuous foreplay, sometimes speaking, or merely staring at each other in the intent optic cannibalism of fascinated strangers. Now *he* seemed to be 'home', and the mattress, the shadow-flickery room – being extensions of him – were 'home' also.

'I want to stay here.'

'You can't. It's damp and disgusting, and the rats make a godawful row crashing about outside when it's dark.'

'I can't go back to the house. Angel said—'

'One night,' he said, 'is all. Tomorrow I'll go to Jallow. Anything'll do, so long as it's under his stinking auspices. I'll find a room for us on the Levels or somewhere. Then, when I've got enough together to see us through, we'll move out, travel, find some other town.'

Eva flinched slightly, guessing it was Steel's possible return they would be travelling away from. This very event she had ached for and felt would never come about she now both anticipated and dreaded.

'I don't want to go back to the house,' Eva said sullenly. But she began to dress herself because he looked as if he might become distraught, and she felt in some odd way she had done him harm as well as brought him pleasure by coming to him.

He walked her back among the graves, holding her hand. She expected things to jump out on them. Once in the streets she saw knives glint in the shadows, rifles level out of broken windows. She was not sure who the enemy was, but the world seemed full of him.

At the house door Sail said: 'I'll meet you at midday. Outside the Jallow Arms.'

'Will you be there?' she said. 'Who will you be with?'

'No one.'

'I may not be there.'

He made a gesture of appeal and despair to the black-green sky.

'I shall be there,' he said laboriously. 'I shall be standing there, biting my fingernails and asking every stray man, cat and whore: Have you seen a crazy blonde girl going up this way.'

'Don't forget me,' she said.

'I'll tie a knot in something.'

He kissed her lightly and opened the door.

'Come in with me.'

'And risk Amazon-Lil? No thanks.'

She went in and slammed the door on him. He battered on it loudly. 'Bolt it!' he shouted.

Eva leaned on the inside of the door, feeling it shake. Finally he stopped and she heard him swearing. She slipped the bolts home at once.

'You cow,' he said outside, slightly laughing. 'Well then, I'll see you tomorrow, madam.'

'You may.'

She slunk up the stairs and crawled into the unfriendly bed. Soon moonlight struck white sparks from the brass rail. Wheels spun in her head, she felt giddy, uneasy and joyful, and occasionally physically sick. At last she slept. She dreamed of rats. Rats ran and scampered, squealed and fought and racketed and rowed. One jumped right through the stained glass window and sank its fangs into her neck as she lay on Sail's mattress. It was neither unpleasant nor frightening. So she stroked its narrow head.

Ten

In the morning she opened her eyes and remembered everything.

She ran about the house singing, and with a queasy feeling in her guts. Making up her eyes she spilled a drop of blue shadow on her blue velveteen lap and only laughed. She painted her toenails a time-consuming scarlet. At the last minute it occurred to her to take certain possessions with her, for she might never need to come back, or even have the option. She flung bits and pieces into a blanket and her black dress on top, and wrapped it all up into an untidy bundle secured with knotted fragments of ancient string. There were a dozen things she might have taken that would conceivably have proved more useful than those she selected. She left knives and sheets, and food to rot in bins, but did not forget her hairbrush or eye-liner – such were the symbols of new-found glamour to her that they seemed the stuff of life.

She ran down the stairs and out of the house and slammed the door behind her. Then came a moment of panic in which the whole interior of her body seemed to turn over.

She walked fast across the grass, faster up the streets,

finally slower and with heart thuds, worn out already by nervous dread and a raging determination to hope. It was a little past midday when she reached the Jallow Arms. A cat rolled in the dust by the door, but Eva was too sick to caress it Inside a few men sat drinking, and a thin woman gave a saucer of green gin to an enthusiastic and fierce-looking mongrel. Sail was not there.

Eva lay back on the wall, her legs dissolving.

People passed her, went in and came out of the pub. To begin with she glanced up at every one. Later she shut her eyes and took no notice, simply half-lying there in a kind of trance. Three toughs offered her their attentions but gave up when she showed no response, and a very old road-sweeper asked her, surprisingly, if she were all right, then? After centuries that must have been about an hour and a half, she opened her eyes again to find that she was crying. When she rubbed the wet from her cheeks her hands came away black from running mascara, but it seemed to her that the waters in her body had been poisoned like the Foulmarsh pump, that she shed black tears.

Time had altered the light, which was now softer. She picked up her bundle and held it to her. He had not come. He had not wanted or needed to. He had ensorcelled her, had her, used her up, squeezed out of her every drop of sexual liquor he fancied from her, and then lost interest, discarded her, forgotten. No doubt there was some other girl sharing his mattress at this moment, or else still in the process of being hypnotised on to it. Just as Angel had said.

Eva wept angrily now. She stuck her claws in the blanket and thought her tears would turn red as blood. Fury stiffened her body, gave it new life. Clutching the bundle, she began to march with wooden arched feet, snarling to herself, up the Levels, not knowing where she was going. If she had met him then, as she expected to at every second, she would have flown at him and torn out his eyes.

But she did not meet him. She met Annie, shuffling half-crippled up the street, leaning all over on one side, with her old face clamped into certain lines caused by the habitual distress of moving.

'Annie!' Eva screamed at her.

Annie looked up and halted. Her toothless old mouth was turned down at its corners. Eva ran up to her and flung down the bundle, almost hitting her with it.

'Where is he – that bastard – that bastard!'

Annie only blinked at her.

'You know! Tell me! He's a liar and a bastard! Where is he?'

'Who's that?'

'Sail!' Eva shrieked. She found she could not stop shrieking it. Annie reached out and shook her with a crab-shaped paw.

'Where do you think, girl, eh?'

'Oh, I know. I *know*. Like with me.'

Annie changed her shaking to clutching. Using Eva as a prop, she said: 'That's all you know. Thought a lot of you, he did. An' you're the one's got him in trouble, I reckon.'

Eva only shouted some unintelligible expression of hatred.

Annie matter-of-factly hawked and spat.

'I'll tell you where he is,' she said. 'Jallow's got him. Or

Jallow's boys is more like it. Trying to get his foot in, he was, to get some money to keep some silly bit of a girl on her arse. Never done that before, he hasn't, not since that stuck-up piece he come here with. Now that Johnny starts something. Johnny's never liked him, never liked the way he could get any girl without lifting a finger when Johnny has a problem getting one of the tarts to take him on. Johnny starts it, and they all join in. Say he's nicking stuff. Say they're going to do him up and fix him, and let's see him look after the girls then.' Annie fell silent, still leaning on Eva.

Eva stared at her and whispered: 'I don't believe you.'

'Oh, you don't never believe anything, do you? You didn't never believe *him*, did you? That lovely boy. I wish I'd had your chances. I know 'cos Janice at the knocking-shop told me this morning. There was a fight in the street, six of 'em, and Sail used his knife on a couple of 'em, but he hasn't got their weight nor anything and they just slung him in the fag-shop and none of 'em came out. Only wanted an excuse, they did, to keep Jallow happy with his big ideas of justice. The bloody stinking buggers.'

Eva, half leaning back on to Annie now, averted her eyes from the whirling white and blazing jigsaw of the street where every bit seemed out of place, and every tall block about to fall on her.

'He's dead then?'

'If not, soon will be. I don't know how I'll get along. Used ter help me, he did, and I needs it.'

'Annie, what shall I do – what – what?'

'What do *you* care? You're all right, ain't you? I reckon as you've done enough. Why didn't you stick to your other

feller if you was so sure he'd come back? I stuck to my
Sandy for twenty years. Even when he got sick and couldn't
do nothing for me, I never went with another man. Well,
hardly ever. And you, you come here and mess him up
good and proper. It's all because of you he's where he is,
and then you come running up calling him names—'

Eva pulled free. She left her bundle lying at Annie's feet
like some kind of propitiatory sacrifice.

She ran off the Levels on to King's Walk, and past the
nailed-up sign saying JALLOW. She had run right up to the
door of Jallow's Ash Emporium before confusion and a
sense of futility mowed her down.

The sky turned black. Suddenly. She thought it was her
eyes. Then pieces of rain crashed on the bridge. Driven by
the rain, she huddled in the shop doorway. The rain
stabbed in after her. To get away, with no constructive
thought or desire in mind, she thrust open the door and fled
under the tinkling bell, into the musty, weed-fume smelling
shop.

The walls were red. A red velvet drape, like the swathes
in the windows, hung over the entrance to the stairway. In a
canvas chair, his feet propped on the counter, sat a narrow-
eyed villain, his lips stoppered by a pipe.

'Yes? And what do you want, little girl?'

Eva pushed her dripping hair from her face, and looked
round wildly.

'I want to go upstairs.'

'What for?'

'Is Sail up there?'

'What if he is?'

Eva clenched her fists impotently. She ran towards the curtain, but the man was up and there before her. He held her back, laughing, the pipe belching in her face.

'Now, now. I asked you a question. Didn't your mum teach you no manners?'

Eva struggled.

'Is Johnny there?' Eva cried, changing names with an instinctive, psychological appraisal.

Oh, yes. *Johnny*'s there.'

'I want to see Johnny.'

'Johnny's busy.'

Eva kicked him. The high wooden heel caught him on the shin bone, and she was free and by him, past the curtain and running up the stairs. He came yelling after her almost at once. She passed a devastated lavatory and came to a landing with two shut doors. Frenziedly she threw herself against the nearer and exploded through. Faded chairs and tables stood about. From a back window the weed fields could be seen blowing in the savage emerald rain.

Johnny sat at a card table, eating chicken legs and drinking cork-rotting Sauterne out of the bottle. He gave a greasy, leering, malignant grin when he saw her. Then pipe smoke and pursuit commandeered the doorway.

'Getting careless, aren't you, Berry?' Johnny inquired, lazy with brief power.

'I'm sorry, Johnny. Little bitch kicked me—'

'Oh, she's a nasty little piece, this one.'

'I'll throw her out now, Johnny.'

But Eva eluded him. She reached Johnny and leaned on him, and put her hand on his neck under the black welter of hair.

'Let me stay,' she said.

'Why should I?' asked Johnny, nevertheless suffering her to caress his neck.

'She came asking for Sail,' said Berry venomously, 'like the other one, earlier.'

'Oh, they all come asking for Sail. You know what they say, don't you, Berry? Once they've bin with him they never want to go with another bloke. They sort of *catches* him. Like a dose of the clap.'

Berry laughed.

Eva said: 'I'm thirsty.'

Johnny took a swig of the Sauterne and put it back on the table.

'Have to suffer then, won't you?'

Eva slipped her hand on to his back under his shirt, and leaned down to his ear.

'I want to talk to you.'

'Talk on.'

'Make him go away.'

'Why should I?'

Eva slid between him and the table, her back to Berry. Her knee rubbed gently in Johnny's crutch. She looked at him, her head on one side, coiling her damp hair round her fingers. His body responded instantly. He licked his lips.

'All right, Berry. You can leave the lady and me alone.'

She heard Berry laugh unpleasantly, and then his feet going downstairs.

'Well, what are you being so nice for, eh?' Johnny asked her, but his eyes were half shut, lulled by the mounting rhythm in his groin.

'Where are the others?' she said, smiling at him.

'Oh, they've gone to get Jallow. Down river. Won't be back till dark. Thinking of asking me to let your sweetheart out, are you?'

A hard bright whiteness opened a door in Eva's mind.

'No,' she said. She put her hands on his shoulders, and let him unfasten her dress. 'What did you do to Sail?'

'Not much,' Johnny murmured. 'We saved the best till later.'

'Jallow likes things done properly,' said Eva.

'Shut up,' said Johnny.

'I want to help you get Sail,' Eva said.

Johnny paused, amazed, his hand hotly moist on her skin.

'You what?'

'Get Sail. I want you to fix him.'

Johnny laughed.

'When you fix him,' Eva hissed, 'I'd like to watch you do it.'

'You are an evil cow, aren't you?' grinned Johnny. 'What did he do to you?' He poked his fingers into her, specific and painful.

'I want a drink,' she snapped petulantly.

Swearing, but still good-natured and amused, he passed her the bottle of Sauterne. She drank.

'Did you get his knife?' she demanded.

'Oh, yes.'

'I want it.'

'Tough.'

'If you give it me, I'll tell Jallow I saw Sail stealing off his stalls.'

Johnny laughed again. Suddenly he reached back behind

himself and drew out Sail's knife, and held it up delicately for her to see.

'Why d'you want it?'

'I'd like to use it on him, the bastard.'

Johnny flipped the knife up in the air, caught it, and tossed it away across the room.

'You want it,' he said, 'you earn it, you warped little cunt.'

He rose, dragging her with him, pushed her on to the nearest sofa, and did her, quickly and thoroughly, with no concessions.

'Let me get up,' Eva said.

'Wait,' he growled.

'I feel sick,' said Eva. 'I'll be sick.' She managed easily enough to heave.

Johnny moved and thrust her away.

'Mind Jallow's sodding carpet.'

He lay on his face and ignored her.

She ran to the card table. She snatched up the wine bottle. She ran back and smashed it over his head. The glass showered, the wine ran out like yellow yolk from a ruptured crystal shell. It barely stunned him. He surged up and around at her, reaching to grab, and in a paroxysm of hysterical terror she stabbed him with the jagged stump of the bottle, once in the throat, once in the chest.

Johnny goggled at her. She had always managed to astound him. Now, astounded yet again, he fell back and bled among the Sauterne-soaked cushions.

Eva raced into the corner where the knife had fallen. She could not find it. She began to sob. Finally she cut her fingers on the blade and ran with it out of the room.

On the landing she listened. No sounds of alarm or impending investigation reached her, only the sharp drumbeats of the rain.

The other door she saw now was bolted several times on the outside.

Feverishly she started to drag back the bolts. She remembered how he had shouted at her to bolt the door of the house. Everything seemed in reverse, and she could hardly breathe. Two bolts moved smoothly, one broke her nails and tore her fingers freshly. The last was too high for her to reach. She ran back into the other room. Johnny's life-empty eyes glared at her; he was still bleeding. She tried to pull one of the huge armchairs out of the door, but it was somehow too big. Finally she seized the flimsy card table, tipped the plates off it on to the floor, and set it up outside the bolted room. It sagged and swayed when she climbed up on it. She held it together by a passion of silently screaming will-power. The bolt shot back. Eva jumped or fell off the table which buckled and thudded down the stairs.

With a suppressed and almost noiseless shriek, she thrust open the door.

The room was all darkness and a smell of woodworm. Outside the boarded window, the rain now sounded like a million tiny tin horses galloping on each other's backs.

'Sail,' Eva said. The frightened tears ran down her face as she groped for his corpse on the ground. On her knees she crawled behind the door and found suddenly an ice-cold hand which fastened immediately on hers.

'Eva?' His voice sounded far-off and inanimate, yet surprised, as if she had called him up by witchcraft from his grave. 'Eva – is it you – or am I dreaming you?'

His hands were tied. She slashed the string awkwardly, for she could barely see, and the hands fell apart, away from her.

She found his body on the end of the hands. He jumped violently as her fingers negotiated his ribs.

'What is it?'

'Nothing. Only the memento of a boot or two.' His voice came more strongly and he took her shoulder, 'How in Christ did you get here?'

'I—'

'No. Don't tell me. Just get out. Run. Don't get dragged into this bloody awful mess. Who let you in?' Her eyes made out his abruptly, next, his face, daubed with dried blood and bruised black along the left cheek. She saw fresh blood marks on his shirt from her murdering hands.

He looked down where she was staring, then up at her.

'Eva – what have you done?'

'I killed Johnny. I stabbed him with a bottle.' She gazed around her, dazed and crazy-eyed. 'I got your knife,' she said, and handed it to him. She bowed her head and wept piteously. 'When you weren't there, I thought you'd left me.'

'Oh, Eva,' he said in tones of amusement and as if his heart were breaking. He caught her to him and held her fast, both of them shaking as they had at first among the graves.

There came a sound from below.

'Johnny?' a voice called up the stairs.

'He won't answer,' Eva cried, as if this were astonishing.

'No he won't, will he? You answer.'

'What?'

'You. Go to the door and call out to him – tell him Johnny wants him – anything.'

The knife was moving in the gloom, and she saw that they had also tied his ankles together, and he was now slashing the cord.

'Johnny!' Berry yelled. 'What's going on up there?'

The knife stopped moving and Sail stood up, leaning on the wall and cursing softly. Eva ran out.

'Johnny wants you,' she called from the landing.

'Oh? What for? What's all that noise up there?'

'Come up and see,' Eva shouted.

'Eva,' Sail said, 'go and stand by the window.'

She did as he told her. Shortly they heard footsteps, a heavy stumble and oath as Berry met the broken card table outside the lavatory. After that he came on faster. His weasel head appeared above the stairs, next his torso and legs. The pipe no longer filled his mouth, which hinged open as he saw the unbolted door, and then Eva standing in the room.

'Johnny!' Berry shouted. 'She's bloody got him out. *Johnny!* Where's he hiding, you cow? Eh?'

Eva cowered back and Berry ran into the room at her.

There was a swift movement behind him as he passed beyond the door. Berry yelped and tried to turn himself round, but fell down on the damp floorboards instead. It occurred to Eva that Sail had efficiently knifed him.

Sail wiped the knife and sheathed it.

'Are there any others here?' he asked her. His voice sounded disgusted, as though what he had just done to Berry had disgusted him.

'No.'

'Then let's get out of here, Eva.'

On the landing, in the gin-coloured rain-light, she saw the bruises on his face and body with agonizing clarity, and stopped in her tracks.

'It's nothing, Eva. Come *on*.' He took her hand and they got down the stairs. She watched him trying to appear as though it did not bother him, limping with a sort of stiff nonchalance, his eyes almost white with pain.

In the shop they waited, listening. Rain galloped.

Sail pushed open the door.

They went along the bridge, through the rain. Nothing and no one moved except a paper streamer drowning in a gutter.

'The river,' he said, although she had not asked him. 'There's a boat or two. We can ride with the current. There's a marshy place just past Jallow's fields. If they follow us, they won't want to go beyond that.'

'Will they follow us?'

'Possibly not. But my inflated ego tells me they may. There's a way down here.'

They had got behind the shops and brothel, and now there were slimy steps, and a bank full of rot and rat-holes. They crept down it, cautiously. At the bottom an unravelled knitting of small dead trees stretched on the water and held up two big row-boats in their arms. Sail holed one with its oar, and watched it fill with bubbles and go under, hanging on to the branches with a grey face.

After a moment he said to Eva: 'Can you row?'

She shook her head.

'Oh, god. No. I didn't think you could.'

Rain slopped and popped, and a white fire-crack opened the sky, and the water seemed all scales from the individual penetrations of the deluge.

He pushed the boat free, and in among the scales, sending out great spasms of ripples. He climbed into it and grasped the oars.

'Get in,' he said, and she flopped into the boat, making it duck and bob while she cried out in alarm. 'Watch me,' he said. 'I can't keep this up long, you'll have to take over. Hardly chivalrous, but you won't have to row far. The current gets stronger farther down. Oh Christ,' he said as he pulled on the oars, and then: 'Oh bloody Christ,' as he pulled on them again. She stared at him, her hands clenched and her teeth sunk in her lip, enduring it with him. Another lightning. She saw he had shut his eyes, but his face ran sweat, loosening the blood into a new virulent red.

'Let me do it,' she whispered frantically.

'I'm all right. Wait your bloody sodding turn.'

She looked away, finding it unbearable, and stared instead across the down sweeps of dead branches, luminous with growths, as they pushed with a sloshing water sound through the tunnel of storm sky and boiling river.

Eleven

Later, the rain stopped, but the sky retained its darkness. The funguses gave a confused light.

He had not yet given up the oars. The river ran faster here, and he rested on them, letting the water move the boat on.

Eva gazed downwards at ripples and bubbles. She felt bewildered and afraid. All security seemed gone for ever, and he had shut her out.

'What—?' she began.

'Shut up,' he responded hoarsely.

'Why?' she cried.

'Ssh. Because I hear riders up the bank.'

She fell silent at once.

'Were the rest of Jallow's gang in the town?' he asked her softly.

'No, down river—'

'You never mentioned it,' he muttered. 'Didn't it occur to you we'd run slap into them coming back? Never mind.' He relaxed wearily. The oars made no sound.

Eva caught the thud of hooves, on the right bank, farthest away from them. She waited, a horrified audience of one, until suddenly a shadow horse and shadow rider burst out from cover ahead and galloped through dim green toadstool luminance along some invisible path, making back towards Oiltown. No sooner was the shape gone than two others followed. A snatch of foul language and laughter eddied unmusically in the stillness.

At this point the boat was pulled free of the concealing branches by a twist in the river's tail.

The riders seemed oblivious of the boat. Eva willed them into blindness.

Not blind, a man moved his head.

But he did not stop or call to the others. He grinned. Clearly he did not realize who was in the boat nor for what purpose, yet caught unexpectedly by this scene which emanated in essence from some summer Sunday uncountable years before, he bared his fangs, derisively tickled. And then rode out of sight among the crowded corpse-trunks.

'He didn't know you,' Eva breathed.

'No. He wasn't with the others this morning. Lucky.' Sail leaned on the oars; the river now ran with great determined surges. His eyes were open and very palely bright. 'We might even make it. You must be a talisman.'

Eva, accustomed to un-understanding, merely trailed her hand in the black water. A slight froth was starting to appear on it, and it had a slimy feel like some curious oil-slicked animal under her fingers. There was a smell too, faint, acrid, sour – it reminded her of the Belmort shack and the noisome and noisy swamp beyond the wall.

'The marsh,' she said. She shivered and drew out her hand, away from an abrupt acid-green welling just under the surface.

Between the claws of forward branches she made out a curve in the river wending leftwards. Trails of the green stuff in the water led to and converged upon the curve. Tall bald foggy trees rose from the far bank with dripping wigs of lichen.

A sound came from behind them, up the bank. At first she thought the rain had begun again. Then, once more unmistakable, the wet heavy beats of horses with men on their backs.

'Sod it.' Sail grabbed up the oars. 'I knew that was too good to last. The bastard must have told his friends.'

It seemed now a whole herd of horses was bearing down on them. A voice shouted, wordless, imperative.

The oars strained in their sockets, the river heaved. Gelid cascades ran down the banks, creating whirlpools, so that the landscape seemed to catch the urgency of flight and pursuit.

There came a sharp explosion out of the air. Somewhere a piece of metal death leapt, and then fell back cheated, with a whining ricochet among the trees.

'Keep your bullets to yourself,' Sail said. The oars, caught in an insane cross current, bucked and wrenched in his hands.

Another shot came over them in a howling shriek to split the river into a dozen broken mirrors.

'Get down,' he hissed. '*Eva!*'

She threw herself on the boat's uneven floor, and bit her fingers with fear.

The swing came suddenly as the curve took them and swept them away. Dimly she heard men cursing and horses floundering on the borders of the marsh, unable to proceed. And then another voice shouting his name after them like a malediction.

'Hard *luck*,' Sail ground out above her. But a final burst of firing fell through the sky. The boat gave a great pitch. She thought one of the bullets had hit it, but the steady swing continued and a deep quiet drew in on them.

She picked herself off the bottom and sat up. Sail was staring back up the river at the men and guns now hidden and made impotent by the bank.

'You bastard,' he whispered, 'you fucking bastard.'

Blood was running all over his left arm, swimming in the rain-wet shirt.

'They hit you.'

'I don't know where,' he said. 'I can't seem to feel anything.' He lapsed back against the side of the boat. 'You'll have to take the oars now, Eva,' he added.

She crawled along the boat and passed him dragging himself the other way. He lay down, still half propped up by the limited space. She was afraid to touch him, as if one finger out of place might send the bullet spinning deeper and more deadly into him, rupturing, severing. She took hold of the oars instead, and such was her skill, that the boat flung itself widdershins and almost capsized.

'Eva, Eva,' he said, and began to laugh. She had never heard such laughter; he might have been crying. Finally he murmured, 'Either I'll bleed to death or you'll drown me. Which?'

She sat bolt upright and forced the oars to move. Vertebrae in her back seemed to break free and tumble up and down her spine at each thrust. Her huge eyes were fixed on him. Cobwebs of mist drifted from among the marsh trees and wove around the boat. The water lost its impetus, sluggish suddenly, and slow. There was no sound.

'Don't die,' she moaned.

She began to pray, unknowing, her lips moving awkwardly around the unused words. He did not speak to her. After a time she became convinced that he had died and she, like some mythical ferryman, carried him into the country of the dead, into a marsh Hell ruled by a bone king.

She rowed and rowed, her back like a broken rod.

She could not stop.

The prayers withered on her mouth. She ceased to exist, or so it seemed, and her soul went out of her.

The marsh fog rolled down and smothered the trees, the river, the boat.

At some time during the darkness she fell asleep. Dawn woke her patting her face with pale red light. She was stiff and ice-cold, her hands locked to the oars. Somehow the river had drifted the boat very gently through the marsh, which was not Hell after all, but merely an interlude. Now it lay before her but behind them, a distant blur of shapes where something was giving a coughing scream.

Eva's eyes went down the short length of the boat as though it were a long stretch of many yards. She half expected him not to be there any longer, dissolved by the corrosive acid of her sleep. But he lay as before, almost still, yet she could see him breathing.

She leaned to him. Her shadow fell over his face. The blood was a dry crust, a kind of black armour on his body;

the rest of him seemed completely colourless. She touched his cheek and he turned his head away and said something she could not make out.

She went back to the oars but her arms seemed to have come out of their sockets in the night. She gave up, and turned herself round to see where the river was taking them, but trees still hid the vistas of the banks. The water was like warm red wine, but frost spears dripped from boughs.

She stretched out to him again and touched him again, but he was burning hot despite the cold. She remembered a man at Foulmarsh who had burned like this under his skin when a snake nipped him. After a day he turned black and died. She did not know what to do. She sat by Sail and held his hand tightly, trying to hold him back from pain, or the Skull King of the marsh, who even now might ride after them on a rattling horse, to demand of her what he considered his.

'Sail,' Eva said to him at intervals. He did not hear her.

Much later in the cold red morning he opened his eyes and looked at her.

'Where are we?' he asked distinctly.

'Out of the marsh. But I don't know. Are you better?'

'Yes. But it won't last. You don't look real. You've got a halo all round you.'

Eva stared at herself, and when she looked back at him the tide had pulled him away from her once more.

Later he held a conversation with someone who was not there. She could not make out much of it, but he seemed angry. She held his hand more tightly and her tears ran between his fingers.

* * *

With an almost metaphysical whim, the river suddenly split two ways. Faced with a decision, Eva managed to guide the boat into the left hand channel a moment before it rammed the dividing bank. Why she chose the left she had no idea. It was sheer desperation, and possibly because at first she had tried to go right. Having accomplished her task, she sat by the oars, yet facing down river. Soon the separate river branch was out of sight. It was noon, a dull sky full of clouds piled ever more deeply overhead. Suddenly something loomed on the left bank.

'Sail!' she cried, forgetting he no longer knew her, or cared.

Through a dried-out chainmail of willows, she saw a three-storey building with endless ranks of broken windows, great broken glass doors facing on to a wide verandah and long jetty. Cake-icing terraces of ruinous crazy-paving held the pile above the river. A battered tin sign cracked and creaked on a pole. All paint was gone from it, plus all identity, and with every lurch of the wind it came a little closer to its final descent into the water.

As the boat ran alongside the jetty, branches hooked it, angled it sideways, and brought it against one of the underwater piers with a bump, after which it sat almost immobile, consentingly trapped.

For some minutes Eva did not move, sitting in the slightly bobbing boat. The deserted and pillaged façade of this riverside inn filled her with both a longing for shelter and a dread of abandoning flight. For pursuit was by now so tangible to her, she seemed to feel the strong breath of it blowing down river after them. Besides, she was not certain how they would get out of the boat, up the jetty, through the remains of doors.

She put her hand on him gently and called his name. It seemed to her he would never hear her, as if she were calling out to someone sightless and deaf across a great abyss.

The cloud swelled in the sky, and a spatter of thin hail stung her hands and the nape of her neck.

In desperation she managed to lift him up to sit against her, and he came to suddenly, and said: 'I think he knew I took it off him.'

'Try to stand up,' Eva coaxed, 'please, Sail.'

'Stand up,' he said. 'No, you don't understand. When I took the money he felt it. He wasn't sure, though, or we'd know about it already.'

She somehow got both of them to their feet. He seemed to be able to stand. While the boat dipped and sidled dangerously they achieved the jetty. She found herself kneeling on the dank wooden platform with Sail half lying against her, his eyes wide open and looking round feverishly after some ancient enemy.

'Please,' Eva said, 'please try—'

But he only agreed with her that they would have to split up and that Frank could deal with the man.

Hail slashed her face with twenty sharp needles.

She dragged him upright and to his feet again, and held on to him, with her teeth cutting through her lip, and her eyes burning holes out of her face. He was not so much heavier than she was, but it was difficult, for his steps wove in every direction except the right one. She sank her nails into his side in her efforts to keep hold of him, and bits of the jetty received her Oiltown heels with sick soft depressions. Presently the wood splintered and snapped the right heel so that thereafter she was a limping cripple with one leg three inches higher than the other. She dared not stop to undo the shoe-straps and be free; she could not let go of him because then she would never be able to take up the struggle again. The door came towards her weaving, and with torturing slowness. The bullet wound, which seemed to be in his shoulder, began to bleed again, drenching her left hand. He kept talking to her about the pick-pocketed man. It drove her insane.

'Shut up!' she yelled at him.

Inside, a survival of plastic oak beams arched overhead. A curving bar backed by smashed mirrors, a few broken tables, a chair or two, and the remains of old sofas now despoiled of stuffing. Jagged shards of bottles carpeted the floor, evidence of previous human infiltrations.

Eva, in her instinctual quest for defensible shelter, rejected the open-work room. She manoeuvred them behind the bar and somehow, incredibly, half way up a narrow staircase, before he slid out of her grip. She sat on the stairs on the worn carpet, holding him, for ten minutes before she could dredge enough strength from her apparently melting wax body to haul them both to the top. While they sat she found a baby's rattle wedged among the banisters.

In the passage at the stair head were several doors, some kicked down. And there was a bedroom with a boarded-up window, huge pieces of walnut furniture, an unbelievable double bed with a chintz cover still on it, and a door – not only entire but possessed of lock and key. She got him to

the bed and on to it, ran back to the door and forced the
rusty key around. She was so exhausted she scarcely knew
now what she did, or what was happening to her. She lay
down beside him on the bed, but could not sleep or even be
still. She nibbled at her nails and hair, and sometimes got
up again to pace about the room. She had reached a total
impasse.

There was nothing else she could do, or think of to do.
Her distress had become so complete she no longer felt it.
The hail-storm flagellated the roof for a while, then fell
silent.

Gradually the light changed into bronze and then into
black through the cracks in the board.

She fell abruptly asleep by the door, and was woken in
the core of the night by Sail's voice calling out to her by
another name. She stumbled to the bed and he was looking
at her perfectly lucidly.

'Caroline,' he said, 'can you get me some water? I'm
burning up.'

'My name isn't Caroline,' she spat at him, unbearably
robbed of identity along with all the rest. But he did not
hear her.

She hated to unlock the door, but she scraped the lock
open and ran along the corridor into various rooms.
Kitchen taps blotched with rust spoke of forgotten water-
mains, but there was now no water here except the
corruption of the river. She went down to the bar. Dry
pumps mocked her. A bottle of crème de menthe had long
since bled out its sticky soul. She found a cellar beneath like
a little dungeon, and rattled and crashed about among its
crated prisoners. But she was not the first. She cut her

154

hands on broken glass; she could not see what she was doing. Eventually she found a group of bottles unviolated in a corner.

In the orange moonlight of the bar she peered at dark liquid, and smashing off the top against a beer pump, she gulped a blazing surprise that made her cough unbearably. Nevertheless she carried it back to him, having found nothing else. But he was unconscious again and took no notice of her wheedling to drink.

Later she drank some more herself, because it warmed her, and at last slipped over in a drunken sprawl beside the bed.

She dreamed she was in Foulmarsh, and Steel a black silhouette on the roof of the Moss shack, but it was Sail not Jezubal who fell back with a bullet in his brain, and oceans of blood ran down the street and swept her away with them.

She woke feeling ill and depressed in an unbearable late afternoon glare, the night and most of the day having bypassed her. Her eyes watered and her bones hurt. She went and stood by the bed and gazed at him as he lay there bleeding almost imperceptibly to death, inch by inch, drop by drop. She felt such pain in her then that it transcended any emotion or hurt she had ever experienced. It was beyond grief or prayer or reason. She had no room for it in her fragile narrow confines; it seemed to burst her open, being too large for the vessel that contained it.

Somewhere outside, in the huge void of the world, a horse whickered.

Eva froze, every muscle, nerve and pore strained to catch again that terrible sound. For several minutes she stood there rigid. Then came a hoof beat, brief on ground followed by a faint, dry rustling among the willows. They had caught them up. Jallow's men had found them. Whimpering she began to heave an ancient wardrobe along the wall to cover the locked door. It made a lot of noise, so that during the agonizing move, while she seemed to tear all the fibres of her body in pieces, she could not hear what was taking place outside and around the building.

At last she leaned on the barricade, sobbing for breath.

They had been close all the time, as she had sensed. They had clearly come overland, galloping on the horses while the boat drifted slowly. Even negotiating the marsh had given them little trouble.

There was a crunch of footsteps through the broken glass below.

'Oh no,' Eva pleaded, whispering, retreating to and crouching by the far wall. 'Please, no, no . . .' But the feet were on the stairs now. Only one man coming up. Perhaps he would not think to try this room, would go away. Perhaps—

Outside, in the corridor, the feet halted.

In the pause, the world stopped spinning, and every angle of it congealed in a burning silver stasis before Eva's eyes.

Then the handle of the door was rattled, only once, after which there came the shortest shift of movement, a brief click, and then a shattering concussion which seemed to bring the building down round her ears. Plaster sprayed fine as pollen from the ceiling, but no bricks. She uncovered her face and realized he had shot off the lock, and was now thudding at the door.

The wardrobe, rotten at the back, began to splinter, and totter.

'No!' Eva screamed, trying to hold it in place by mental frenzy.

But there was the soft disintegrating moan of wood, and the great walnut monster tipped and toppled slowly forwards and down, just missing the bed, cracking open on the floor, to spill a welter of intense dusts and odours. It had cost her so much effort.

Eva got up and stood facing the door which now swung easily, almost casually open. She was prepared in her terror for all Jallow's gang, for rape, murder, pain, for what they would do to Sail, while they held her shrieking.

But she was not prepared for what she actually saw. For Steel was standing in the doorway, the ivory rifle smoking in his hands.

EVA AND
STEEL AND
SAIL

Twelve

To Eva, a situation burst ready-made into the room. Nurtured as she was on feuds and jealousies and cruelty, she could see only in a black and white fashion this scene projected from some ancient play, or from more recent episodes in the settlement. Not that Steel in the least resembled any village man, he had become rather, in his absence, like some figure out of myth or from the Bible. But she barely saw him at all, only what she thought he represented, and such was the frightful purity of her vision that she sprang to Sail and snatched the knife out of his belt, and stood over him with the knife pointed at Steel.

This then was how she welcomed him back to her. She, who had begged and implored him not to go, she, who had lived off his life like some parasitic plant, who had learned every angle of his face by rote, who had hung on the tail of a running horse in order not to be left separate from him. If it disturbed or troubled him in any way, or even pleased him obscurely (having satisfied some assessment he might have made of her), he did not show it. He merely leaned the rifle on the upright of the door, and stood looking at her. She had forgotten or mislaid her memory of his elegance; it astonished her, the way he stood there, as if nothing had ever passed between them.

'I won't hurt you,' he said. She had forgotten the sound of his voice also. He did not look at Sail, only at her. 'Either of you.'

It offended her sense of values. She could not fit his noncommittal mercy into the jigsaw she had already assembled.

'Don't touch him,' she said.

He said nothing but his eyes went slowly around the room then, and came to the torn-off ruined crow-black shoes lying in a corner which he had given her when he left her, a million years before.

'Did any of Jallow's men come with you?' she rasped insistently. 'Did you bring anyone?'

'No.'

'When did you come back then?'

'The day you left,' he said, and this time his eyes found her eyes and poured into them such a blue coldness that she felt glaciers clashing in the room. She fell back, yet still holding the knife, then sat on the edge of the bed, for she was extraordinarily tired suddenly, as if his presence had released her from some responsibility.

'He'll die anyway,' she said flatly. 'They shot at us. There's a bullet in his shoulder and he's bleeding to death.'

'Yes,' Steel said. He said it without inflexion, indifferently.

'You'll watch, I suppose,' Eva said, with bleak triumph. Then, proudly: 'I stabbed a man in Jallow's shop.'

'I believe you,' he said.

She glanced up and found he had somehow crossed the

room and was standing over the bed. His shadow fell away from the boarded window in a black transparent gash across Sail. Steel was looking at Sail for the first time. He was looking as if observing something entirely new, original and unique, but not as if it interested him.

'What are you going to do?' Eva asked, tensing.

'Break his neck,' he said. 'Naturally.'

She missed the bizarre and empty humour, and tried to slash him with the knife, but he caught her wrist effortlessly and took the blade neatly from her scrabbling fingers. Eva began to scream and tear at him, but he pushed her away and held her there.

Such was the effect of his touch on her that she became eventually still and almost quiescent.

'Is that whisky, on the floor there?'

She turned and stared at the broken bottle she had drunk from on the previous night when Sail had called her by another name. She picked up and handed Steel the bottle; he sniffed it and set it aside. His movements had been calculated and slow up to this moment. Now he leaned forward and ripped the blood-caked shirt off Sail's body, and the terrible sound of sundered material charged the air with violence and horror. Eva cried out. It might have been actual skin that he had violated so abruptly.

'What are you going to do?' she yelled at him again.

'Get the bullet out. I presume you want him alive. Otherwise you have a choice of haemorrhage, blood-poisoning or gangrene. Whichever sets in first.'

'You'll kill him,' she shrieked. 'You'll kill him.'

But he took no notice of her, bending over the atrocious mess of wound and flesh with a passionless carved intensity.

'If you want to help him,' he said, taking up the whisky bottle, 'find some more of this.'

She saw the knife glitter in his fingers. She felt powerless and appalled, like the helpless witness of some unspeakable calamity either hundreds of feet below her or many miles up in the air, unable to prevent anything, yet forced visually to participate in all. So overwhelming was the sight of the tall figure of Steel bending over Sail's undefended body that she could no longer bear to look at it. Steel might have been a ghoul or vampire or some savage animal reared up on its hind legs. So she turned and ran out of the room and down the narrow stairs. Her feet were sliced by broken glass. She fled out into the open fires of earliest sunset. Everything seemed to be in flames, the river, the trees, the shattered windows, and now her own self ignited like tinder as her inflammable whiteness struck on the air.

She skidded down among the willows. She ran into a tree and fell over, half cordoned off by shadow now from the blazing conflagration that was the world. Here she whimpered, waiting for the sky to fall on her. There seemed no other possible resolution to her existence now she had betrayed what she loved to what she loved.

In the twilight he emerged from the building, and found her sitting limp and expressionless against a tree. She would not look at him.

Steel said, 'I didn't kill him, Eva. Why should I?'

She could not find words to explain to him that by her own inexorable creed there was every reason why he should. She bowed her head and picked at her skirt.

'He won't be able to leave here for two or three days,'

Steel went on, 'and I imagine you want to stay with him. Where were you planning on making for, the two of you?'

'I don't know,' Eva managed to answer.

'Jallow's men are liable to arrive at any time,' he said. 'They'll come down river. They imagined I'd shoot both of you when I found you, and they allowed me a margin to do it in. But they'll follow to make certain. I'll stay here until you're able to get away.'

Her head jerked up and she stared at him.

'Why?' she asked, incredulous. '*Why?*'

But there was nothing in his face to help her. He said: 'I have the time.'

Almost with anger she said, 'Don't you care about it – that I slept with him, that I ran off with him?'

'Yes,' he said, 'I care about it.'

He was smiling faintly.

'You're glad to be rid of me,' she accused him.

'No.'

'Yes. Once I thought you'd poison me to get rid of me, anything so I shouldn't be in your way. Now you're happy that I'll go with him.'

'Very well,' he said. 'Consider me happy.'

He extended a hand to help her to her feet. She seemed only able to remember him in fragments; the hand and the iron strength of the hand surprised her all over again. When she was standing he let her go, and began to walk a little ahead of her towards the inn.

'Steel,' she said.

'What is it?'

But he did not turn to her and she could think of nothing to say to him.

Once inside he sat in one of the abandoned chairs, his long legs stretched out, the rifle across them, its ivory parts pale in the gloom. She hesitated, hovering before him.

'Go up and sit with him,' Steel said.

She began to cry again, silently.

When she reached the room it seemed indefinably different because Steel had moved about in it, some of its entirely non-physical chaos reduced to order. He had found a lamp and lit it, and left it by the bed. The fallen wardrobe was upright against its wall. Finally she looked for Sail and for a moment could not find him, because the bed had been opened and Sail put inside it with his head on the pillow and the covers over him. She somehow shuddered at this, visualizing Sail being lifted up and replaced, for Steel could lift him as easily as a child, as easily as he had lifted herself. It seemed in some perverse way that the whole necessary act carried out in this room had been a form of intimacy between them, while she was shut out.

She went to peer at Sail's face, and it had again that look of death on it that once before had moved her to intolerable pity. Yet now she felt repulsed.

She thought of running down the stairs again, of seizing Steel's hands, but it would be like flinging herself against a rock. He would not give an inch.

So she sat beside Sail and disliked him in varying degrees of intensity, until an hour had passed, and he opened his eyes and looked at her, and said: 'Eva.'

'No,' she sneered, '*Caroline*.'

At which he seemed so troubled and lost and uncertain that her hostility left her immediately.

'Does it hurt you?' she finally whispered.

'Yes. Funny, it didn't hurt at all before. I thought there was someone here,' he added vaguely.

'A man came,' Eva said carefully. 'He helped me. He got the bullet out, and you'll get better now.'

'A man? Not one of Jallow's—'

'No.'

He sighed.

'Someone tall. There was a shadow and a bloody awful pain. I thought, This is it, mate. The Angel of Death in all his magnificence. There was a feller used to live with my mother. I can remember him bending over me when I was a kid, a great tall bastard. He used to like to smash me from one end of the house to the other.'

Eva began to shiver uncontrollably. Sail caught her hand.

'You're freezing. Come in here, with me.'

But she struggled, and looked all round the room, as if hundreds of eyes might be ogling from the walls.

'What's the matter? Is he still here, this man?'

'No,' she said, 'no, he's gone.'

'He's bandaged me up nicely,' Sail said, surprised. 'Why did he do it?'

'No reason,' she stammered.

Sail's eyes were fixed on her, and she began to notice that they seemed to have become greener, as if illness and pain were sliding their bottle glass over the light blue lenses underneath. While she stared fascinated at this change, he said her name three or four times, very insistently.

'Eva, for Christ's sake. Who was it?'

'Who?'

'This man—'

'No one.'

Suddenly he let go her hand and said, 'It was him, wasn't it?'

'No,' she said, shaking her head vehemently.

'Yes,' he said, 'your Steel. Christ,' he breathed softly, 'Christ. The Angel of bloody Death.'

'But he didn't hurt you,' she cried, 'he helped. I didn't know what to do.'

But the wonderment of it seemed to have submerged him. She saw that he was touching at the bandages.

'He's still here,' she said, to bring him back to her. 'Downstairs.'

'Oh,' he said. Casually he said, 'Waiting for you?'

Her teeth were chattering.

'He doesn't want me.'

'But you want him.'

They paused.

He said, 'Then go and find him. I'm not stopping you. I'm sure you can get round him. Somehow.'

She had not anticipated venom from him. It was a mark of her regard for him, perhaps, that she expected him to be, while never being so herself, noble in defeat.

'Sail—'

He moved away.

'Go to hell,' he muttered.

And so, dismissed by both of them, she went to sit half way down the stairs, outwitted.

Sometime later she heard movements below her. Outside, the wheels of a wagon rolled and horse feet clicked. These sounds disinterred various memories, so that she sat on the stairs remembering things that had happened when she was travelling with Steel. She felt like an old woman, remembering, and that was strange, for she had always somehow known she would never grow old. It did not surprise her that Steel had got the wagon through the marsh when Jallow's men faltered at riding through it.

Eventually the smell of cooked food came drifting to the stairs.

She had not eaten for three or four days. She had a picture of herself as an animal, slinking down, seizing something from a dish or out of a pot, and running out into the trees to devour it.

So she slunk into the bar room, and halted among the broken bottles. He had brought in a stove from the wagon and a pan sizzled on it. She found herself intimidated by his tall figure and could go no farther. After a moment or so he turned and came up to her and handed her, without a word, a fried egg between two slices of bread. She wolfed it down so fast that she did not feel appeased and went up and stared at what he was eating, until he glanced at her and handed her the plate. She had never felt so hungry. Perhaps her grief had made her so.

Steel said, as she licked the last crumb off her fingers, 'Take him that.'

She turned and saw that there was soup heating. She wanted very much to say: He won't take it from me. But somehow she could not. She filled a bowl and went upstairs with it.

Outside the shattered bedroom door she paused. She felt a malevolent desire to pour the soup down the bathroom pipes. She crept into the room, hoping he would be asleep. But he was lying on his back in the bed, the lamplight making his face into a mask. He did not look at her. She presented the bowl.

'Eat it,' she said.

'Where did you go?' he asked her, his eyes coming suddenly to her face, so that she was surprised and unnerved by their candour.

'Downstairs,' she said.

'It's all right now, then,' he said, 'between you and him.'

'Oh, yes,' she said. She put the soup down carefully on the floor.

He looked away and said: 'I'm glad, if that's what you want.'

She had an urge to kill him, but did not.

'I'll go in the morning,' he said, 'get out. Jallow's lot may still be after me. I'll be strong enough tomorrow.'

'You won't be strong enough.'

'Well, I'll have to be, won't I, because I'm not hanging round here.'

She stood staring at him hopelessly, and he said gently, 'Piss off, Eva. I'm very tired.'

This time she did not go to sit on the stairs, for she had grown aware of the symbolism of this act of half way. Nor was she unaware of having become the tenuous link between the two of them. She found another small bedroom down a previously unexplored section of the passage. In the pitch blackness she lay on the broken surface of a mattress which she stumbled over on the floor. The night seemed unpeopled by demons, but she did not expect morning, for morning would presumably take Sail away from her, and ultimately Steel. She had a dream in which she saw the two of them riding off together, leaving her behind. It had a kind of obscure justice, but nevertheless, she wept with jealousy and pain in her sleep.

Morning came, fresh and pale, to spite her.

Partly because of the dream, partly because she could hear no sound in the whole building, she began a half-believed pretence that they had both already left her.

The presence of each of them caused her hurt and disquiet, though each in a different fashion. Now, alone, she seemed to have gained a certain freedom.

Steel was not in the bar room. It would have been hard to explain him away if he had been there. Outside, the day had been cold, and was now warm, and shattered laces of ice revolved in the river.

She went down the jetty and looked at the boat still hooked among the willows. She wondered if she should step into it and row away, and felt bitterly satisfied at leaving all and everything behind her. But then she thought of the wide and inhospitable world of dark-haired, dark-eyed hatred where she would become again a freak, and a prey to all the various lusts and malignancies and boredoms and agonies she had known in Foulmarsh. So she looked beyond the boat and wondered whether or not to drown in the river instead. Death held no positive fear for her. It was not that her imagination stopped at death, but simply that it continued in an oblique direction. She did not ask what death would make of her spiritually or mentally, if there were a god or a hell or a blotting out, a nothing. To Eva the continuation was purely physical. She imagined herself a waxen corpse, a graceful decay, ultimately clean bones. In fact, in death, she saw herself at last impersonally.

But she heard the whicker of the horse from beside the inn. She looked back irresistibly, and saw this horse standing with its nose in a bag the way the first horse had stood. It might have been the first horse in appearance. She even wondered if it were, conjured up by some magic of Steel's. It occurred to her he had been outside, feeding the horse, unseen, while she lingered by the river, and this seemed to give the lie to her make-believe more directly than if they had actually met. With her tongue slipping into the hollow of the missing tooth, she went back up the jetty and into the bar room. He was thrusting wood into the stove. She wanted to run to him and encircle the dark hard body with her arms, and place her cheek on the coarse silk of the hair, but now her spontaneity had grown uncertain. She took half a step forward and at this moment Sail appeared behind the bar. She could remember the children in the settlement performing little plays of endless adventure and demise, but in which nobody knew their cues, and rescuers and villains were always running in too soon, disrupting someone else's instant of action. She wanted to shout at Sail to go away, but the second she looked at him total confusion overcame her, because she had the same overpowering desire to embrace and be one with him that she had just experienced for Steel.

Sail's eyes met hers. He shook his head at her and half smiled, an impossible manumission both generous and meaningless. Somewhere above he had found a belted jacket to replace the ripped shirt. It was too large. He had rolled up the sleeves but it hung like a sack round the frayed belt, adding something humorous to his otherwise completely tragic appearance. His face was white and he looked ill and drained and hopeless and, as she had seen once before, this seal of death invested him with a heart-clawing beauty and romanticism. He leaned on the bar counter because that was the only way he could keep himself upright, and contrived to look nonchalant. It was impossible to her to think of him crawling off into the dead trees. But he was looking at Steel now, whose back was still turned. There was an expression of puzzlement and unease on Sail's face, as if he were not sure what Steel might turn out to be. Steel shut the stove door, straightened and turned round. He must have been aware of the dual presence in the room, for they had both set up by their emotions a sort of fiery cross current among the broken bottles. He looked at Eva first, then at Sail. Steel's face was quite blank; she had expected nothing else, but Sail cleared his throat nervously.

'Thanks,' Sail said. The word hung absurdly between them. As if it had been made visible by uniqueness, they all seemed to be in some way staring at it. 'I mean,' Sail said with desperation, 'bloody thank you for saving my fucking skin. And now,' he added, angling himself off the bar and around it, 'I'll be on my way, lady and gentleman.'

'No!' Eva cried.

'Oh, why the hell not?' asked Sail, starting exhaustedly to negotiate the room, making for the doors.

'You'll die,' Eva whispered.

'I'm quite tough, basically.'

She planted herself in front of him, but somehow could not touch him. Aware of Steel, panic began to choke her.

'Please,' she said.

Sail stood and looked at her unhappily.

'You are making this unnecessarily difficult,' he enunciated carefully, but he had started to unbalance and, released by instinct, she was able to catch hold of him. His head subsided, down, down, on to her shoulder.

'For Christ's sake, let me get out of here while I can still walk.'

'No,' she said, and held him more tightly.

Dimly she heard the crackle and rasp of a piece of furniture on the smashed glass floor. Then she and Sail were both somehow seated on one of the bulky, de-stuffed sofas.

'I gather,' Steel said, 'you don't know that Jallow's men are about. You wouldn't make more than a mile or so, assuming you could get that far in any event.'

'He said you could stay here,' Eva told Sail, 'and he'd be here in case they came. Didn't you?' she pleaded.

'Yes,' Steel said.

An unequivocal silence tried to swamp the room.

Sail said: 'What is this? I mean, what is it with you?'

Steel sat on one of the chairs and looked at him. After a moment Sail looked away.

'OK,' he said, 'since I don't have much choice. But you bloody bother me, Steel-whatever-your-name-is.'

Steel said nothing.

Sail seemed compelled to fill the silence.

'And if I'm here, don't worry. I won't come after your girl,' he said bitterly. 'I do get the picture.'

'Obviously not,' said Steel.

Eva began to cry. Sail stirred awkwardly beside her.

'All right. So I'm thick. What glittering facet have I missed this time in the original and stimulating situation?'

'He doesn't want me,' Eva cried out. 'I told you last night.'

Sail seemed to find firmer ground.

'For Christ's sake,' he said. He looked at Steel again, and said, 'The soiled goods bit now, is it? You went off and left *her*, remember, mate. What did you expect her to do, sit round and spin all bleeding year? Why didn't you buy her a chastity belt while you were at it? And how many bits and pieces have you been screwing on your travels? I bet you never went short.'

'Don't,' Eva said frantically.

'All right,' Sail sneered, 'I can see he's bloody seven feet tall and one blow of his iron fist is liable to smash me straight through the wall. The fact remains that he just can't chuck you over because you went off for one night.' He leaned forward and glared at Steel. 'It's all my bloody fault. Do me over, and take her back, you bastard.'

'She happens to want to go with you,' Steel said, and behind the immobility of his expression there seemed to quicken the faintest trace of grave amusement.

Sail subsided, apparently surprised.

'Eva,' he began.

But she jumped up and left him.

'No,' she said, 'no, no.'

'I told you,' said Sail.

'No!' shouted Eva.

'I'll go,' said Sail.

'Wait,' Steel said. 'Eva,' he said, 'be careful. Do you know what you want?'

She went, crying, biting her mouth, to stare out of a broken window, up river.

'Ah, leave off,' Sail grated. 'She's told you, hasn't she?'

Eva clenched her fists and stared out of the window and realized that what she had been staring at was in fact a distant rowboat with three men in it, and the sunlight glinted on the ripples their oars made in the river, and on the rifles across their backs.

Thirteen

She could not seem to tell them what she saw, but Steel had looked where she did. He lifted the rifle off a chair.

'Upstairs,' he said, 'both of you.'

'I'm staying here,' Sail said.

Steel turned. Leaning against the window frame, he angled the rifle casually to cover Sail.

Sail looked at it, got up, swore and walked out of the bar door. Eva ran after him. But neither of them attempted to go up to the bedroom. Sail sat on the fifth stair up; Eva, compelled unbearably to know what would happen, stood by the closed door itself, looking through a crack in the wood into the bar room.

Steel had moved to the broken doors. He thrust them open and went out, the rifle balanced lightly in his hands.

She found she could see along the jetty. The three men were coming out of their boat, stumbling and cursing on the soft planks. One jerked his thumb back at the water.

'The boat's there,' he shouted to Steel. He shambled up the jetty and stood grinning at Steel with grey teeth. 'Boat's there. They came here then. Like Miller said.'

'They came here,' Steel agreed.

The man with the grey teeth laughed and slapped Steel's shoulder.

'You got 'em, did you?'

'You don't see them around,' Steel said.

The two other men joined them, grinning. The rifles seemed to twitch, almost alive, on their backs.

'Led you a dance, didn't she, that little blonde bitch of yours? Get her too, did you?'

One of them said, 'She must've been the one got Johnny. Christ what a mess.'

Grey Teeth edged by Steel and came into the bar room. His eyes went round the plastic wood walls, and up the smashed mirror-back of the bar. Momentarily, unknowing, his chilly probing flicked Eva, and she began to shudder behind her door.

'Any drink left?' the man asked. He touched the old stain of crème de menthe. 'Never could stand that foreign muck.' His eyes rested again on Eva's, through the door crack, quite blankly. 'Where'd you put the bodies, eh? Not just left 'em lying about, I hope. Most unhygienic.'

'The river,' Steel said.

'A watery grave,' said Grey Teeth. 'How very romantic. What's up there then?'

He walked behind the bar and Eva sprang back from her hiding place. She was almost noiseless, but not quite. Grey Teeth cocked his head.

'Rats here, eh?'

He gave the door a thrust and stood looking at Eva speculatively.

'Blonde rats at that,' he said, and Steel shot him in the back.

Eva could no longer see what was happening in the bar room. Instead she watched the intruder fall forwards on his face, as though in supplication before her. Outside came the ominous greased click of two rifles.

'What you do that for?' a man asked, with a kind of moronic astonishment amounting to humour.

Eva took several steps forward in the strangling silence which followed, but at the door someone brushed past her. She had not heard Sail come down the stairs, had, in fact, forgotten his presence. She shrank back, and then, because she could no longer see where any of them were, she ran blindly out of the doorway after him.

She had the briefest impression of the two men standing with their guns directed at Steel, before the scene changed completely. The head of each jerked round at her abrupt entry and one rifle swung in continuity. Before the annihilating blast transfixed her, however, there was a spasm of light or movement on the air, and a knife appeared as if by magic in the gunman's throat. His whole body shocked upwards, and the shot went off among the plastic beams. Then the shot uncannily sounded again. She looked for the other man, and saw him falling slowly into the broken glass.

There was a stillness of settling.

Eva began to giggle and managed to stop herself. Sail went around the bar, retrieved the knife, wiped and sheathed it in his makeshift belt. More than any of them he seemed unnerved by their moment of defensive camaraderie.

Steel hung the rifle on his back, and the smoke of it curled up behind him, in a clear, prussic-blue stencil.

'We no longer have a choice,' he said, 'any of us. We get out now.'

They carried things to the wagon. Eva embraced the horse. She was not really aware any longer of danger, only that indirectly she had got what she wanted – both of them, together, and with her. For however short a time.

Steel carried the stove out last, and tipped its smouldering wooden entrails back across the bar room floor. It appeared a clean and necessary action that they should depart, as once before, in fire.

She got into the wagon with Sail, who slumped immediately against a roll of blankets and shut his eyes, and appeared to fall asleep. She crouched beside him awhile in the moving wagon gloom, looking around her, not in the least marvelling that this interior seemed identical to the last wagon Steel had owned, even to the crated coals and the bolts driven now through the feet of the stove. She was again able to touch clothes which belonged to him in a chest. There were also books, though less of them than before. She fluttered their pages reverently. A strange luminous happiness settled on her. She kissed Sail's cheek as he lay asleep, neither desiring nor resenting him, then pushed open the flaps and edged out to sit beside Steel on the box, something she had never done since the very first.

They drove in silence up a track between the misty trees while below the river ran sinuously parallel, intermittently shrouded by smoke blowing from the burning inn. She turned around, clutching the wagon's canvas, and stared back at the inn, now an open rose of flame.

While Sail slept behind them in the wagon, they rode side

by side but did not speak. She felt no unease this time. There was nothing strenuous in the silence; besides, she had of late grown more accustomed to aloneness and lack of sound. Her thoughts skittered and milled through her brain, not unpleasantly, not really reaching any conclusion or agreement, but never demanding much emotion from her, or any pain. She watched the land change as they veered away from the river.

There was eventually an old road, some vague outer portion of Oiltown, now divided off by the marsh. It was as wide as the highway she had known at the settlement, perhaps even wider, but it had experienced upheavals and also conceivably explosives, for there were several craters. They passed under the remaining parts of many collapsed concrete bridges, set at ten minute intervals.

At first trees and great brambles edged the road but eventually these petered out and left only the vistas of upward-sloping dead fields. Once they went by a beautiful preserved cow's skull lying on the tar, and Eva stared back at it until it was out of sight.

As the light thickened with a looming, warm, crepuscular menace, the landscape seemed to respond in mood. It stretched itself out, downwards now, into valleys, so that Eva could look away and away into ever more murky distances where nothing at all seemed to be growing, and the predominant colour was black of every intensity and hue. When the sun finally staggered under the horizon in a series of drunken smeary lurches, the fume of night seemed to crowd up from the ground instead of down from the sky. Stars showed. Somewhere off the road, from a last stand of briars, something screeched and chattered devilishly.

181

Steel stopped the wagon and lit the swinging lamp. Light fluttered up. She held out her hands to it as if to warm them, though the night was sullenly hot. He came back and swung up again on to the box.

'Are you afraid?' he said.

She shivered.

'What's here that I should be afraid of?'

'It's a desert,' he said. 'You may see anything. Don't let it surprise you.'

'Jallow's men won't follow this way?'

'I doubt it.'

A raw cindery hot wind came blowing suddenly across the open valleys.

'What was here?' she whispered.

The horse began to move forward again and the lamp swung bright.

'Farms.'

'What now?'

'Anything at all.'

Outside the circle of light the dark pressed close. She glanced back towards the inside of the wagon, but did not retreat.

'He's still asleep,' Eva said. She paused and waited for herself. She said: 'He came from a settlement. Like mine, I suppose.'

Steel said nothing.

'You,' she said, 'where do you come from?'

He did not answer. 'I know,' she said, 'a *place*.'

'A place,' he said.

'Why did you leave?' she hazarded.

'I had no choice,' he said.

'What happened?'

He glanced at her. But a sudden film came over the backs of his eyes. It was what she had expected.

'Tell me,' she said.

'No.' But then, as she stared at the ivory rifle across his back, 'Clever Eva,' he said softly.

Her attention was distracted then by a great loping shadow beating across the road about twelve feet in front of the horse, which stamped and shook its head in alarm.

'What was that?' she asked him.

'An animal of some kind.'

She shuddered again, and suddenly turned and went back into the wagon.

Letting go the flap, she crept over to Sail. To her terrific amazement, she found his eyes were wide open and looking straight at her.

'What's out there?' he asked her quietly.

'Desert. Black fields.'

'I'm thirsty.'

Familiar from before with the wagon, or its layout, she reached for one of the slopping leather bottles and passed it to him. He unstoppered it, tipped some liquid into his mouth, then choked and spat. He glared at her.

'Lamp-oil!'

She tried another bottle, which turned out to be water.

He did not drink much. Setting the bottle aside, he lay back on the blanket roll and looked at her remorselessly.

'This is a damn stupid situation you've got me into,' he said.

She smiled enigmatically.

He amazed her again, this time by laughing. Then he

caught her hand and pulled her over to him.

After a moment she tried to push away.

'No,' she spat, 'not *here*!'

'Where then? Out there in the fields?'

'Not in his wagon. No.'

'Why not? He must know. If he's so bloody magnanimous, let's see how far it goes.'

She hit him and he promptly hit her back. There ensued a comparatively silent struggle marked only by their panting, the creaking boards, and Sails suppressed but potentially explosive curses on the two occasions when she managed to bite him. In the end he let her go.

Instead he put a hand on his shoulder and pulled a face at the pain.

'I don't care,' she said, and turned her back on him.

He said: 'There was some story about him – your Steel – That he goes after certain men, to kill them—'

'Yes,' she said.

'Really?' he said. 'Why?'

'Oh,' she said. Her hands shook a little, so she tucked them together.

'Christ,' Sail said. She heard him turn on his side. 'Sleep tight,' he said sarcastically, but very soon she did.

When she woke up it was light, the wagon was still, and Sail had contrived to get his head on her shoulder and was deeply, serenely sleeping. Disgusted by his almost angelic appearance and this somnambulist plot of his physically to link the two of them, she thrust him off and scrambled outside.

They were parked on the topmost rise of a sweep of rises,

still on that ominous dishevelled highway. About twenty yards farther on a huge vehicle lay on its side under decades of brambles.

By daylight the landscape was even more forbiddingly and nightmarishly beautiful. Its straightly sloping ebony lines seemed impressed like a wood-cut on the bottom of a sky. Eva looked for Steel, even called out for him, but he did not appear. The horse turned and stared at her and stamped its feet, and its hooves made metallic pockets of sound in the wooden quiet her voice had failed to stir.

She began to walk along the road, and went past the derelict mobile. Ancient tins lay tumbled among the briars. She thought Steel had for some reason gone down the highway. It therefore seemed logical that if she kept on walking she would eventually meet him coming back.

After a while the road curved away on itself. She stopped and looked back round the bend and saw first the prehistoric vehicle, then the wagon silhouetted blackly on the sky.

'Steel!'

This time an answer came, though not from him. Somewhere in the black fields something squalled at her.

These sounds deterred her. At the curve of the road she hesitated, and probably would have gone back to the wagon. Then she looked the other way, and saw, a long distance from her, the form of a tall masculine figure, standing static as herself.

She walked round the bend and then up the highway towards him.

When she was rather nearer, something struck her as odd about the way he was waiting there. She began to run to get to him more quickly. There was only about twenty feet between them when she suddenly realized that this was not Steel after all.

She stopped, staring.

His white hair was very long; she had not seen before. He wore clothes of dark skin, but was mainly clothed in his own, also very dark and strangely metallic. It was by the look of his skin that she knew he was a mutant. What had misled her at first was his enormous perfection.

His ribcage was colossally enlarged, and his eyes, she now noticed, had over them an inner closed lid, almost transparent, and under that there was no white only a fluid gleaming golden-blackness. It came to her that he had also perhaps mistaken her for someone else. Now he turned and moved back along the road away from her at an easy controlled and loping run. She thought of the mutant in the silent woods who, Steel had said, would supplant her. Now she had seen it to be true, and had seen transience – her own.

In this state of mind she turned back towards the wagon, and her brain translated the images in her eyes into a curious and ephemeral hallucination. The highway seemed fallen away, the brambles were forests of thorns. The wagon, when she reached it, was a hulk, a skeleton, and presently only a smoky ghost suspended in the air.

She felt a shift in her life, quite distinctly, as if some bone of her soul, which for seventeen years had been rattling disjointedly about in her, had suddenly snapped home into its socket.

There was an aptness also in this shift, for today was her eighteenth birthday, though she had forgotten.

Steel came suddenly around from the back of the wagon.

For the first time ever she looked at him impersonally, unemotionally. He seemed to be aware of the content of her scrutiny. His eyes touched briefly on hers and in the cold waste at the back of them she saw, for one second, a glimpse of terrifying ordinariness. And though only for a second – for he was really very far from ordinary – it came to her that he and she were initially built out of the same material. Surprised, she became aware that he also, as Sail and she were, was merely a human being.

Fourteen

Sail was still asleep in the wagon. He seemed feverish again, his skin dry and hot and himself moving restlessly, so that she sat with him for a time until he grew quieter.

Later she sat again on the box with Steel, and saw how the road swooped down ahead of them into a tangle of curious dead growth, part of which seemed to be trees, some fallen, part the ruins of buildings. She had a premonition of something horrible as they advanced towards this place.

'Must we go through there?' she asked.

When he did not answer, she became aware in their direction of a continuance of his searching. Somewhere ahead his quest went on, his mysterious work, or only need – to kill. Why did he do this? What grudge or vision drove him? Could it ever end? It came back to her that he had once said: 'One killing gives birth to another. Once begun it can't be stopped.'

Black shadow enveloped them.

She found she could not make herself look left or right and that she had narrowed her eyes so that she could barely see ahead. Her tongue curled into the socket of the absent tooth.

'I don't like it here,' she spoke, trying to let nothing else hear her. 'I don't like it.'

Neither did the horse like it. It tossed its head and shied at nothing. Steel unslung the rifle and held it across his knees.

In the air was a smell of rust and dankness, and through this came occasional dim stenches. Eva cowered. At last new light broke out ahead, pale yellow flames of dayglow. Because she had her eyes fixed on these and would not look aside, she did not at first properly grasp what happened.

There came a brutal, brutish crashing, and a strong gorge-knotting odour, both at once, as if sound had assumed a smell, or smell a sound. Eva had an impression of part of the black wall heaving up and over her forward line of vision.

Then the wagon was flung upwards and sideways, bucking and subsiding and the horse danced screaming on its hind legs with something like a large blanket tossed over its back.

Eva, confused and frightened, found herself clutching the canvas to save herself falling off the box. A deafening blinding eruption in the air confused her further until she realized it must be the rifle. With a jolt the horse, and what had settled on it, sank on the roadway. The blanket – something of dark, scabby hide, still formless – slid away. Released, the horse kicked feebly, now under a red lacework of impossible, horrifying injuries, inflicted so swiftly, still uttering ghastly screams at its pain. Steel swung quickly from the box. Eva bit her hands and shut her eyes. This time she did not mistake the shot. The cries ceased and the wagon gave a final shudder and stopped still as if it too had experienced the bullet. She let go her hands and sat limply with no feeling in her, not even the desire to cry.

'What the hell is going on?'

She turned and looked incuriously up at Sail, who had appeared as if conjured, by her shoulder. He seemed better again, she vaguely noted. He slipped an arm around her; certain situations elicited certain appropriate responses from him.

'Go inside,' he said. And this too seemed automatic, and, if anything, irrelevant.

'It doesn't matter. I saw,' she said.

He let her go then, and jumped down, and walked to where Steel was still standing.

'What a mess,' Sail said. He bent and quickly flicked a piece of hair out of the horse's open death-glazed eye. It was a useless gesture, yet oddly touching in its superfluous tenderness. Steel had turned back, and was getting the dead body free of the wagon. 'Do you want this harness off her?' Sail asked casually.

'Yes,' Steel said.

Sail set about the task.

'Any more of those things likely to be around?'

'It's possible,' Steel said.

'Eva,' Sail said, 'keep an eye on the trees.'

Eva scarcely heard him. She leaned to Steel.

'I'm a jinx on your wagons,' she said solemnly. 'You lost the last because of me.'

But at a sound, she recollected, and stared round at it. A small unspecified shape hovered near the road edge, perhaps drawn by their movements, or more likely by the smell of blood.

'He hasn't lost the wagon, yet. Shoulders to the wheel,' Sail said with debonair sarcasm, and in an accent not his own. He put the harness past Eva into the wagon, rather as if she were not there. As Steel started to drag the corpse of the horse off the road, he went to help him.

'Leave it,' Steel said.

'Ah, come on. Quicker with two.'

'You'll open the wound,' Steel said shortly.

'So I'll bloody bleed.'

Eva, marooned like an audience on the box, watched the two of them regard each other across the ripped and matted death. All her sorrow and sickness burst suddenly forth in huge, slow, soundless tears, but even through running water, she continued to peer at them, fascinated, sensing abruptly a personal isolation that had little to do with where she sat. After a moment they began to pull at the dead horse in unison. It bothered her. She had an urge to jump down and add her own strength, but could bear to go no nearer.

She wished that they could bury the horse. The thought of so many little nearby mouths filled her with disgust and fear. She called to Steel but he did not hear. The body fell upon crackling undergrowth. Sail and Steel emerged from shadow and stood on the road in front of her.

'Now what? Push the jolly old wagon?' said Sail.

Steel took up the rifle and came to her.

'Get down, Eva. Walk behind us and shout if you see anything bigger than a cat.'

She got down.

Sail, going past her, hesitated, and gently brushed the large round tears away from under her eyes.

'I take it I'm honoured by inclusion in your work gang?' he said to Steel in the other voice. 'All push together, old boy, eh?'

Steel said nothing. The three of them walked behind the wagon.

In the shadowy back-lit gloom the physical similarities of the two men seemed absurdly highlighted. The differences became unimportant, even, in some peculiar way, seemed to accentuate their sameness. She was struck suddenly by a weird and faintly terrifying thought that they were merely facets of one thing – which would shortly conjoin and then dissolve, leaving her alone in the wilderness.

Mesmerized, she stood on the road.

They set their right shoulders against the hulk. Wheels creaked. Sail swore.

At the next thrust, the wagon rolled protestingly forward.

They moved slowly and laboriously in this manner towards the open sky ahead, Eva trailing behind them, glancing nervously from side to side, but more often at them, in a miserable and suspicious silence. She could not explain to herself what she felt, or why; she was aware again of that curious jealousy which she had felt at the inn.

It took a long time to reach the light. The broken stumps and skull-eyed walls fell behind slowly. At last only the black hills rolled beyond the road. Eva scarcely looked about her. She looked at them.

They leaned against the struts, simply breathing after the exertion. Sail had shut his eyes and grit his teeth. Then she heard him say: 'You were bloody right. It's torn wide as a barn door.'

Steel opened Sail's shirt with one hand and looked. Eva watched him. Steel went up into the wagon and came back with clean strips of cloth. He packed the linen against the wound and bound it up again while Sail leaned on the wagon strut, white-faced and slit-eyed.

'Thanks,' he said hoarsely. 'Sorry to give you the trouble twice over, mate.'

'We'll stop here,' Steel said. 'There's some kind of settlement over those hills. They may have horses, or dogs.'

'You know everything, don't you? Could get to be a bad habit.'

'Smoke. That's how I know.'

Sail turned, but Eva did not, still watching only them.

'Oh, I see. Clever. Christ, I feel as weak as a nit. Somehow I'm going to have to crawl back up there. It's fucking silly, but I don't think I can even make it . . .'

Steel had not moved away. Now he simply lifted the other man up and placed him on the ledge at the wagon's back.

A red-hot, icy and oddly shameful tide ran down Eva's body. One of those sudden dry winds ripped across the road and raised the hair from her burning face. She coughed harshly and then gave a burst of fox-barking laughter. Sail, sitting facing her now, seemed abruptly to remember her. His hollow curious eyes flickered away from hers.

Steel said to her, 'Stay here. Stay in the wagon.'

She snarled at him.

The rifle across his back, he turned off the road and began to walk along the roll of the slope towards a new line of hills over which separate spasms of smoke were drifting. It alarmed her neither that he might be walking into danger nor that he had left her in it. She scrambled into the wagon almost eagerly, but not for protection.

Sail sat against the canvas now, drinking from a leather bottle. He half looked up at her, and offered it.

'Brandy,' he said.

Still without understanding her feelings and still burning hot with some inexplicable shame or rage, she struck the bottle out of his hand, and then struck him across the check. As if a sequence of events must be re-enacted, he caught her hand and pulled her down and somehow turned her as she fell and was on top of her.

'Be careful,' she sneered, 'mind the bullet *wound*.'

But she had no scruple now concerning Steel's wagon, and was also amazed to find herself unbearably sexually aroused, not only by this violence and Sail's body against hers, but also in some oblique way by the episode outside. The thrust of his entry into her made her gasp and clutch at him, as if to rip the flesh off his bones.

In the middle of the afternoon there was a sudden storm and rain crashed from ruptured incendiary clouds. Afterwards a glare hung on the wet road, reflected from the magenta sky.

Eva drank some of the brandy which had not been spilled, and lay dozing and discontented. Sail reclined on the blankets reading one of Steel's books with apparent absorption and understanding. She resented this bitterly, not having properly understood at any time anything that Steel read. They did not speak to each other.

When the rain came she got out drunkenly and let it soak her, keeping her eyes rigidly away from the ruins where the horse was doubtless being eaten. When the downpour ceased she climbed back into the wagon, stripped and towelled herself, and put on one of Steel's shirts in lieu of her dress. She seated herself not far from Sail and began to brush and comb her wet hair with long elaborate strokes, humming to herself and taking care to splash him. As the droplets of rainwater flew off her hair on to the pages of his book, darkened and smudged across incomprehensible words, she began to laugh intermittently and softly, but he took no notice either of the wet or of her, and so eventually this game left her unappeased.

As the magenta rain-glare deepened and pulsed in slow irregular beats towards a magenta sunfall, she began to think that perhaps Steel had abandoned both of them and would never come back.

'Read to me,' she said to Sail abruptly.

'No,' he said.

'You'll be going soon, won't you?' she asked in a bright clear voice. 'Like you said before.'

'From the sound of it, I've outstayed my welcome,' he said, not looking up.

'You said you'd go.'

'I seem to recall you asked me not to.'

'That was before. You were ill then.'

'Oh, yes,' he said, 'you had a touching concern for me then.'

'I dislike you,' she suddenly said, quite irresistibly, 'I dislike you intensely.'

'Thanks.'

She was suddenly afraid that he would get up and desert the wagon and walk off up the road, leaving her entirely alone. She was also afraid at what she had actually said.

'I didn't mean it,' she told him.

'Oh, you meant it all right,' he said, and looked at her, and for the first time she saw actual malice in his own eyes directed at her. 'So, having established your brainless little opinion, you can shut your mouth and let me read this.'

She dreamed of Foulmarsh and of Belmort her father who, with a grinning and congested face, raped her repeatedly on the groaning bed he had formerly rocked with Old Woman. The horror of the dream was not so much in his actions as in her own irresistible yet simultaneously revolted pleasure. She dreamed, after, of the impenetrable wall and Jezubal's spinning face, and woke with an agony of cramp in both her legs, screaming in fear and pain.

Just beyond the wagon flap a man cursed gruffly.

'You keep a zoo in here? Wild animals?'

She did not know his voice, and, instantly alarmed, looked about her for Sail, who was not there.

'My sister,' another voice said. The words made no sense, though this time she recognized Steel. Then the flap was pulled back and she found herself looking straight into his extraordinary face, which, even now, she still found an unnerving experience. 'What is it?' he asked her.

'Nothing,' she said icily.

'There are three men from the village out here. They lent us a bullock to get the wagon across the fields.'

'Where's Sail? I suppose with you,' she said disdainfully.

'As you see,' Steel said. He pulled the flap a little wider, and she saw Sail and a big, rough-coated man squatting on the wet road in a raw amber twilight above three flat stones. After a moment, the man pointed at the middle stone.

'That 'un there. She's it.'

Sail flipped the stone up, spun and caught it one-handed.

'Well, I'll be,' said the man thoughtfully. 'Where is she then?'

'You tell me,' Sail said winningly. 'Double your coin if you can get it.'

The man pondered.

'There.'

The stone flew up from the empty wet.

'Damn it,' the man said, goodnaturedly enough, 'I should've known better than to try you out.'

From under the third stone Sail drew a silver coin, tossed it, appeared to catch it, and showed the man his empty hand. After this, he drew the coin from the man's forehead. The man laughed and shook his head, rising up from the amber puddles and towering over Sail.

'You owe me two more like it,' Sail said.

'Pay up, Ed, you've lost good and proper,' the first voice said, from round the side of the wagon now.

'The gentleman has already paid,' Sail said, with all the elegant swagger of his incidental profession, holding up two further silver coins. His victim swore, but stayed sweet.

'I'll have to watch myself round you.'

Sail caught sight of Eva, bowed to her and said: 'Legerdemain.' Purely as she thought to insult her, for she did not know what he meant.

At that moment there was a lurch and a stamping sound from the bullock at the wagon front.

'All set,' a third voice called.

At once the wagon began to move in heavy ponderous rushes, off the road into the rain-drenched desolation of hills. Steel and Sail, letting the villager drive his bullock, fell a little behind, walking with the rough-coat, Ed. He seemed good-humoured, if a little slow. His build and swarthiness showed him a typical product of the villages. Fascinated by Sail's sleight of hand, he kept on at him, in a slurred coaxing voice, for more tricks, like a large and amiable child or some endearing big house dog after bones. Occasionally Sail would oblige. Eva, awed as she would have been long ago in Foulmarsh by his sorceries, considered him cheap in her present mood. It nagged at her, too, that Steel had called her his sister. Probably for her protection, yet she would rather have been claimed as his woman – it was like him not to do that. She wondered if he had adopted Sail into this makeshift family. Physiognomy would back up such an assertion, certainly. Staring at them out of the wagon-back, she became aware that Ed was now looking at her, smiling shyly and trying to catch her eye. There seemed no demand of any kind in his look. Unlike the men of Foulmarsh, whom he so closely resembled physically, there was nothing brutal or sly in his face. She smiled back at him, yet supremely and loftily. Some part of her perhaps had thought this village would be peopled by creatures like the one she had met earlier on the road. Yet she should have guessed they would not be found in mere village groupings. Like phosphorus or clouds, they would simply come and go, appear and disappear, or so it seemed to her. Ed, so earthbound, both disappointed and reassured her. And she could be lofty with him.

Mist was rising in milky green streamers from pits and shallow dykes. She heard the bullock puff and grunt, and the other two men encourage it. She let the flaps fall.

The village was a strange one, when they came to it. It had the usual defensive wall, brick and sheet iron, bolstered up in places by dismembered furniture. Thorns and briars, trained to grow along its top, had by now taken over most of the vertical plane as well. But inside the wall the village was graced by more than shacks and lean-tos. Tall houses towered up in the last traces of twilight. A deserted duck pond lay choked but lovely with saucerine flowers. Three churches sidled past, many more pubs with thick yellow oil-light in their windows. A few shops, mostly closed and dark, one with a lamp in the window still, all apparently in daytime use, a couple labelled above their frontages: BREDS, and KEMIST.

It seemed there were neither horses nor dogs currently going spare here, but presently would be from horse-dealers passing through. (Pearson had bought a mare off them last year, a good lass with strong lungs and a lot of pull in her.) Meanwhile they could stay, providing they would work or pay, or both, for no settlement could support outsiders gratis. Janet would put them up for a bit at the Fly's Eye if they liked. She kept a room or two for 'guests' – mostly god-speakers or salesmen. Janet would see them all right.

Janet, however, seemed not so sure of this. The public house she ruled was already open to drinkers and had probably been so all day. It was a leaning wayward building, patched up in haphazard fashion by slats, bricks and nailed planks. The wagon drew up on a paved space at the door. Ed and the other walking man, Barney, went into the pub, and, after a while, Janet emerged alone from the doorway. She was a plumpish scowling harridan in a floral dress, with an incongruous white silk flower in her bottle-curled tresses. She put her hand on her hip, and Eva saw that she favoured scarlet nails but not much renewal thereof.

'What is it you're wanting, then?' she asked in a familiar yet unfriendly voice. It seemed she had met them many times before and that they did not improve with repetition.

Barney appeared at her elbow, clutching a dull glass of murk.

'A room, Janet. They want a room.'

'Maybe. But can they pay for it?'

This last was apparently addressed to Barney, even though Janet was staring straight at Eva now.

'Course they can,' said Barney.

'Well, I want to see the colour of their coin first.'

Barney brought this curiously insular conversation to an end by translating to Steel: 'She asks can you pay her?'

'Yes,' Steel said.

Janet looked him over, then Sail.

'Well, you don't seem a bad couple of blokes. But we get all sorts here. Have to be careful, I do.' Her attention was abruptly diverted. 'Barney! Now look what that bullock's done! And this paving only cleaned off an hour ago.'

Fifteen

There were three guest rooms above the interior of the pub. The rooms all possessed interconnecting doorways, one of them now minus a door, so that privacy was doubtful. They faced across the corridor a large linen cupboard and a bathroom, which, though devoid of plumbing, was still used as such, water being lugged up from below. Also from below drifted the scents of liquor and cooking in continuous, alternating gushes.

The wagon had been stored in a barn and the doors locked. Eva saw Steel paying Janet an advance on their stay in the lamp-yellowed dark. After that she showed him some respect and deference, and referred to him as the 'gentleman upstairs', which incredible historical title could only have sprung from some novel she had consumed behind the bar. To Eva she scarcely spoke, but when she did so under pressure of circumstances, her little bright mascara-ed eyes said quite plainly, I'll be polite because it's my business, but don't think I don't know *your* sort. To Sail, as Eva had expected, Janet exhibited a motherly yet flirtatious concern. At first she did this as though it took her rather by surprise, acting like a woman hypnotized, or under a spell. But in the end all reserve was swept away, and Eva would shudder at her hooting laugh, the response to Sail's jokes. At other times her voice was frequently audible, and she also sneezed a lot in raucous bouts that somehow seemed struggling to be genteel. Altogether the sound of her drove Eva to frenzy.

Once upstairs Sail had taken himself and what he had borrowed or appropriated for himself from the wagon into the last smallest room, where the door was. It seemed unspokenly agreed that Eva and Steel should share together the vast double bed in the first room. The bed depressed Eva immediately. Under its moth-mutilated canopy, it seemed to her like a box of old black sin, a complex in which endless murders and perversions had been performed. Useless to see the plastic newness of its posts; its rotten curtains had convinced her of diabolism and age.

The first night she lay on her back, several miles away from Steel, wondering dimly if he would caress her, speak to her, or in any way intimately communicate with her, though she thought it unlikely. Twice she turned and looked at him, but it was too dark to see his face. She touched his body but it was cold and still. She imagined him in that trancelike, vampire sleep to which she had once grown accustomed, but which now filled her again with fear. Sail did not go to his selected room. She listened for his door. To begin with, last bursts of sound came from below. After these were no more, Janet's own personal sounds vibrated and faded. Then there was no clue left as to where Sail might be in all the tumbled preserved skin of the pub. At last, mainly empty, the pub itself made noises, rubbing old wooden bones together as if for warmth.

Later, a moon shone in from the cracks of a loosely-bricked-up window. For the third time she turned and looked at Steel, but his face was blanched intolerably by the moon so she slid away from him in terror.

Earlier they had eaten below, towards the back of the bar room, the three of them and Ed and Barney too, the bullock driver and his beast having been primly cursed off into the night by Janet.

A girl laid the table, Janet's daughter by some bygone male Janet claimed as her spouse. This girl was commonly addressed as Sel, her real and unclipped name being a flight of cultural fancy on Janet's part, now mostly forgotten by all save Janet herself. Sel had black hair reaching to her waist, but was in other ways quite unlike a village birth. The swarthiness of the village skin type was in her transmuted to a creamy fawn, her body was little-boned and attractively overlaid, all curves, her eyes a fierce and amazing blue. Janet's daughter was a cut above the rest, no doubt Janet had hammered that into all of them. Only her hands, like her name, had been degraded by the pots, pans, ovens and general montage of coarseness and hard work in which she lived. There was something touching about her hands. And also about herself. When the farmers yelled for her around the bar, thumping their fists for drinks, she answered them in a soft, almost inaudible voice, and went to serve them with soft amorphous gestures.

As she put cheese on the table, her hair swung past her face.

'What *is* your name?' Sail said to her.

She blushed and looked down.

'Oh. Selene. It's silly.'

'Why?'

'Well . . .' she said and glanced at him under her rook-black lashes.

This fragment of conversation passed again and again across Eva's squeezed-tight eyes as she lay in the black box of bed with a vampire sleeping at her side. Also other conversations, conjectured at because unheard, for Eva had watched him afterwards sitting by Selene, talking to her as she washed glasses at the bar. Generally the girl did not look directly at Sail, but continuous colour dyed her cheeks, so that she seemed to become progressively more vivid, feverish, glowing, like a lamp full of untapped and waiting flame. And her sapphire eyes, becoming more startlingly blue by contrast, darted to him and away like blue birds. Once, apparently by mistake, they crossed over Eva's, and Selene flinched.

Eva felt old and wizened and hideous in the bar, for this was the effect the scene produced in her. As Selene flamed, Eva dulled and finally went out like a fire with no fuel. Later she actually felt her body in nervous apprehension, fearing sudden wrinkles, tightenings and lapses. Something like a briar grew inside her and left her no room to breathe. Altogether she seemed suddenly to have little space.

And the sound of Sail's remote door never came.

The second day broke and burned. The sky was brass, and distant indigo hill sweeps crouched above the village. Three or four of the loose bricks levered from the window space enabled her to see all this, also a white sun and the white heat it induced blearing and blaring in the valley bowl, picking out the white tufts of pickets and thickets, and pockets of workable land which the village contained, and brakes of dead trees resting like black gauze. Below, in the yard, a man was sluicing his head at the pump, cursing to himself.

She had dozed and slept finally, and woken to find Steel gone. It seemed only that she had gone back in time and he was in Jallow's fields, while outside lay Oiltown, corrupting in the sun.

For a long while she lay where she was, fantasizing herself into this past. Then she heard unmistakable soft footsteps outside, and soft sounds round and about the linen cupboard. She imagined Sel-Selene there, like a dark mouse, and a blind, gut-clenching fury took hold of her. Selene timidly folding up clothes with her raw hands, downcast china-doll eyes, and the last traces of Sail's lust inside her. Eva jumped from the bed and slung open the door, and glared across at her. Selene responded with a nervous convulsive half turn, instantly regretted for it brought them face to face. Sensing her power, Eva lounged in the doorway. Her white slept-in hair and the rumpled petticoat in which she had crawled to bed combined with her narrowed yet enormous eyes and look of incalculable contempt, to make her appear quite definitely and dangerously mad.

'What time is it?' Eva said.

'Early,' Selene whispered.

Eva flipped a languid, nail-bitten hand.

'I want some food, and I want a bath.'

'Yes,' said Selene.

'Now.'

'Yes.'

207

Never in her life had she either been able to address, or thought of addressing, anyone in this fashion. Now her latent hubris broke out, for Selene was obviously afraid of her. (Libby, Libby, there's a ghoul—)

'Well, do it,' Eva snapped. 'What do we pay you for?'

Selene shut the linen cupboard and sidled away and down the stairs.

After about ten minutes she returned and set bread and cold meat on the sideboard with leaf-tea in an eye-blue pot. Nibbling and gnawing, Eva watched her stagger twice upstairs with buckets of hot water to fill the bath. Selene was pink from exertion now; Eva, standing like a crazy ghost, combed her hair, half-lying against the doorpost.

'That'll do,' she said, when the fourth bucket had been emptied, and going in among the steamy chrome, she waved Selene out and slammed the door in her face.

This episode afforded her amusement of a kind. She lay long in the bath, going over it.

Later she put on the blue dress and thought with nostalgia of her high-heeled Oiltown shoes, lacquered nails, and the lost blacking for her eye-lashes.

She heard Janet incessantly below, sneezing and commanding.

At noon the pub grew more generally noisy. Men joked and laughed in the yard. Looking out, she saw Ed and Barney eating meat pies. Ed glanced up and found her at once.

'Where is Steel?' she called down.

'Up on the Shoulder.'

'What shoulder?'

'That 'un.'

Ed pointed up the sweeping bowl to some indefinite point among the fields.

'I don't see,' Eva complained.

'He's working, lass,' Barney said, 'like a good 'un.'

They did not speak of Sail, she did not ask, but a constriction took hold of her suddenly, of loneliness and fright. She gripped the brick so hard the old cement flaked down on Barney's head.

'Never seen a window there before,' Ed commented gently.

'Take me up to Steel,' Eva said to him – they had identified the name at once.

'If you like,' he said. 'Half an hour before we go back.'

'I'll come down.'

They turned, their pies finished, to drink their beer in the bar cool. Selene came out by them into the yard to the pump. Sail followed her.

It seemed to Eva he must know she was there above them, watching. He merely slid one hand under Selene's hair, stroking the nape of her neck, then worked the pump for her. He said something to her Eva did not hear.

'Oh, you're mad,' she said, laughing in a soft admiring way.

His white hair was streaked across his forehead. He wore a faded cream-coloured shirt unbuttoned, flapping. It reminded Eva of how she had seen him once before, and she wondered if he had been lopping thistles for Selene's mum. She pushed another of the willing bricks out of its slot and it crashed in the yard a few inches away from them, though she jumped back from the window too quickly to see it.

On the stairs going down to meet Ed, she met instead Janet, sipping lemonade and fanning herself.

'Oh, yes,' Janet said to her with a bright little smile, 'I'd be obliged if you'd refrain from asking my daughter to bring up your bath water. We run a business here and I'm afraid my regular customers must come first.'

Eva felt her throat and eyes and skin clench in one spasm of cowardly malice. Before she should think better of it, she managed to say: 'She's a slut.'

Janet swelled visibly, and Eva, regretting immediately, hurried down the stairs.

'Why, you dirty-mouthed little tarted-up—' Eva heard begin behind her, but she fled into the bar, ran across it and out to where Ed and Barney stood waiting in the sun-fired dust.

'Quickly,' she hissed, and walked swiftly up the street.

Clicking their teeth, the two men followed.

Janet emerged too late at the door, her lips compressed to thin cerise lines, but she said nothing further, presumably fearing to bawl the rest of her sentences up the street after them. Eva did not turn. Ed looked back once and then at Eva and then away.

The sun droned white in Eva's eyes.

The street curved, bisecting dykes of jet-black shadow.

Beyond, fields lay peeled and bleached. All the world sizzled in bone-white tension, and a few insects of great size dazzled their armour in brief bleedings of shade.

Men were scything an acre or so of coarse blond stalks, wheat of a kind in an impossible mail-coat. In a distance divided by fences, two trudging cart horses gleamed like onyx.

Barney went away among the tall stalks, and Ed led her on with one big hand on her arm. She was shivering in the heat but had not noticed. After a time she began to ask him fevered questions about Sail. Was he working for Janet? Had he shown them all that he could juggle several objects at once? As far as Ed knew, Sail had taken over Janet's savage garden, at which Eva winced and said, 'Thistles. Bloody thistles.'

As for juggling, Sail had done some tricks with six glasses that had held the bar spell-bound, and Barney and Parker had lost half their week's wage. At which Eva snapped: 'Watch your pockets, or you'll lose all of it.'

Ed seemed faintly shocked. In a velvet and reproachful voice he murmured, 'Him being family and all.'

'Oh, he's not my brother,' Eva said. 'He's just a thief.'

Ed fell silent and thoughtful. Then, after a long pause, he said with great compassion and as if it explained and excused all: 'He's only young.'

'*Young!*' cried Eva, practically demented. A distant dog, alarmed at her shout, began to bark across the fields.

'Looks isn't all,' said Ed.

Eva ignored this trite yet oddly relevant statement.

'Where's Steel?' she demanded.

Ed pointed. Off the road, directly to their left, two men were standing in a scythed field under a dead yet spreading tree.

'Pearson trying to get rid of his mare,' Ed remarked.

Even as they turned into the field, Pearson made the gesture of despairing amazement common to all failed

211

would-be sellers of shoddy goods, and walked off. Steel turned and saw them.

'I brought her up, she was asking to come,' Ed said. He let go Eva's arm gently.

Steel looked at her, but his face and eyes seemed more remote than ever before.

'Saw Pearson trying to sell his old lady,' Ed remarked. 'She'll not pull you far.'

'No, she wouldn't,' Steel said, 'she's lame as well, or hasn't he noticed?'

Ed laughed softly and shook his head, and turned and walked away again back across the field. Steel stood looking after him with apparently sightless eyes, while the sun nicked unexpected little flames from the shorn stalks.

'Are you angry I came after you?' Eva rasped.

'No.'

'This honest toil, I suppose, is fulfilling,' she said acidly, slipping unconsciously into a parody of Sail's vernacular. 'And brings back memories perhaps.'

He looked at her, this time intently, his eyes very blue and blank in the heat.

'Why did you come?'

'I'm tired of being left alone always, always.'

'I see.'

His shirt was opened as Sail's had been.

'He went with that girl,' Eva said abruptly, 'that stupid slut.'

'Possibly.'

'You would be glad,' she said furiously, 'if he left me. Then you could both leave me. You've always hated me.'

There was a huge scythe leaning on the tree. He picked it

up, and she thought for a moment, in terrified smugness, that he was going to kill her with it. Then she saw that he was merely beginning to walk back across the decapitated field to join the other workers farther away.

She ran after him and took hold of his arm, next of his body. He stopped, shifting the scythe before she cut herself to pieces on it.

'Please,' she said, 'don't leave me now. You don't have to work for them. You paid them,' she added with a return of ridiculous pride.

'They waited for this weather,' he said. 'They probably prayed for it. They have two, maybe only one day to use it. I know.'

'Please,' she said, still holding to him and trembling violently.

'What do you want?' he asked her suddenly, letting go the scythe because she was struggling against him in a kind of blind panic. He held her arms and she thrust her head against his skin and seemed to try to weep and find she could not.

He picked her up and carried her back under the tree and put her down there in its black and stretching shade. Still she would not let go of him. It seemed to her that if she once gave up her hold she would lose him entirely and for ever. Almost absently he began to stroke her hair, and, as always in the past, his touch was unutterably soothing to her. She shut her eyes and began to relax inch by inch, with little sharp crackings of sinews and an inner creaking in all her bones. At last she lay quiescent and close to sleeping in the shade of the tree while his fingers repeated a rhythm like breathing across her skull. She wondered vaguely at his tenderness, but soon forgot even that it was a human living thing which induced these waves of peace and silence.

When she woke again the rays of the sun were slanting and red, and Steel was sitting against the tree at her side. It seemed he had not left her after all. She said his name and he looked down at her.

'Will you take me with you when you go?' she said.

'Yes,' he said. He stood up and walked away from her to collect the scythe still lying in the stubble.

As they walked back along the road, she took his hand as sometimes she had done before and, as before, he neither rejected nor accepted the caress of her fingers on his palm.

The sun coloured the fields in red stripes.

'I told Janet Selene was a slut,' Eva said. 'Will she let me in again?'

'Probably not,' he said, and suddenly laughed.

'I'm sorry,' she said softly, 'I am sorry.'

But the sun was warm on her as it went down.

That night they ate alone, the two of them. Selene did not bring their food but another girl with large clumsy feet. Later Janet came in lime-green silk and a good deal of very sweet scent.

'I am afraid,' she said, addressing herself entirely and obviously to Steel, 'that you will have to make other arrangements.'

'So I gather,' he said.

'You understand, I need the rooms. I've no complaints, though your *sister* has caused rather a lot of fuss and bother with her wanting things at all hours of the day.' Janet paused, awaiting some form of comment or explanation which was not forthcoming. 'Well, then,' she added, 'I shall expect the use of my rooms by midday tomorrow. I think that's quite fair.'

'Quite,' said Steel. Something in his manner – unapparent to Eva – seemed to unnerve Janet. She made a little supplementary sound and clacked away on her town-bought heels.

Sail was not about in the bar, but later Eva heard Janet's hooting laughter from some room at the back.

Not long after the advent of Janet, Ed came and leaned on Steel's chair.

'You could try the old Duke farm – not much, but she won't need do for long. You could look at her. If you like, I'll take you in Barney's cart.'

As the two men moved towards the door, Eva followed, but Ed shook his head at her.

'Don't you come, lass. It's already turned. There'll be snow. I can feel her coming.'

Eva did not want to remain behind, in this camp of her enemies, but they would not let her come, and outside the air was still and sharp as a knife, the sky dotted with tangerine stars. So she slunk back as the cart rattled away behind the blowing earless horse, and sneaked up the stairs to the bed.

She dozed only fitfully in the cold. A wind came up and slashed at her through the unbricked window. At last in shivering misery she got up and tried to put the bricks back. Mostly they fell and smashed in the yard, terrifying a procession of men coming to and from the wooden lavatories. Much later still, as she lay curled like a frozen foetus, she heard Sail's outer door grate open and close, and shortly, unmistakable sounds of lust and enjoyment. Filled with unbearable frustration and pain and staggering on her numb feet, she gained the closed connecting door and flung it open, and screamed through it an unintelligible stream of abuse and distress.

Gasps and curses came from the bed. Someone fumbled to light a candle, and presently she found herself confronted not by Sail and Selene but by Barney and the large-footed girl from the bar, framed in a welter of shocked blankets.

Sixteen

Duke farm stood in a copse of dead elms, still with the damson dabs of old and wind-raked nests caught up in their pointing tiers. It lay across hilly, scabrous and useless fields, yet still within the village wall. Part of the roof was gone and rats sometimes ran about the upper storey. Below, a stone-flagged kitchen was large enough to serve as an all-purpose room, and a warm one once the range was alight and the window shutters nailed in place. Outside a pump stood green with old water and refused to yield new. Steel and Ed worked on it for an hour while Eva dragged wood about the stone floor to feed the fire. Investigating the stairway she met a gigantic rat and threw a branch at it, mainly because it reminded her of Sail's room behind the church.

The first snow fell at noon, another denser fall in the sluggish twilight. They brought things from a wood-shed where Steel had stored the wagon, and left them in the kitchen. Eva watched Ed and Barney's cart and horse beating back through the drifts, and experienced a thrill of isolation. The village street was perhaps a mile away, but she could not see it or hear it. It, together with Janet and the Fly's Eye, Sail and his china-doll girl, might have slipped into a chasm in the earth and been covered over by the blessed yellow snow.

In one of her crazy bouts of domesticity, Eva scrubbed and broomed the kitchen, cooked, even baked bread – and burned it – made up their mattress bed each day, and sang as she chased rats up the stairs.

They lived mostly on packet food as in the wagon, though once or twice Ed struggled over the fields with vegetables in horny skins and meat pies bought under false pretences at Janet's.

Once a man from Warren stopped at the farm, and held out a brace of dead rabbits. He bred them for their flesh, and usually got a good response, but Eva sent him away, appalled by the actuality of their deadness, their dangling ears and limp white paws. In Foulmarsh Old Woman Belmort had dealt with such things.

Of the horse-dealers there was no sign. The snow had put paid to most travelling and roaming. And it seemed set to be a long snow. Four weeks passed, and Eva grew accustomed to the sound of Steel's axe felling trunks and splitting logs, and to the sight of Steel's long black figure clearing new falls from the door, or wrenching the reluctant and moaning pump back to life. Some days there were icicles to be boiled. On clear mornings she would walk a little way from the house and over the rise, and see a dim far-off mirage of a village with a pall of smoke on it under a green-glass bubble of still air. At first old poisons would stir in her blood but later she forgot them. Occasionally she made snow balls and pelted them angrily at the distance, and then ran back and cried as her hands thawed by the range. Ed, when he came, never spoke of Sail. And she never spoke of Sail at all, though at first the need to speak of him had been urgent.

Through all this time she revelled with a sort of fearful delight in the nearness of Steel. At the beginning they had said little to each other, but after a while, by intermittent nagging, she got him to read to her again from those books which she never fully understood, yet which always stirred and entranced her. She also set about seducing him in a methodical and inventive spirit, for she deemed his lack of interest in her sprang from a remaining aversion to her time with Sail, and all times with and thoughts of Sail it seemed to her imperative she must destroy. Though when finally Steel took her glistening body from its lasciviously splashing tin-bath activities before the range, and fulfilled its yearning for him so definitely on their mattress, he seemed only giving in yet once more to the inevitable. She sensed no great passion or pleasure on his part, but then she never had, while it pleased her inordinately that he should want her again, as in the past. For indeed it seemed now they were in full measure living in their own past together, to such an extent that she felt once more that niggling, haunting dread that he would ultimately leave her.

In the fifth week the snow fell continuously for two days and the sky seemed to press on the tops of the elms.

On the third day Ed came in Barney's cart while Steel was on the hillside getting wood. Ed hoisted in a jar of village-brewed beer and a sack of black potatoes.

'Doing all right?' he asked Eva, in a soft coaxing tone. 'I

brought you something.' And he handed her a folded up bundle of paper, which Eva opened on the kitchen table to reveal a white silk dress, straight out of an Oiltown window. Eva could hardly believe her eyes. The blue dress – tattered and scrubby from hard wear and much washing – was now as abhorrent to her as her old Foulmarsh frocks.

'Oh, Ed,' she cried, but he forestalled her.

'She isn't from me.'

It had been long enough that her eyes widened in a moment's genuine bewilderment before she narrowed them, dropped the dress as though it were not merely white but white-hot, and said: 'If it's from him, you can give it him back.'

'Wait a bit. Took most of his week's wages doing work round the village. A man came by from Warren – he gets stuff like this from the towns, but they'll cost you.'

'Let him give it,' Eva said, 'to *her*.'

Ed looked away and down at his feet.

'Well, there's bit of trouble there,' he said slowly.

Eva went to the jar and poured him a drink and handed it to him with such fury that most of it slopped over both their hands.

'Did he say give it to me when Steel was outside?'

'He never said how. Just give her.' Ed sat down and cradled the remains of the beer. If he had ever guessed at what kind of relationship really existed between the three of them, he had never verbally referred to any of them as being other than brothers and sister. That Steel and Eva seemed at all deviant was no matter, for incest was indulged in here, as in most places, and not taboo.

'It's bad for him,' Ed murmured, 'he gets laid up, you

know that, in the cold. Plenty do. And his shoulder still healing. And then there's the thing with Janet.'

Eva, quickened and sickened with unanalysed emotion, would not look at Ed, only stonily out of a shutter-slit at Steel's dark shape still splitting logs about thirty feet away from the house. She could hear the axe blows, but only remotely. She wanted to call out to him for help, but of what kind she scarcely knew.

'You see,' Ed went on, 'you see how it is – Janet's not a bad sort, but this feller now, he put her in the cart sixteen, seventeen years ago, then run out on her. And she's done her best with Sel, and now the same thing's up and on with her. Don't think Janet'd've minded if she hadn't taken, but there you are. Not many girls take now. Wouldn't make no difference here. Plenty of men be glad to know she could.'

'You mean,' Eva snapped, 'Sail's put Janet's idiot of a daughter in the family way and Janet wants them to be god-joined and Sail won't. How sophisticated,' she added malignly. She had a sudden recollection of Libby Moss with her big stomach, deriding her at the black-running pump in Foulmarsh. Women who conceived seemed to her generally foolish; her own barrenness she had nearly always taken as a voluntary and clever state.

'That's how it is,' Ed said. 'Will you tell your brother?'

'You tell him,' Eva said. And she sat by the range, until Steel came in.

Ed spoke more directly to Steel, and immediately. Steel said nothing as he set down the wood. When he straightened, Eva spat out: 'He wants to come here. Well, he can't.'

'He can,' said Steel. 'Presumably there's nowhere else.'

Ed nodded; he seemed relieved, for somehow he had invested himself with Sail's problems. As Steel paid him for the potatoes, Ed looked at Eva uneasily. When he left she turned her back.

Through that evening Eva would neither look at nor speak to Steel. She threw aside domesticity, crouched at the range, and finally went out across the snow and walked in circles past the elms till the cold and some wild and savage animal yowl sent her running for the safety of the farm.

In the dark, as she lay rigid, back to back with him, she found herself staring at the white silk dress still lying on the table, where Ed or Steel must have put it. At last she got up, intending to thrust it into the fire, but the beautiful texture of it made her think twice. Ultimately she stuffed it out of sight beneath their mattress. And then, still, she could not sleep at all for anger and a curious despair.

The next day, knowing that sometime now he would come, she paced about the kitchen, sick with anticipation, unable to eat, talk or be still. Outside, twigs snapped off from trees under snow-loads. Each time this happened she jumped and sprang like an animal from one place to another. Steel began to make candles, for the lamp-oil was low. When not engaged in actions necessary to the upkeep of the room, he read, though no longer to her. She gnawed her nails to the quick and lay awake all night, for Sail did not come that day.

The next day a fine rain sent snow slipping off the ruinous farm roof with heart-stopping crashes.

Steel went out at noon, and up the hill for wood.

She was washing her hair in the tin bath before the range when she heard the very distant sound of a horse across the fields. Expecting Ed, she listened for cart wheels but they never came. Instead, after a wait, she heard footsteps crunching and sliding through the copse, too light to be Ed's. The soap ran down her face and into her eyes as she crouched above the bath in a halo of froth, listening. Suddenly, very close, the footsteps came to a halt, and simultaneously she jumped across the room and shot home the solitary bolt of the door.

Instead of coming directly to the door, the footsteps moved along the front of the house, then back, hesitating. She heard him circle the pump and finally come up the slippery track Steel had cleared.

She ran back, as if to get the tin bath between herself and the doorway, and clenched her hands violently, one on the soap so that it shot out of her grasp and hit the far wall.

Outside someone began to cough. It filled her with mixed passions, mostly fury, as once before. Then the coughing stopped and he knocked with incongruous courtesy on the door. After a moment he tried to open it.

As the soap had shot uncontrollably from her hand so her voice now shot uncontrollably from her throat.

'No!' she shrieked. 'I won't let you in. I won't.'

Silence came through the door. Then he said huskily, 'Eva, for Chrissake.'

'Go away!' she shrieked.

'Eva, oh Eva,' he said. 'Eva, it's a long walk.'

'Not for you! Ed brought you. I heard the cart.'

'Only across the fields.'

'Go away!'

Again came silence, then a sound as if he were leaning on the door.

She rubbed the smarting lather from her eyes. For a time neither of them moved, then a fresh explosion of snow reverberated the house. As the concussion faded, she heard Steel's unmistakable footfalls. She strained her ears but heard no word exchanged outside, only a fall of wood against the wall. Presently Steel said: 'Eva, draw the bolt.'

Not speaking, she shook her head at the closed door.

'Eva,' he said, and his voice seemed full of menace. Reluctant yet cowed she had half risen to obey, when he set his shoulder against the door and burst it open.

She dropped on her knees beside the bath and watched them come into the room, Sail first, Steel after, carrying the wood. Sail's eyes flicked to her then away. He looked even thinner than before and haggard with illness, but she had expected it of him, as she had expected the sound of his coughing. She classified it as an act, an expert bait for compassion, and so felt no pity or concern at the indelible signature of death written so clearly.

Steel closed the door. Sail sat on a chair against the wall, distant from both of them, staring at the floor.

With emphasis Eva lied: 'I *burned* your dress.'

Then let down her head to sluice the soap from her hair.

As the hours passed the rain set in to slash away the snow, making background music for the fire-crackling silence in the room. A dark storm-light only punctuated by dull red glares from the range separated each of them as if in fog.

Steel had stacked the wood, and now sat at the table shaping candles with his long and imperturbable hands.

Eva rubbed and then incessantly combed her hair. Its silver electric gleams and sizzlings added new character to the silence and the gloom. Sail sat now with his back against the wall, his eyes shut. None of them looked at the others. None of them spoke.

Perhaps three hours later Steel rose and made black tea from the muddled hoard of provisions Eva had piled up on shelves. They drank it from chipped mugs found five weeks ago in cupboards. Oddly, conveniently, there had been three. Into Sail's mug Steel tipped a brief cascade of alcohol.

'Thanks,' Sail said. It was the first thing any of them had said for so long the kitchen seemed to ring and howl with echoes. He drank and coughed, and tried not to cough, and said, staring into the tea, 'I won't be here long. I just needed somewhere – I'll have to go back and sort it out somehow. God, what a mess.'

'Yes,' Eva shot at him viciously, 'and you so clever.'

'Be quiet,' Steel said to her without expression.

'No, let her dance on my grave if she likes,' said Sail. 'I was bound to come unstuck sometime. I deserve it.'

'A shotgun wedding would be hard to enforce,' Steel said, 'under the circumstances.'

Sail shook his head.

'No, it's not that. It's Selene. She's so – so bloody young to get messed up like this. And I was the first. Christ, her first go at it and this happens.'

'You should be pleased you're potent,' Eva crowed, rasping the comb brightly through her hair.

'Oh, for god's sake,' Sail said, and lapsed into silence.

'So you'll go back,' Steel said eventually.

'Yes. Give me a day or two here. Just to think.' Sail got up suddenly and began to move rapidly up and down in front of the chair. 'It's all so bloody stupid. It wouldn't matter if she didn't think I was somehow important to her – priceless, isn't it? She's built a kind of fantasy around me—'

'What about *me*?' Eva jumped up and caught his arm and shook him. He stopped still and stared in her face and she saw that his eyes, so close to hers, had grown deep lines about them like those of a very old man.

'I'm sorry, Eva,' he said. 'I never lied to you about what I wanted with you.' And then she felt Steel disengage her hands and put her aside.

'You're welcome to stay,' she heard Steel say, 'get some rest. There's another mattress in the wagon we can use.'

'Thanks,' Sail said again.

Eva watched him sit down on their bed, then ease himself full length and fall abruptly and helplessly asleep.

'He said he loved me once,' Eva said, 'but he lied.'

'He didn't lie,' Steel said.

In the dark she could no longer see either of their faces.

He brought a second mattress in from the wagon and another supply of blankets, but she lay down exhausted on it without him.

Sometime in the night she half woke and saw him sitting at the table, cleaning the ivory rifle in faint candlelight, the range a garnet smoke behind him while the rain still slashed the snow.

In the morning the fields were thick with mud and full of seeping rainlakes that glittered back the sky.

Eva woke, and Steel was gone, Sail still sleeping. She

226

found she could no longer bear the enclosure of the room, and went out, picking past great puddles to the pump. She worked the handle to fill their all-purpose cauldron, looking for Steel on the hill. Instead she made out the tall shaggy outline of Ed, on foot, coming through the elms.

He took over the pump handle and filled the cauldron, then carried it brimming to the step for her.

'I was taking the cart up Warren way tomorrow. Would you want to come with us? She's been a long time snowing. Give you a break that would.'

Eva stared at him suspiciously, but his face was open as it always was, and creased in a kind of compassionate concern she did not understand though felt entitled to.

'I'll ask your Steel, of course,' he said, 'but there's shoes and beads and stuff there, going cheap enough. Nice to see you prettied up.'

'I'll go,' she said, 'you needn't ask Steel. I'll tell him.'

It was her defiance against him, against both of them, and the claustrophobia of the room.

'I'll come by early, then,' Ed said, and left her. Yet, walking back the way he had come, he met Steel and she saw them talking together.

She could not stay in the farm that day. She slopped about the muddy fields and little clusters of musically dripping woods, looking vaguely for berries as she had done once in Foulmarsh. And, as at Foulmarsh, she lost all track of time, and came wandering back in the final rank pink skeins of afternoon light, with a white weed-flower or two to stick in a jam jar. The open air had cleared some of the miasma from her, as had Ed's invitation to ride to Warren, but a horror came on her as she neared the farm.

When she left, Sail had still been sleeping, silent and immobile. Now, when she pushed open the door, she found him and Steel together, playing a lethal card game at the table. Her jealous soul writhed within her, for, more than any other thing it seemed, this incomprehensible dealing and challenging and stealth bemused her and shut her out.

She slammed about the kitchen, thrusting at the fire, boiling water, kicking off her shoes, but could not seem to distract them. Steel's enigmatic guile and Sail's limitless reserves of cunning, made them ideal and effective adversaries. And while there was nothing particularly glad or irresponsible in Sail's manner, yet he was totally absorbed. They were also playing for money, and it angered her unbearably that this was how they should spend the last of Sail's time.

She sat by the range, and attempted to drink all the beer, until her head swam and her eyes shut, and she reeled to bed.

Even then, once or twice, some snatch of their conversation broke into her dream-swept mind. They seemed to be talking about the rats above, though it was possible she imagined it.

Seventeen

She got up early to go to Warren with Ed, though not earlier than Sail.

Eating bread, leaning by the range, she said to Sail: 'I suppose you'll be gone when I come back.'

'Yes,' he said. He seemed better but his eyes were still lined and burned out to that colourless almost-green which had once so surprised and moved her.

Strung with inexplicable tensions, she waited and waited for Ed, while Steel and Sail moved variously about her and the sky grew great pillars of brown cloud. But Ed did not come. It seemed unforgivable that he should desert her also, and so she swore at him aloud.

When she finally heard wheels it was almost midday, and she flung open the door and ran out to him. He brought the cart to a halt near the pump, and sat looking down at her and his face stopped her in her tracks, for it was full of a most unspeakable grief and distress.

'What is it?'

'Wait a bit,' he said, as if to calm her, and then: 'Are they both here?'

'Steel!' she cried before she knew it.

She heard Steel approach almost at once behind her.

'It's him should know,' Ed murmured, looking beyond Steel, and then away.

Eva took several steps back from the cart, cringing before the aura it seemed to have acquired.

Sail came out of the house and stood looking at Ed.

'What am I supposed to know?'

'Janet's girl,' Ed murmured, his whole face working to produce the words. After this he could seem to say nothing else. Eventually he got down from the cart and began to stroke the earless horse along its neck. Staring at his hands he then said, 'Reckon she took something – to sort herself out, thinking likely you'd gone off. Something to bring herself on.'

Another silence fell.

Sail stood looking at Ed with his hands loose at his sides, while Ed carefully stroked the horse.

'Janet fetched out Barney in the night, to get the doctor from Warren, but it wasn't any good. Sel'd gone.'

'Gone?' Sail repeated harshly. 'What in fuck do you mean?'

'I mean she's dead,' Ed answered him, looking him in the face for the first time.

Sail frowned as if this still made no sense, then convulsively turned and stood facing the other way, across the fields.

'It's Janet, you see,' Ed said to them. 'Sel meant a lot to her. She's got it in her head to come running up here. Barney and a couple of 'em tried to stop her, but she won't be stopped. I came after in the cart. She wouldn't listen, not her. Never seen a woman look like she did, like she was out of her mind. So I came on ahead.'

He stopped stroking the horse and got back into the cart, and sat with his head hanging as if he had fallen asleep. Plainly his agony was entirely theirs, he felt for each of them who still had something to bear of it. Eva began to tremble, remembering her hate, and thinking of Selene as she would look now, as she had seen a woman look long ago – shrunken and bled out and empty, with her blue eyes like dusty glass.

Then there came an incredible and intolerable noise. Eva stared up at it in nauseous horror, and saw a plump woman come running along the brow of the hill, where Steel sometimes cut wood, her arms spread out as if she were somehow trying to fly. She stumbled and skidded in the mud, and her face as she ran nearer was all a wide-open, smudged red mouth. They stood watching her as if waiting for her by appointment, as she careered down the slope towards them. A man's figure appeared on the rise above her, trying to run and catch her up, but he had none of the violence in him which was her impetus. Seeing where she had got to, he came to an immediate standstill, outlined against the uneasy sky.

Janet stopped only when she was in their midst, a few feet from Sail, and having only for him eyes which were running and red from weeping.

'You,' she panted, spit bubbling on her lips, 'do you know, do you know what you've done – my little girl – god's taken my little girl because you put your filthy hands on her. It needn't have happened if you'd left her alone.'

Sail stood staring at her, slightly frowning again, as if unable to understand.

'And then to run out on her – that's why she did what she

did, because you ran out, you rat—' and she began to scream at him without words, and raised her hands, and Eva saw that her nails, now completely pared of lacquer, were like the long yellow horns of a ten-headed beast, ready to gore and shred their way through human flesh, if it were necessary to assuage her pain. But as she raised her hands to tear at Sail, Steel suddenly stepped between and hit her across the face. Her awful screams subsided, and she fell back moaning and holding her cheek, and the horns were pressed into her own skin.

'Your daughter died,' Steel said, 'because of your ham-fisted attempts at abortion. She was too easily led, and mainly by her mother.'

Janet's face, held rigid until now, seemed to collapse inwards until only the red stricture of the mouth was left intact.

'You bastard,' the mouth whispered at him, 'what do you know about it?'

Steel said nothing, but a huge darkness fell instantly on all of them from the sky as if some gigantic bird had spread its wings overhead.

'You know nothing,' Janet cried out. '*Nothing!* She did it herself because he—'

'Who told her to do it?' Steel said.

Before this final inexorable statement Janet's stiff gorgon mouth melted and ran into itself.

'You bastard,' she sobbed again, 'what do you know about it?' But she turned and almost inadvertently began to pull herself back the way she had come, her feet slipping in the mud. The sky cracked when she had reached half way up the slope and the rain fell blazing through the elms. The climb became even harder for Janet in the rain; near the end of it, the man who had paused to wait above edged down a little and helped her to the top.

Eva felt her hair twitching flat to her scalp. She looked at Sail – the rain ran across his bowed skull, moulding the hair to it in silver-grey strips. His shirt was already soaked through. As she stirred she felt the rain heavy in her own dress. The sound of it was of a vast river running downhill. Sail lifted his hands and let them fall, the rain burst round his feet. He moved suddenly away across the mud and in through the farmhouse door. Eva looked up at Ed, still immobile in the cart, then, as Steel followed Sail into the farm, she ran to follow. Yet she found herself unable to cross the threshold, and so hung there in the doorway, rain on her back, gazing in at them like a ghost in a book. Sail sat down at the table and set out both his hands on it, as if to examine them. Then abruptly he put down his head on his arms and began to cry.

A great and agonizing desire to hold him to her like a child swept over Eva but, glancing up, her eyes met Steel's across the table length, and there was something in his face and in his eyes which pushed her backwards from the kitchen door and suddenly, almost in panic, sent her running to Ed as he waited in the cart.

'Take me to Warren,' she called out at him, and the rain splashed in her eyes and mouth.

Ed raised his head a little and looked in her face. Then he leaned and lifted her up beside him, and clicked his tongue at the horse.

Without a word they jogged across the slope, while water drenched and drummed.

* * *

It rained for an hour. She barely noticed it, nor the way to Warren over the hills and dark brown fields. After the rain came a cold dull afternoon in which Ed gave her a faded tartan rug and told her to wrap up in it, and in which also she suddenly recollected and exclaimed: 'I never asked him for money.'

'Gave me some for you,' Ed told her, 'yesterday.'

'He never trusted me with coin,' she generalized bitterly.

Yet her dread had strangely faded by the time they reached the village of Warren, which in content seemed similar to though rather less than the one she had just come from. Ed took her to a pub where she drank hot spirit in a pewter mug and stared at a round pie he had bought her, and which she could not eat. He appeared concerned, and when he left her to visit the latrines, she hastily cut up the pie in segments and stuffed it in the mouth of a ravenous dog lurching past her chair.

Ed had business with a man or two in Warren. He handed her Steel's money in a leather pouch – 'Look after her, mind' – and turned her loose in an alley littered with incredible, awning-covered stalls of town goods.

At another time she would have revelled in this financial liberty and choice, touching and fingering and staring. Now, she wandered up and down, her hand tight on the leather pouch, almost blind, stepping into puddles, until a man approached her thinking she might be after custom herself, and she busied herself with a black spider-web shawl. On its strands were strung little silver beads which tinkled. She shook and prodded at them, mesmerized, yet not really aware, so that the stall woman leaned forward and asked her if she were buying or only messing up the goods, and Eva, in fright, bought. After this, in a state of bemused guilt, she felt obliged to purchase everything she touched, even inadvertently, and the money was soon gone.

Not once did she think of Steel or Sail. Her mind seemed quite closed to them, as if they were chance acquaintances merely.

Ed found her at the door of the pub, aimlessly holding several packages. He bought a little bottle of whisky, and bread and cheese for himself, for she still had neither the desire nor the ability to swallow food.

As they drove back, an early dusk came round the cart. He had wrapped the rug about her again, and from time to time passed her the whisky and made her gulp some down. It made her cheeks burn and her ears sing. They rarely spoke. Once she heard an animal howl in the distance as starless darkness swamped the world.

Nearing the farm, Eva's dread returned and coming down among the elms as she saw the outline of it black on black, and apprehended in a burst of curious fear that there were no lights burning, physical sickness took hold of her.

The cart pulled up, but she sat where she was, mainly paralysed.

'Best get down,' Ed advised her.

'Not yet,' she said.

'Yes. Be best you do.'

With weak arms and trembling legs she got herself off the cart and across the muddy space where they had stood in the daylight and watched Janet run towards them. Behind her, Ed still waited in the cart, not moving off as yet. She pushed at the kitchen door. It swung open on a faint, dim pulsing glow of old and almost-extinguished embers in the range, which also seemed to have filled the room up totally with a scent of burning and charcoaled things. Standing on the threshold once again she recaptured her feeling of intrusion and the sense almost of a barrier across her path, but she forced her way through it, and was in the darkened room, though her hands were knotted as she clutched her packages.

The kitchen at first seemed empty. A rat pattering above brought a reaction to every trigger of her body. She took a couple of steps across the stone floor, and a little gush of lavender flame swept suddenly through the dying fire. For a moment she could make out every angle and detail of the room, after which she saw them. It was merely an instant. Immediately the light sagged and crumbled and ashes popped tiredly, yet the information she had received held perfectly still and defined before her eyes as the shadows recommenced.

There was no movement between them, they might have been asleep or possibly dead, but even in the now motionless and passionless attitudes they had adopted, it was at once apparent that they had each become for the other what she had been for both of them: a lover.

She neither spoke nor breathed. She took her steps backwards with infinite care not to brush any object in her way. She was trying in fact not to touch even the motes of dust and dull light that filled the air.

At the doorway she slid out backwards, and continued to walk backwards away from the farm, her eyes fixed on the half-open door, as if some monster would emerge from it to pursue her, though she was already irreparably in its power.

She started when the horse blew softly near her ear.

'Ed,' she whispered, and then again. 'Ed, Ed, Ed.'

Whether from observation or from instinct, it seemed he knew everything. He lifted her again into the cart where she sat bolt upright, her hands still tight on her packages from Warren. For a long while she said nothing, then she said: 'I am alone.'

'No, lass,' he said.

'I must go with you. Do you have a woman? I'll be that.'

'Hush, lass,' he breathed, 'hush.'

'Take me with you. I won't stay here.'

'If you'd rather.'

'Do it now, quickly.'

But as the horse began to move up the hill, she heard the dead elms straining through the pitch-black night, and the rhythm came to ache and shift in her, and when they were free of them she leaned sideways from the cart and vomited into the abysmal muddy dark. After her sickness she was so weak she scarcely knew where she was or the reason for anything, and the jolting of their passage shook her into a strengthless whimpering, for it seemed to have no end.

Long ago, Ed and his brother Colin had built a shack for themselves on one of the overgrown tracks leading off and up from the village street. Later Colin had injured his hand on some shears, contracted blood-poisoning and died, so that now Ed lived there alone.

There were two rooms, one up some rickety stairs, and it

was in this upper room that Eva lay on Ed's incredible wooden bed for five days.

Colin had made the bed. He had also made and carved scores of animals in wood, and these were scattered up and down the walls on nails, or else suspended from bits of cord as though hanged. They were, too, animals Eva had never seen except sometimes in books. She stared at them for hours as she lay on her back, and on the second day she came to imagine that she was lying in an improvised court, such as had occasionally been organized at Foulmarsh, and that the wooden animals were trying her for some crime she could not remember.

At first she was ill. She shivered, and was sick at intervals with monotonous and bizarre regularity. But after the third day she could tell she was no longer ill at all. Ed was so gentle with her she felt neither shame nor strangeness. She had never in her life known such curious and unhuman compassion, for his kindness came so easily to her and demanded nothing of her in return. But when her sickness had gone, and he brought her a thin broth in a wooden bowl, she pushed it away, and when he urged her to eat she said: 'Why?'

For it seemed quite pointless that she should. She had no idea this time of creating her own death to achieve some posthumous vengeance, for she felt – though only dimly understood – that the two who had caused this breaching of her soul had put her so far beyond them in the very act, that it seemed now nothing she could do would touch or in any way ever affect them again.

To begin with she did not even think of them; they had so alienated her that this was very easy. But later she would emerge sometimes from bouts of delirious sickness and long for one or the other of them to be there to comfort her, as if she were a child, having briefly forgotten what she had seen in the glare of the fire. Later still, when she recollected how they had lain together on the mattress, lying over, in fact, the crushed white silk dress Sail had sent her as a bribe, she strained internally. They had made her redundant, superfluous. They had formed together a world where she could win no place. Where she was invisible, non-existent. Had she been meant to find them as she did? At no time did she speak to Ed of what she felt; it was perhaps her sense of inadequacy that kept her silent.

In the end she began to eat a little, and got up, and went to sit below in front of the stove. Day in, day out, she existed on the fringes of living. She began to have that look about her of something kept for ever locked away and out of the light – some impossibly fragile ornament, or a plant grown in the dark.

Initially Ed seldom left her on her own in the shack. Later, when he was absent for long periods of the day, she fell prey to a dreadful fear that Janet would seek her out there – but she did not tell him this, and certainly, Janet never came near her.

She had no plans for her life. She did nothing of a domestic nature in the shack, but he was well used to taking care of himself. He slept on a mattress in the room below, and though he made no sound, she was aware of his presence under her in the dark.

One night he came back with Barney, both of them a little drunk, but Barney seemed embarrassed by her, and soon went away. Eva got up and went and stood at Ed's elbow as he sat by the stove. It was the first move she had made towards anyone of her own volition for days, and it surprised her.

'Do you want me?' she asked him. 'If you want me to go upstairs with you, I will.'

She said it passionlessly, tiredly, primly. Perhaps she felt she should repay him for something, or needed to be reassured of her own existence, she did not know at all.

'No, lass,' he said quietly. There was a pause in which he seemed to be listening intently to the crackle of the stove. 'Not that I wouldn't like,' he murmured eventually, 'but there wouldn't be no point to it.'

'I have nowhere else and no one else,' she said.

Seemingly irrelevantly he said: 'Horse-dealers came yesterday.'

At first it made no sense to her. Then she remembered, and a wave of fresh sickness went over her, illogically, because it no longer had anything to do with her whether Steel went away or not.

'Why tell me?' she said, when the nausea faded. 'It's nothing to me.'

She had been with Ed for nine days. She was seated on the unmade wooden bed, combing her hair, while transparent crenellated sunlight came and went across the spaces of the room, the wooden animals, and her own bone-white fingers. Combing her hair had become for her a mindless, satisfying ritual. She spent hours on it, for it filled the spaces of her life in much the same intermittent fashion as the sun now filled the room. Dimly, in an unreal way, she heard a door open and Ed come into the lower area of the

shack. She sensed rather than heard that Ed was not alone.
It was not Barney, who was noisy, and incompetent at
negotiating furniture and stove; it seemed to Eva that it
might be a woman he had brought with him, and for a
second she thought of Janet once again, and came to her
feet in terror. Then she heard Ed move up the stairs, alone.

There was no door to the room, but he hesitated at the
top step and called her name before coming in. It was a
formal courtesy he had always shown her.

She was standing in the middle of the room, the sun
catching her hair alight like a white bonfire, the comb in her
hand pointing at him in an uncertain and dangerous
gesture.

'Who's that downstairs?'

Ed looked at her, and then out of the window, and then
at his feet.

'Not Janet?' she said, combing the air frantically, yet
standing otherwise quite still.

'No. Not Janet, lass. Not Janet.'

'Who then?' she asked, lapsing from fear to vague
distress, for something in his manner disconcerted her.

'Someone wants to see you. Shall I bring him up here to
you?'

'Who?' she shouted, but she had already begun to back
away from him, as she had backed away from the kitchen
door of the farm.

'Best to see him,' Ed said. 'He's come a fair way.'

She could tell then that it was Sail. Ed spoke in that
strange and sympathetic manner in which he had spoken of
Sail before. She did not understand it, and now found it
unforgivable.

'No!' she shouted.

'Best,' he said, and she hated him for his blindness and stupidity.

Realizing then abruptly that Sail could hear her as he waited below, she said: 'There can be nothing he could possibly want from me.'

But her heart began suddenly to beat in her throat. As if he heard her momentary indecision along with her words, Sail called out her name from the foot of the stairs.

'Stay there!' she screamed at him immediately. 'If you come up I'll kill you.'

Then came silence, and she felt both Ed and Sail waiting on her words and actions, and she crumbled before the onslaught of their waiting, and because she knew suddenly she could not bear him to go now he had come to her.

'Let him then,' she hissed to Ed. 'But make him wait.'

And Ed turned and went downstairs and she stood in the middle of floor and began to cry but no tears would come. She had a desperate need to be in the same room as Sail. Her emotions now were nameless.

Soon she thrust the covers over the bed, then fumbled under it for her Warren packages which still lay untouched and mummified in their wrappings. Staring in a cracked mirror she powdered her face and blackened her lashes and reddened her cheeks with stuff she had bought in the market. She painted her toenails, but her hand shook and she did it messily. She put on high-heeled blue shoes and draped around herself the black and silver shawl. Then she sat on the bed and again began to cry in dry racking gasps, without tears, and in the middle of it choked herself into quiet, for she heard Sail coming up the stairs.

She found she could look straight in his face, and yet not see him. And it seemed he was struggling in reverse, for he only glanced at her and then did not look at her, and yet appeared to see nothing but her.

The effect of what she had done to herself was unnerving, for the coloured paint and bright silver beads imposed on her thin, sick, dispirited frame made her look impossibly unreal and doll-like, and yet at the same time extraordinarily beautiful.

'Eva—' he said, and then nothing else.

She stared through him and said: 'What is it you want?'

'I thought you were crying,' he said.

'Oh, no.'

He came up to her and gently brushed at her hair with his hand and she stared straight in front of her, and presently he left her and went to the little window through which the sun still swelled and faded.

'He's gone,' he said eventually.

A wave of sickness came over her again, thick in her throat, white before her eyes, but she said nothing.

He said: 'He got a horse off the dealers. Caroline and me, we thought we were the greatest at getting horses cheap, but Christ, Steel could've made mincemeat out of us. He must have left in the middle of the night. That was two days ago.'

'You didn't see him go,' she said tonelessly. 'That's how he left me in Oiltown. And he's gone to kill someone just the same.'

'Eva,' he said, 'we've got to stop him.'

'We?' she said. '*We?*'

'You then, or me. Someone.'

'Why?'

'Didn't it ever occur to you,' Sail said, 'that he was crazy?'

'What?'

'Oh sure, cool, tough, all that. But he's obsessed with death. You set him up like a bloody great god, you silly bitch. But he's a killer, he's spent his life searching out and killing. He's eaten himself alive – he isn't alive. We don't know how many he's settled. Now there's going to be another. Can't you bloody see?'

She said nothing. It was a trick she had learned.

Sail swore and turned and looked at her.

She sat now, facing the empty room.

'Why should I care?'

'Why should you?' he repeated, and rested his head against the window frame.

'You should have stopped him,' she said. 'You understood him so *well*.'

'Eva, you are a priceless fucking cow.'

Suddenly her lethargy snapped inside her. She threw it off in one convulsive ghastly shudder. She stood up and put her hands over her eyes and screamed again and again: 'I saw you! I saw you! I saw you! I saw you!'

But somehow he reached her almost instantly, and somehow got his arms about her and held her tightly to him, and seemed to be trying to rock her and soothe her, though her body was as rigid as a pole. After a time she stopped crying out and her body slackened against his. Because of her new shoes she was, as in Oiltown, as tall as he. She stared past him and now the room was full of shadows. She began quite senselessly to count all the carved animals on the walls, but the shadows misled her; she had continually to begin again. In the middle of this he disorganized her by abruptly clinging to her more tightly even than before.

'Help me,' he said. 'Please, Eva, help *me*.'

And she found that she had put her arms about him, and had begun to caress and stroke his hair, all with a serene yet distracted tenderness.

Eighteen

She had never ridden a horse before, except Steel's when Steel had led it. This one filled her with fright, for although it was rather close to the ground, she was still afraid of falling off. Also it had no tail, and was covered by a perilous, flea-peopled matting of coarse black hair. In addition it did not like her. It liked Sail. It would do anything for Sail. It was in love with Sail. When Sail turned and looked at them the horse would pretend to excellent behaviour, otherwise it would wriggle and swerve, and shy at non-existent obstacles and blunder into obstacles that were there. Eva took to slapping it ferociously, which would keep it briefly in order, though she was always afraid it might bite her when she dismounted. Sail's own horse was slightly larger, if possible slightly uglier and certainly more villainous-looking, yet in point of fact it had no temperament, no personality of any sort, and would trudge docilely under him with its nose trailing on the ground, apparently half asleep.

They had got the horses off the dealers, having followed them to Warren in Barney's cart. She could not seem to wake up that day. The sounds of haggling and Sail's impeccable double-dealing came to her through a grey haze. The evening before she had let him take her back to the farm, and surprised herself because she felt no urge to run at the door. She had even slept beside him on the mattress she had seen him share with Steel. Perhaps because she was so tired, all implications dissolved in air, and pain had become a small and superfluous thing. Possibly his pain was worse, for he could not seem to look at her, and when he did, never into her face or eyes. She lay down without thinking, and fell asleep before the range, and woke in the morning to find they had each put their arms about each other in their sleep and that they were pressed together in a curiously childlike and asexual fashion. Their whole relationship seemed to have been altered, to have settled into strange long-established grooves which, though existing, had never until now revealed themselves.

It was by then an unspoken agreement between them that they should somehow follow Steel. There was no longer any desire in her to argue or debate, it seemed a natural and certain move, more natural and more certain because they would achieve it jointly.

The morning when they left, Eva pulled from under the mattress the crushed white silk ball of the dress and shook it out. Sail came back into the kitchen for her and she said: 'I lied to you.'

He smiled, not looking at her.

Outside, Ed amazed her by gravely shaking her hand. He seemed moved at their departure, but to Eva the village had already become a dream. She waved to him as they crossed the fields, but it was merely a ritual gesture.

They got back on to the highway about noon. The

dealers had said this road crumbled and wove its way across the patchy land, and fell off only at the shambles of rock that marked the coast. Sail seemed to have assumed Steel would take this route . . . or Steel had let drop some hint. It was all they had to go on.

The land was rough and dark and finally deserted. They sheltered in a ruined barn the first night, and Eva's horse crowded close to Sail, seductively rubbing against his body its black thatch leaping with fleas.

She slept, yet not fully. One horse started to snore and one trampled restlessly. In the end she got up, barely awake, and went out and stood on the black and empty road. Dead trees pillared up with phosphorescent fungus glowing between their fingers and joints. The stars whistled silver overhead, and suddenly she forgot where she was and began to run up the road away from something or towards something. Someone caught her and turned her.

'What is it?' Sail asked her, staring at last into her face.

Bewildered, she glanced around her.

'I thought,' she said, and then: 'I don't know where I am.'

'You're here,' he said, 'with me.'

The starlight appeared to shine right through his eyes into a machinery behind. He looked away from her at once and took her hand instead.

He led her back to the barn, and coaxed life into their fire.

'I can't sleep,' she said. 'Talk to me.'

He said apparently flippantly, 'I'll teach you to read minds.'

'What?'

'Yes, really. It's pretty simple. Something Caroline taught me, and it can bring in a lot of money. Sit up and pay attention.'

So he taught her a traveller's magic act in the firelight until she curled exhaustedly away from him to sleep. And after that as they rode up the highway it became a sort of game between them, and they began to laugh together. It was a thing they might have shared before if circumstances had been different. Now it came to them as something stored, something that had been put by for them.

He said to her: 'I have something in my left hand, Eva.'

And she said: 'Does it belong to a woman?'

And he said: 'This is a lady's, yes.'

'A ring?'

'No, that's if the "yes" comes first. Try again.'

'A glove.'

'Better. And what kind of a glove? What colour?'

'White,' cried Eva.

And sometime later they made love to each other, after which he began to look in her face again.

The fourth day there was a kind of wagon encampment sprawled around the road. The itinerants slouched about fires, drinking, and kicking their outsize scabby dray-dogs. Two men with a sawn-off shotgun apiece came wandering down on the road in their path. They wanted coin, they said, or kind; a sort of toll on travellers, all quite sensible and fair. Sail told them they had nothing but the horses, and who would want the horses? The men seemed to agree but were not so certain about the packs over the horses' backs. In the middle of this a big fat woman came swaggering between the wagons and elbowed the nearest man out of the way. Her hair was so black and sleek on her head that it looked like a coating of boot polish. She wore silver filigree earrings and grinned a row of white fangs at Sail.

'Leave off, you coupla sods,' she enjoined the two men, and they retreated immediately. 'You come after the other one,' she said, waving her hand in a large gesture.

'Other one?' Sail said.

'Other white one. With the wagon. There was some trouble, see? My, but he was good with his pretty gun.' She had a curious accent, and she spat suddenly sideways. 'They are a pack of fools, these,' waving about her at the cowering encampment. 'What sons have I been cursed with. Why not a strong lion like that one, or a boy like you,' and she smiled in a particular, lascivious yet not uncharming way at Sail. 'Ah, but god spare me a girl like her,' she added, 'fit only to be looked at. You follow him, yes?'

'Yes,' Sail said.

'He told me tell you no.'

'It's a family affair,' said Sail.

'So I think. Go on, then.' And stepping magnificently aside, she gave them the freedom of the road. Yet as they went past she slid her hand momentarily over Sail's back, and then, detaching her earrings, dropped them on the matted horse fur before Eva, no doubt stunning several fleas.

A little farther on, Eva heard her voice raised to a shout against her wanting tribe.

Knowing now for sure they were behind him, knowing too

251

he had known they would follow him, lent their journey a fresh urgency and strangeness. Eva would not put on the earrings the woman had given her, yet her dark and brutal grace became entangled in Eva's dreams. In the dreams the woman did not let them by at all, and grew to enormous size to prevent them.

They met up with an old man and his son, dealers in pots, pans and other domestic hardware, and travelled with them in their cart with the two horses tied on at the back. That night by their fire Eva and Sail tried out the mind-reading act on them, which went on the whole very well. Sail also hooked them with the trick of the three stones she had seen him catch Ed with before. At first they were surprised. Later they grew stubborn, and kept on and on at Sail to try them again, try them again, certain that this time they could outwit him. Naturally they came consistently to grief, but it was Sail who had to bring the fleecing to an end for the night, and in the morning they were at it again.

The road was by now disintegrating into pits and crevices laced up by brambles. The occasional fallen bridges lay in great heaps which they picked over or around in the tracks of previous adventurers. They passed above a river of black and stinking stuff, and about two miles beyond it the land began to patch into great wastes of white and porous rock, sharp with raucous winds.

They came through a stockade the second evening, in among a collection of ruined barns, lean-tos and farm machinery. Dogs howled and women haggled round the cart.

The guests' sleeping place here was an extra large and vermin-infested barn, and to earn a share in it Sail and Eva used the magic act a second time. He let them choose their own blindfold because it helped convince them there would be no cheating, but Eva did not like having her eyes bound up in a black bit of scarf.

'I can't remember! I shall mess it up.'

'You do and I'll murder you.'

But because it was his voice talking to her across the crowd she found she could respond to it, and do even better than before, her memory honed by adrenalin. They did altogether excellently, but when he was unknotting the blindfold, her eyes, though dazzled, suddenly made out a little pucker-faced man staring up at her. She clutched Sail's arm but by the time he looked round the man had gone. He was really a most unremarkable man. She only recalled him because of the pain that he had brought with him for her when last they met.

At Oiltown she had tried to keep him out, but he had got in. He had found a man for Steel to kill, and Steel had gone away.

She told all this to Sail, and they tramped about the makeshift settlement in the dark, searching, but did not find him. They asked after him, too, but their hosts were a thick-witted reticent lot. A woman, smiling at Sail, said she thought there had been a man about a day or two before, come from the coast, and his horse gone lame. In the end they went to the barn, tied the horses up among straw and debris, shared bread and beer with the old man (the son was off with some girl), and slept.

Eva woke in a pre-dawn chill because in past days she had grown very receptive to the movements of Sail, and now he had woken and was sitting up. He shook his head at her to be quiet. Nearby the pot and pan merchant was grunting, but at the far shadowy end of the barn, someone was creeping around the horses. Sail stood up and slipped the knife out of his belt. There appeared to be a length of string going towards the horses and tied to his waist. Cat silent he moved down the barn and into the dark, and suddenly there came out of it a jerky little cry.

'You should know better than to thieve off your own kind,' Sail murmured. 'Failing that nicety, you should watch out for string.'

Sail reappeared, driving before him the little man, who stared mournfully and apologetically at Eva. It was how she remembered him.

'My friend and yours, I take it,' Sail remarked. He still balanced his knife delicately in the fingers of one hand.

'Yes,' she said.

'You know a blond man, white-haired, like us,' Sail said to his captive.

'No. Not me. You're making a mistake.'

'What did you want the horse for?'

'Yes. Shouldn't have done that. My own went lame.'

'Going to or coming from the blond man?'

'I don't know—'

'She knows *you*,' Sail said.

The little man stared sideways, piteously, at Eva.

'Yes. S'pose she might,' he said.

'Where is he?'

'Going to the coast, perhaps.'

'Where on the coast?' Sail asked levelly.

'Town perhaps. Old resort it was – Ship Bay, used to be.'

'Does the highway go there?'

'Turn off bit farther on – side road, still tar and stuff on it.'

'All right,' Sail said. He sheathed the knife and came to sit beside Eva. He put his arm around her and she began to tremble.

The man stood uncertainly, fidgeting, not sure what they would do now, this unexpected jury of apparent twins.

'I take it there's a man there he'll kill,' Sail said eventually.

'Yes. Yes, that's it, perhaps.'

'You've helped him find them, or some of them,' Sail said. 'Why?'

'He paid me,' the man said, but he stared at his feet and fumbled his hands together.

'Let me rephrase my question. Why does he want them? We'd like to hear,' Sail said, very softly, and Eva felt him tense as a sprung wire beside her.

'Can't tell you anything,' the man muttered, drooping there.

'You can and you bloody will. It's not unknown for horse-thieves to get cut up in the act.'

The man rubbed his eyes. He took the little flask from inside his jacket as once before, but this time swigged deeply from it. His eyes when he looked back at them were red-rimmed and accusing.

'Shouldn't ask me.' He shook his head. He sat unexpectedly in front of them and stared at the dirty straw on the ground while the barn dawn-quickened through every hole and slit, and the old pan salesman snored.

'It's not that I know anything, not properly. I used to see him as a kid, sometimes. His father was nothing, he had some land, all stones. But his mother, the woman – she was a mutant woman. She had those eyes, closed over on the inside. But she was lovely, in a strange-looking way, really beautiful. There was a drought, it got hot, and no rain. I'd been doing some work there, in the village and the fields. The father, he had these two ivory-handled guns, and all you could hear all day was him shooting at some stones, or at the sky – then one day he shot a man. I don't know why, I didn't see it. But they strung him up, and the woman – they raped her and they killed her. He was only a kid, about seven. Got sent off to an aunt, clever woman, reading and everything. But she was a bitch. She had religion. And then, years later I meet him when he's a man. Like meeting his father and that white woman all rolled in one. He could shoot, too. He says to me, Do you know any man anywhere, this way, tall, thickset, eyes like this, or this? I say no. He says, But you remember them, how they were. You were there. You can find me just that kind. He says, I haven't seen a man like those for three months. The last one I saw, I killed him. And then he describes one or two others, and then he says, if I find him some men like those he'll pay me. He was young, about seventeen. He talked more then than now. I asked him what he meant by it, because I was drunk. He sneered and quoted the Bible. Said the mutants would inherit the earth, and the rest of us were on borrowed time, we couldn't alter, but he'd make that borrowed time go quicker for some of them. Well, I went off, but it happened a day later I did see a man. He was like I remembered. Nothing to do with it, the ones that killed Steel's mother – but like, a thin bastard with a nasty way to him. I went back and caught him up and – I told him.

And he asked the name, so I gave him that. It was a different name, of course, not the name of the man this man was like. But any way he went after him then, and he shot him. He just shot this man. I said, What happens, when you do that? He said, One less. That's all he said. *One less.* You see, he doesn't think they're the same ones – the ones got his father and the woman. He knows. But it's – the *types* he wants, and he likes to have the name. Then he kills them. Quick. One shot. I'm not the only one he has out looking. He's always on the move himself. He never stops long anywhere. One day someone will get him. Word gets round. But how long have any of us got? *One less.*'

The dawn was now bright and cold in the barn.

The man said, cajolingly, 'I can go now, can't I?' And when no one answered, he sidled away from them.

Sail said very quietly, 'We'll find him, Eva. We will.'

But she felt a terrible futility. If they found him, he would still be lost, shut in some prison of the mind. They could call him through doorways, glimpse him through window-slits, touch him even, momentarily, but never get near.

'It won't matter,' she said. 'There's nothing we can do.'

'There is,' he said, and gripped her fiercely, and the light spilled round the filthy barn like milk.

Nineteen

They left before the settlement was properly awake. The old man still snored, the young one, dissatisfied with his night, groped about the barn to find the remains of the beer. Outside, light slanted through the dreary yellow glass pane of the sky. Steel's man had vanished.

The highway stretched brokenly out in the dull sun. The turn-off, when they came to it, an old side road winding down between gaunt wire walls of briars, had only kept its facing in parts. Occasionally drifting mist obscured horizons and holes.

Eva hung her head. She and Sail did not speak to each other except in brief mechanical bursts.

'Perhaps he lied,' she said finally. 'Perhaps Steel took another road.'

But Sail ignored her, and eventually the road degenerated into a track which on the whole was easier to manage.

It was possibly ironical that in the late afternoon Eva should be the first to see Steel. They had had no particular hope of catching him up, he was, after all, three or four days ahead of them. Yet some detour, some measure of waiting, probably for the man they had also inadvertently met, had

259

slowed him. At a point where the track spilled down from the crest of a hill, she saw something moving and alive, a little jolting speck of a wagon pulled by a microbe, which was a horse. She herself had dismounted, for Sail was prizing a stone out of the hoof of her own horse – it had probably picked it up to get his attention. And now, for an instant, Eva held back from telling Sail what she could see, for in another minute the foggy distance and the black bone trees would hide Steel from both of them. And then at the last moment she cried out irresistibly, and Sail dropped the hoof and ran and looked down.

They stood like this, as if petrified, their eyes following the wagon into the trees, impossibly constrained.

'We shan't catch him up,' said Eva.

'He'll have to stop sometime,' Sail said.

'He won't. And he goes nights without sleeping.'

'Shut up and get on your horse.'

So the pursuit began.

Somehow Sail urged speed out of his somnambulist beast, and dragged Eva's by its bridle. Bullied and coerced the terrible horses now showed themselves capable of a sustained and rather fast jouncing. For hours it seemed they ran over the track into ever-increasing sallow limbos of mist. Once they saw him again, taking an upper curve of the track ahead.

In the end, in a thick bank of fog smeared externally by maroon sunset, the horses slackened and slunk together coughing damply.

'We'll lose him,' Eva now moaned. 'He'll leave the track.'

'He'll have to leave the wagon then. The ground's mud and marsh from here on by the look of it.'

They came out on the other face of the fog into a star-pierced afterglow casting every aspect of its feverish reflections on each side in sluggish water wastes. The track broke up into slippery rocks, and at last became a causeway of sinking blotchy brick. Ahead on the farthest horizon, a pin-point pale star swung irregularly.

'If these damn things will only move we'll get to him in an hour,' Sail said, but Eva, overpowered by sudden panic, shook her head.

The lie of the land gave them always now a slightly downward vista, so that the far-off light faintly surrounding the wagon swung perpetually ahead. Eva began to think of stories of witch lights, leading travellers to unintelligent muddy doom. Maybe Steel was leading them similarly, anxious to be rid of them. As so often before she found it easy to fantasize him into a demon. Her back ached and her head swam tiredly; she wondered if she could manage to fall off the horse. But then, she felt she could not rely upon Sail to stop. At that precise moment he did. She in turn jerked at her horse and finally brought it to a floundering halt a few yards ahead of him.

'He's not moving,' Sail said.

She stared, and saw that the light no longer fluctuated nor dwindled.

'He must know we're behind him,' Sail said.

For a second or so they both sat non-plussed, oddly restrained by this apparent invitation. Then Sail's horse was suddenly rushing past, and she, in a frenzy not to be left, kicked so viciously that the four-legged woolly rug leaped under her and took off up the causeway nearly leaving her itself.

Riding like this, the wind thrusting the hair off her face and blinding her with tears, she thought she would collide with the wagon-back, or else might never reach it. It had become a sort of race between Sail and herself. They were rivals as well as lovers. She almost began to hate him again. Then there was a man ahead of her on the causeway. It startled her, and, of course, startled the horse. They ran about in a circle and she screamed at it furiously, and then found it had jerked to a standstill, ridiculously facing the way they had come. Aware of events behind her, she cursed and slapped it, and eventually slid from its hide in defeat.

When she turned, she beheld Steel standing in front of the wagon-back. He seemed taller even than before. The aureoles of light coming around the sides of the wagon made him a silhouette. Only the white hair and the white parts of the rifle in his hands shone like frozen mirror, and behind him a sky full of cold white mirror stars.

Something came into Eva's head from the book-read past at Oiltown.

'Ill met by starlight,' she said.

'Moonlight,' Sail said automatically, after which silence fell crushingly on both of them.

Initially Steel said nothing. He seemed not even to be looking at them. It was like confronting a blind man. At last, when he did speak, his voice was toneless and objective.

'I left you a message on the road.'

'Oh yes,' Sail said, 'your gypsy duchess. Quite dramatic.

A touch of the Gothic to liven up the trail.'

'I intend to make this journey alone,' Steel said.

'You'll find that difficult. We're pretty persistent, she and I.'

Steel shifted the rifle very slightly. Its round eyes tilted and glared. Eva clenched her hands.

'Go back the way you came,' Steel said.

'We met a man,' Sail said casually, 'that last settlement on the road. A friend of yours.'

Eva sensed Sail poised on a tightrope of words, the rifle swinging. Her nails in her palms, she said: 'Don't tell him.'

'He knows. For god's sake. You get it, don't you, Steel? Someone handed us your secret on a plate.'

It seemed to Eva that the rifle took on a life of its own. She hid her face in her hands, and Sail said: 'She thinks you'll shoot us with that thing.'

'She could be right,' Steel said softly.

'*Oh* no. Don't try to kid me.'

'Go back,' Steel said.

'Back to where? And where are you going back to when you've finished in Ship Bay?'

Steel turned and looked at him, and for the first time Eva made out eyes in the silhouetted mask-face. The eyes were cold and dead. She remembered how he had looked at her first. She remembered how she had materialized in front of him, laughing and recently afraid, a shadow with white hair – perhaps, momentarily, as much an undead for him as he had been for her.

'He can't hear you,' she said to Sail. 'He doesn't know we're here. He thinks he's imagining us.'

Steel looked at her then.

'Don't analyse me. I told you before.'

'I'm alive,' she said piteously, holding out her hands to him. 'I'm real.'

'Get on your horse. If you turn back now, the two of you can make the settlement before dawn.'

'Stuff it,' Sail said. 'You're stuck with us.'

'Don't lay odds on that,' Steel said. He walked away, round the wagon, and out of sight. Presently horse and vehicle began to move, leisurely, almost silently. The light picked out distant stretches of water and occasional leprous trees. As neither Eva nor Sail made any immediate attempt to follow, the light grew fainter and worked its magic stencilling farther and farther away. They seemed to be losing it altogether. She experienced a very primitive fear at the loss of the light. It was like the fear of sunfall and night, the terror of total eclipse, sleep and finally burial. She caught at her horse, got on it, and beat it with her hands until it began to advance in the right direction. This time Sail came after her.

They were about forty yards behind the wagon, which was moving like a snail. She expected momently that Steel might turn and shoot them both; she saw things altogether in a more naked and barbarous way than Sail, for she had never acquired his veneer of civilization. But in the end she was so tired she no longer expected anything.

'Wake up,' Sail said.

'I'm not asleep.'

'You've been asleep for bloody hours.'

She opened her eyes and yawned ecstatically, not remembering where she was. The overhead sky was still

black, but a faint corrupt glow edged the horizon.
Discontented with the scene she began to burrow again into
the warmth of the blankets, but Sail caught her and dragged
her into a sitting position.

The çauseway appeared to have petered out. On the rim
of the sky the land rose and ended in the stripped poles of
trees. Among the trees was incredibly parked Steel's wagon.

'Yes,' Sail said to her, 'that's what I thought. And you
were rolling off your horse every ten seconds. So we tied up
for the night. But I just took a walk up there, and it's Steel's
wagon all right, but he's taken his horse and gone.'

Eva began to laugh.

They packed their gear together and walked their horses
to the wagon. Eva's was tied on the back, carping, while
Sail wheedled the other big sleepy beast into the shafts. It
had been easy for Steel, with his disregard of possessions,
to leave the wagon behind, and equally hard for them to
ignore it and its elements of familiarity, security and
shelter. They had been *meant* to take it. They grinned at
each other with sour amusement as they sat on the box and
cursed the horse into movement, and fulfilled Steel's geas
on them.

The morning wind blew like splintered knives, carrying
with it a feeling of vast and interminable emptiness. They
came from the trees and passed a stone house with crippled
sides and smashed interior, evidence of gales blown
through at front and back, and a fossilized bush sprouted
from the chimney. Beyond the house the land plunged
down to meet the wind and abruptly stopped as if
something had bitten it off. At the margin of nothingness
were a few twisted iron railings. Beyond them lay the

evidence of emptiness felt in the wind, the end of the world, the void – yet not quite, for something moved in the void, a great amorphous spasming and sounding.

Sail pointed.

'That's the sea,' he said.

At first she could not reconcile this image with the pictures she had seen of it – for she had not thought it would move and make noises. The representation had become the real thing, and reality something obscene and unnatural.

Breaks appeared on the distant skirts of the sky, and the sea became lit up similarly. It was not green, as she had always supposed, but black. It had an oily filmed shimmer, catching the light; she was reminded of scaled things, of serpents in books, and the armoured reptiles of the marsh. Its smell, too, was dismal and fearful to her. Once it had carried the breath of life, fish-reek, ozone. Although she had never known these smells, some part of her sensed their absence, some race memory of crowded beaches, and the universal panacea of brine and breezes, or perhaps some even older tug of the heart towards the sea-womb from which life first crawled aboard the land. Now it had a hemlock tang and somehow, too, an inexpressible odour of nullity.

She sat rigid and glared at the shifting phantom of the sea as they rode parallel to it beside the markers of the railings. Once they passed steps going down the cliff to the stone-littered shore.

Apart from the dawn there was another light ahead of them on the land. It appeared in faint sprinkles of yellow, white and pink, and soon distracted Eva completely.

They passed a dirty white shelter from which the glass

windows had been removed, also the seats. Houses began to appear, or the rubble of houses. Unable to withstand violent freak winds, walls had fallen like cards. There was a makeshift barricade of bricks and tarpaulin across the path. Most of it had collapsed. A piece of wood on a pole had scratched on it the words: SHIP BAY, and under that: SLOAT/KINGSLEY.

A man was sitting by the wall on the other side, holding a rifle. He glanced up at them, but made no move to stop them or speak. He was a mutant, quite hairless, and his features were blurred together as if his face had been smudged when still wet.

The sun came up, and the sky and the sea caught flame with it, so that now the void was filled with a raging fiery furnace.

Below the rotting promenade with its ornamental lamp-posts, the black sea curled and twitched. The façades of partially derelict hotels were here and there still in place, pale green, pink or blue, like the mummified remains of the ices that had once been consumed beneath their windows. The sea wind wailed up and down the streets and back roads over heaps of cement and tin and bricks and corrugated iron. 'Ozymandias Inc.,' said Sail. But the magic fairy lights were still burning as they came down the promenade. Eva stared at their coloured globes, diluted by the daylight. Then the lights winked out, bank upon bank, string upon string. After which the prolapsed streets lay dead and silent, except for the wind.

Eva stared about her. Nothing moved.

'There's no one here.'

'There's someone here,' Sail said, 'someone who likes seeing the lights go on and off.'

Below, the sea pumped and pummelled. One day the promenade would collapse, and the water would slush in upon the fallen hotels.

'There were two names on that board,' Sail said. 'And a wall, and a guard with a gun.'

A piece of sound came down a side street in front of them. Sail pulled up the horse. A woman came out on to the promenade. She carried a basket of what appeared to be linen, and thin, thin wisps of hair curled about her head. Her body was misshapen and hunchbacked and little. She did not seem to see them, and began to walk away ahead of them, carrying her basket among the ornamental lamps. Sail jumped down and ran after her. He touched her arm lightly, trying not to startle her, but she turned and looked dully at him. Eva could not hear what Sail said to her, nor the woman's replies. She began to bite her nails. It seemed they would never find Steel now, for the ruin-crowded emptiness was enigmatic and concealing. He could even now be looking down on them from one of the endless ranks of windows.

Sail came back to the wagon.

'What did you ask her? Did you ask about Steel?'

'No. For Christ's sake, Eva, he doesn't want a public announcement. I asked her where the local boss-man shacks up.'

This made no sense to her, but, enervated and oppressed, she asked nothing else, and sat meekly beside him as they drove on, presently passing the trudging and uninterested woman with her basket of clothes.

* * *

On the other side of the bay perched on the headland, was an old house. It had been built to resemble a castle, now ravaged by the sea winds and minus several turrets, it leaned backwards into its garden of dead trees as if falling in a swoon.

From the windows of the house came the incomprehensible sounds of a full symphony orchestra struggling scratchily across the surface of a waltz. Eva had never heard such noises and was duly terrorized.

'*What is it?*'

'It's a bloody record-player,' Sail said, caught between marvel and disgust. 'They've got a generator. Jallow had them. But this lot use it for fairy lights and Strauss.'

At that moment the incredible orchestra snagged on its own burnt-out and unwaxed grooves. A phrase was repeated, and repeated again, and thereafter repeated and repeated. To this accompaniment horse and vehicle angled past the house and down a turning, and stopped beside a rubble of steps in the narrow street.

Sail cat-sprang from the wagon.

'Stay here, Eva.'

'No. Don't leave me. Where are you going?'

'That's Kingsley's place. At any rate, so the jolly washerwoman said. Kingsley owns Ship Bay. I'm going to offer my services like any well-behaved clean-nosed itinerant – cut your lawn for you, sir, tile your roof. That saves us getting thrown straight back on the road. In addition, whoever Steel is after is round here somewhere. Find him and we'll find Steel.'

269

'No,' she murmured, and shook her head, but he had walked up the steps.

Faint gushes of plaster fell unexpectedly through the canyon of a boarding house with the mutations of sweet peas.

Eva looked up, and saw an apparition.

It wore bleached jeans and plimsoles, a shirt open at the neck, in which a jaunty yellow-check scarf was tucked, also a waisted jacket of maroon and orange stripes. It was male, and stood swaggeringly, looking at her. An unnerving sense of recollection came over her. She stared at the blunt hairy fingers and the green cigarette poked through them, at the mane of hair which unaccountably sent cold down her spine. More than anything she disliked the eyes, for they were masked behind a pair of ink-black sunglass lenses in spider-web-thin metal frames. She felt something lurking behind the sightless oblongs, some sort of unpleasant animal. A tiny crack bisected the left-hand lens; she visualized it splintering abruptly open and a fanged head breaking out.

'Well, well,' said the man, 'so he finally got here. And bringing his little skinny girl with him too. At it already is he then? No, I don't think so. Not quite yet.'

'What do you mean?' Eva cried.

'The Angel of Death. We must all daub a little lamb's blood on our lintels tonight, as you might say. He's polishing his ivory rifle, perhaps? Cleaning it out, getting it nice. A perfectionist. And you blondie? Where do you fit in? The carnal urge comes on him, no doubt, in the bloody aftermath.'

Nausea roiled in Eva's throat. She did not know who this

was, and yet a familiar fright had hold of her. With unrealized, uncanny relevance, she croaked: 'Why do you wear spectacles?'

'Oh, grandmother, what big eyes you *do* have. You were always a perspicacious tart I recall. I wear the – *sunglasses* blondie, not spectacles, try to get it right – *sunglasses* – to hide my disability from the world. Things are run in a proper fashion in Ship Bay. The useless crap does the work, and the thinking man reaps the profits. They see my worth here. I have my wits about me. But it doesn't do to thrust my little misfortune up their noses.'

Eva snatched something from the immediate interior of the wagon, which was in fact a book. She slung it at the man's head, aiming for the dark glasses. With a hoarse yell he leapt to one side, but, turning his plimsoled foot on rubble, plunged down on his knees. He dropped his green cigarette, the glasses slipped off his face and fell. In a frenzied twist and flapping of hands he somehow caught them before they smacked on the pavement. With bowed head he examined them tapping cautiously at the previously damaged lens, still on his knees. Then he looked up and smiled nastily at her. She saw that his unmasked eyes were round, colourless, swimming, albino egg-white eyes, and she remembered immediately.

'Derry,' she breathed.

'Oh, yes, Derry. Your friend's friend Derry. The mutant. You thought he'd shoot me, didn't you? Do you remember the Bottikelli lady in my book?' He thrust the glasses back into position. 'And my name, which is Willowby? Remember that, do you? Where's *he*?' he suddenly said.

'I'm not with him,' Eva said.

'Pushed you out, did he? Then whose wagon's that?'

'Mine.'

Eva and Willowby turned together. Sail was leaning casually by the extended wall of the old house. Lightly very lightly, he was moving and spinning the knife in his fingers.

Willowby looked at Sail. His mouth quirked.

'Shrunk in the wash, did he?'

'If you want this blade straight through your bollocks, mate, you're going the right way about it,' Sail remarked conversationally.

Willowby's lip twitched and he turned back to Eva.

'Where is he then, pray?'

Eva half opened her mouth. Sail cut in: 'Not with us. What do *you* think?'

Willowby eased himself about on his plimsoles.

'No longer friends?' he asked Eva.

Sail offered smoothly, 'He slung her out, since when she's been with me. Where he is now is his bother.'

'He should be here,' Willowby said.

'Why?'

'Did she never mention his little hobby?'

'What's that then?'

'He kills people.'

'Just like that,' said Sail.

'Certain men,' Willowby said. 'Certain types. One is here. So he'll be coming here, sometime.' Willowby smiled.

'What's your angle?'

'None. Purely an interested spectator.'

'For an interested spectator you've grubbed up a hell of a lot,' Sail commented.

Eva, caught up in his ruse until now, could no longer bear it.

'How did you know he'd come here?' she cried. 'How did you know why?'

'Venus waxes restless,' Willowby said. '*He* kicked me out of a very nice living before I was ready to go. I asked about here and there. Besides, Derry – she will tell you about Derry – knew something and was a trusting soul. One likes to know where one stands. And it isn't so hard to trace our fellow men in these days of insularity.'

'Who's this man then, this man you *say* he's after?' Sail asked. He said it as if he were very interested; even Eva appreciated his logical cleverness, for to be uninterested would be too coy, too transparent, and Sail, in his rôle of successor, would be as curious as Willowby. Willowby tapped his chin. In the background the waltz toiled in its groove.

'Thinking of tipping him off? Don't bother, he's well looked after. One of Kingsley's pets, as am I. Slave-master you might say.'

'But you're *waiting* here.'

'Why not? All roads lead to Rome.'

Sail came past Willowby and swung up on to the box.

'Well, you can give *him* our regards, mate. That's if he ever gets here.'

The reins jerked the forward horse awake. They began to move away. There was a brief skitter as Eva's horse, tied at the back, tried to kick Willowby. Then Sail had turned the wagon around the corner. The wail of the waltz receded but did not quite diminish.

Eva stuck her claws into Sail's arm.

'Where are we going?'

'Somewhere to park this thing first. There was no answer at the house, only that damn record upstairs.' He was silent a moment, his face set. 'He mentioned Derry to me. And Willowby. Why the fuck didn't he polish him off when he had the chance? Keep your fingers crossed we find Steel first.'

Such a sense of terror came over her that she shut her eyes and said nothing else at all.

Later they passed a group of mutant men at work. They were replacing broken fairy lights in the illuminations, while the cracked roads and other decay reared all around them.

'Nobody's going to turn a hair at us,' said Sail, 'providing we keep out of the way of Kingsley's stinking elite.'

They finally left the wagon more or less hidden in a partly collapsed alleyway, the horses fed and tied up in a lean-to at the end, while they holed up next door in a block of derelict flats. They shared food on a broken-down bed, while behind them the glassless window showed black gelid sea in retreat from black scabrous beach.

'When it's dark, I'll go out and have a look around,' Sail said.

In the corner a birdcage without a bird in it wobbled on a stand. Eva began to cry.

Sail put his arm round her. She clung to him, but the emptiness of the beach below seemed to fill her up.

Twenty

Just before sunset a hurricane rose out of the sea. It had six coal-black, gouged-out bellies and six churning, spewing mouths. The yellow sky went black, the black water in places yellow from disgusting upheavals of mud, so that sea and air seemed upside down. Wind screamed. The flats rocked. Venomous spray splashed over the cliff railings and pavement, in at windows, up the stairs, and in gelatinous runnels through the gutters. Pieces of detritus were flung against the promenade. A tree blew over the roof.

They upended the bed and thrust it over the window and the tacked-down mattress bellied and sucked.

After the winds subsided, a sullen glare streaked the sky and reflected on the wet pavements. Distant cones of fog billowed across the sea. And into this witches' sabbat dusk sprang up the sudden gleam of the illuminations.

'There are electric lights on in Kingsley's place,' Sail said.

Having again shifted the bed, they could see the house across the bay.

He had not asked her to go with him, she did not want to.

She huddled in the blankets they had brought up,

kindling no fire in the grate for he had warned her it might attract unwelcome attention. The lights outside painted the room. Many had been damaged in the storm. Whole strands would abruptly sizzle, pop, explode. Some burned with naked elements.

He was gone a long while.

No noise reached her from the lighted house across the bay, but once she heard footsteps under her window. She did not look out until they were fading, and then she saw Willowby walking along the promenade, casual, anachronistic, draped in a huge mackintosh, a late stroller taking the air after the hurricane. He looked to neither side.

She began to believe that Sail would not come back.

She slept. The sea woke her, coming in. She stared down on it, puzzled by its persistence. It moved yet had no life.

It was well into the night when Sail came through the door. He looked exhausted, and was alone.

'As you see,' he said, 'I didn't find him.' He sat on the bed and took her hand. 'I could sleep for a year.'

In her present state of mind she was unpleasantly able instantly to visualize this. She imagined shaking his catatonic body and screaming in his ears to no avail, while miniature ages ground to dust.

'First, though,' he said, 'we're getting out of here. There's a reasonably habitable shop we can use, just behind Kingsley's house.'

They took up the blankets.

'I saw Willowby outside,' she said.

'We'll have to think something up for Willowby,' Sail muttered.

He selected a few things from the wagon and left food for the horses. Eva's horse stared at him, furious at this jilting.

They tramped across the wet backroads and fallen bricks, seeing nothing alive but the neon eyes of three or four foraging rats.

Only one light burned still in the house, high in a semi-gothic tower. From the interior of this light emanated occasional sounds of smashing glass, and once a bottle landed on the pavement. The record had stopped.

The shop had sold curiosities – shells, fur toys, fishing nets, and brass teatrays engraved with Viking long-boats and lighthouses. The remains of its past lay scattered and broken, and upstairs a few rooms crowded together. They lay down on the sad and sag-springed bed and Sail fell instantly asleep.

Eva imagined Steel somewhere in the town, meticulously cleaning the gun.

Suddenly the dark grew darker. The illuminations had been switched off prematurely, or else failed altogether. It seemed to her portentous. She felt the sigh of death pass over the shop. A premonition began to tick inexorably inside her.

The next day Sail watched at the window.

From the window they could see the street below, and the curve of the promenade as it followed the bay and curled by the frontage of the Kingsley house. For a long while the house was silent. Once, two hairless mutant men arrived with a cart, and went in at the front with packages, and then came out and went away. In the middle of the afternoon the scratched record-player began to play, and two ghostly voices, one male and one female, started to sing that some day they would find each other. This optimism, proclaimed so trustingly in the yellow wormwood air, depressed Eva. Although the needle did not catch this time, the entire record was played over and over again.

Steel did not come to the house.

A brackish sunset.

'On clear days,' Sail remarked softly, 'I bet you could see across to France.'

There was a sudden crash from within the house. To Eva it sounded like a shot.

'It's all right, they're only breaking things,' he said. He turned to her. 'I've got to get into the house,' he said.

'No,' she cried.

'Yes. This isn't close enough. He could come in another way and we wouldn't see until too late.'

'Take me with you.'

'You bet I will. We're not risking splitting up now.'

'How will we do it?'

'God knows. Have to trust to luck.'

A handful of coloured bulbs snapped on outside, though the far sweep of the promenade was left in darkness.

Lights eye-opened in the house at random intervals up and down its walls.

Outside it was gusty and very cold. Sail coughed and cursed himself. A wrought iron gate swung open and they pushed up towards the house through the brambles.

One of the upper cracked glass windows was thrust up. An indeterminate shape appeared on the light.

'Clear off, you buggers!' roared a voice.

'Wait!' Sail shouted.

'What? Who's that? If it's one of you bloody mewts—'

The roaring shape was deposed by another.

'What do you want?'

'To see Kingsley. Or Sloat.'

The new shape laughed a little, a curious kind of stage laugh. It had a high male cultured artificial voice, that seemed to be wearing white gloves and possibly an orchid, and did not belong in a million years in a cracked glass window.

'Sloat has hopefully passed on to better things,' it said. 'I am Kingsley. And what can I do for you?'

'We're looking for work.'

'We? Oh yes, and a young lady too. Well, dear boy, the mutant population does the work. We don't have any need of casual labour.'

In the background the record had been abruptly changed. To the accompaniment of a violin, the shape of a woman with high-piled hair insinuated itself into the window frame.

'My dear,' this woman said, in the same unbelievable rhinestone voice, 'you simply can't turn normal people away like that. At least give them something to eat.'

'Thanks,' said Sail humbly, 'that's good of you.'

The woman was staring at him as he stood under the window in its electric spotlight. Then she leaned back in an almost-parody of elegance, and called sharply: 'Flak! Go and open the door.'

Someone, presumably Flak, grumbled from within.

'Do as she tells you,' Kingsley said. Wearily he swung about and vanished, the woman moving slowly after him.

The door opened almost instantly on a large, unlit space. No one was there. They went in and the door slid shut. Eva stared at it in horror. At the head of looming stairs, the woman suddenly appeared, carrying a six-pronged candelabra dripping wax. She wore a long black satin dress, and as they climbed towards her, the candlelight pushed the shadows indecently down her body to her feet.

She was revealed to be all metals and manufactured things, bare white enamelled shoulders and arms, unbare painted plastic doll face, red chinese-lacquer nails, tuba-swellings of brass hair, blown green glass eyes, and with a salivation of apparent diamonds from her ears. She was taller than both of them, and the light refracted and splintered on her hard smooth brilliance. She smelled of roses, as roses themselves would smell no longer.

'Don't let the door alarm you,' she said. She spared a noncommittal glance for Eva. 'An electric eye. We still run it from the generator.' Her accent was in fact not quite so consistent as Kingsley's had been. It could not be directly faulted and yet its polished edge occasionally softened, becoming slovenly. 'My name is Roma. And you?'

'Sail,' he said. He took one of her enamel hands and kissed it. It was a gesture he had always kept by him, a combination of humorous gallantry and cynical neurasthenia, yet it now fitted so perfectly that Eva felt moved to angry applause.

'I'm Eva,' she said clearly.

'Oh, really? And are you related? Brother and sister perhaps.'

Not waiting for an answer, she turned to them her ceramic back and they followed her through the blind dark of the house to a double doorway spilling light.

Years ago this had been a drawing room. Great brocaded armchairs bulged about a marble fireplace. Incredible wallpapers faded on the walls and an ornately gilded white-faced clock stared dumbly with broken hands. Overhead bulbs blazed from white velour shades, a static glare broken up by the flickerings of the fire and of the populated candelabras palpitating from every angle. The record-player pulsed hypnotically on a rosewood table. It was just a box, a turntable. Beyond the window, framed by velvet curtains, spread darkness pimpled briefly by fairy lights.

Two men sat drinking and playing cards, another leaned at the fireplace. Kingsley – unmistakable – sat with an open book balanced across the arm of his chair. He kept his profile turned to them, narrow, aquiline and pale. In his bony fingers burned a green cigarette such as Willowby had smoked. Roma set down the candlebranch and, crossing to him, put her immaculate hand on his shoulder. There was a silence. One of the cardplayers swore softly over his game and there came a clink of glasses and bottles. Yet Kingsley and Roma seemed quite removed from everything now they had come together, like something pristine, still sealed in a polythene wrapper.

'So these are your two orphans of the storm?' Kingsley said at last. He turned and looked at them, first at Sail and then at Eva. His narrow face moved into a little sad smile. 'Oh,' he said, exploring her with creased and distant eyes. 'Such possibilities lost.'

'Jesus god,' a man said suddenly from the card table. A glass skidded and smashed.

'Please restrain yourself, Flak.' Kingsley murmured, not

turning. 'I've had to tell you before about breaking things. What you do in your own quarters is your concern, but in this room at least try to preserve a little decency.'

'That – that mewt,' the man cried out hoarsely. 'Get her out! Get her *out*!'

Eva spun to face him. He was dark and rather tall and wore a grey tailored jacket. A green scarf tucked in at his throat, like Willowby's, echoed the colour of his sick face. He stared at her, breathing hard, and Eva felt a start of panic-stricken hatred, for she knew exactly who he was, and what he had been told, and why he looked at her as he did.

She felt Sail quicken beside her and turn as she had done.

'What's bothering you?' Sail asked softly.

The man shook his head, sweating.

'Both bloody mewts – bloody albino mewts—'

Eva laughed clear and high. The blood drained out of her head and she thought she would faint, but instead she found herself walking across the room to the man Kingsley had called Flak, lifting her white hair in her hands. And when she got to him she looked in his eyes and he trembled like a man in a terrible fever. It was because someone was looking for him. Someone who wanted to kill him since he resembled another. And she was like that killer, a white-haired mutant woman – which, someone else must have said, was what the killer's mother had been. Beautiful; deadly now. The dead returned. The promise of things to come—

'Take her away! Get her out!' he screamed. 'Can't you *see*?'

The other man at the table laughed.

'Better leave him alone, girlie. He gets the jitters lately at natural blondes. Don't you, Flak boy?'

'Shut up, you cunt. She's a mewt. I can't stand them round me.'

Eva shook out her hair. She reached up and stroked Flak's sweating face, and he moaned and grunted and then ran abruptly outside. They heard him begin to vomit, while in the background a woman sang tremulously that her darkest night had been turned into day by a violin.

'Fletcher,' Kingsley said to the man by the fireplace, 'go and get the mutant from downstairs and tell it to clear up his mess. His rooms are already a cess-pit. He is useless to me. I think we might replace him with the other one, Willowby.'

Fletcher went out.

The man at the card table poured himself another drink.

'It's Willowby put the wind up him in the first place. Told him some feller was after fixing him, some mewt with white hair.'

'My dear, this is so very sordid,' Kingsley murmured to Roma. 'Give our guests some food if you want to, or else send them away.'

Clearly they had been dismissed. He raised his book. Roma raised her head and smiled directly at Sail. She picked up the candlebranch and led them out, past Flak, as he knelt cringing and groaning at the banisters, not seeing him with her clean polythene-protected eyes.

There was a stone kitchen. Roma floated about this too. She did not, of course, cook or prepare anything in any way. It was unthinkable. She simply led them to cupboards and stood waiting. There was bread and cheese finally on the dirty table, and also three bottles of white wine. Roma sat beside Sail. He ate and, after invitation, wrenched the cork out of the first bottle. Eva could not eat at all, she pulled the crust off a bit of bread and arranged the pieces along the table. But Sail poured wine into a cracked cup and she drained it like water. A hopeful drowsy warmth overcame her almost at once.

Roma and Sail drank from the same cup.

They drank through the first bottle of wine and started on the second. Eva found she now had to pour her own drinks. Her thoughts were very erratic yet quite absorbing, and she did not mind her sudden exclusion. At first she felt rather happy and made fresh patterns with the bits of crust. From time to time she could hear snatches of conversation. Sail seemed to be telling Roma about his miserable and horrifying childhood. Eva was infinitely amused to see Roma's eyes prismatic with sentimental tears. She also noticed that Roma's accent had now completely altered and that at some point she had undone her hair so that it cascaded over both of them in hard winking metal coils.

But then Eva stared at Sail and panicked. She reached over the table and grabbed at his arm and shook him. The mug he was holding was full of wine which spilled on to Roma's knees. Roma swore at her and brushed at her puddled satin lap.

'You've forgotten,' Eva hissed at Sail.

His pale eyes seemed quite blank. He might have been a stranger she had run up to on the street.

'No,' he said, but it did not mean anything.

Roma was on her feet. She had found a singularly dirty

cloth and was dabbing at herself with it, and now she began to giggle.

'She can get me a rifle,' Sail said to Eva in a low, slurred monotone voice. 'Didn't you hear her say so?'

Eva shook her head frantically.

'Calm down. I know what I'm doing. He won't come here tonight.'

'He might!'

'Don't be bloody daft.'

Roma's hand appeared in white relief on Sail's shoulder.

'I'm wet through. I'll have to take this off.'

'That's a shame,' said Sail very softly.

Roma moved towards the kitchen door.

'Bring the last bottle with you,' she said and went out.

Sail got up, took the bottle and went after her.

Eva was left by the table in hiccuping fright. Such pillars of sanity as she recognized seemed to have collapsed around her.

She pushed a bottle off the table and it smashed on the floor. The sound recalled Flak to her.

She was still very drunk. Her adrift fear had increased the condition rather than sobered her. She bent and picked up a glittering shard of bottle glass. For a moment old envies and angers took her. She was uncertain if it were Sail she would kill, or Roma, or herself, but now, instead of that previous vision of the fantastic lovely corpse, she saw blood and human pain. Then her brain cleared and she remembered Flak, and she went out of the kitchen, leaving the candlebranch to burn for the one or two rats who shortly came to eat her crust.

* * *

Finding her way about the house was difficult. Twice she stumbled into untidy, well-lit rooms vacant of people. In the end she came through double doors and found herself in the drawing room. The men had gone except, that was, for Kingsley. He sat by the fire, his hands resting on the fluttering book pages with an impossible carved elegance that had nothing to do with the act of reading. She wondered if he saw the words at all, or only a picture of himself in a little glass at the front of his brain. He looked up. His eyes were elongated and opaque but they did not alarm her as much as Sail's known eyes suddenly turned inwards, and alien.

'A perfect Ophelia,' he said. He looked at her wild hair and pale intent face and the shard of glass in her hand. 'Or a Fury. Or Atropos. Who are the shears for, my dear?'

'Where's Flak?' she asked.

'Along the passage to your left. And upstairs. Seventh doorway. A sty. And the pig is in its sty.'

'Your Roma,' she suddenly said, 'she's drunk.'

'And with your brother, no doubt,' Kingsley said. 'She has these fancies. Between us, she and me, there is nothing of this sort, and from time to time she becomes hungry, like a dog. You also, I see. Well, go and find your pig.'

Eva realized with insane delight that he seemed to think that she wanted Flak for sexual purposes.

She put the piece of glass behind her now, when it was no longer meaningful to conceal it, and slid out backwards. She saw Kingsley insert one ivory finger in his book to hold his place, rise, and go to poke the fire. It blazed up in sparks, but beyond the window every light along the promenade went abruptly out, as if the movement of the poker had somehow cracked the filaments. It seemed as if a shadow, creeping closer and closer, had suddenly materialized over the house. Eva cringed before a half-heard beating of black wings, but turning and moving along the passage into the dark once again, she came to understand that death's angel was already present, for it was herself.

Her logic was not imperfect. The ticking of the clock of doom had been triggered, like the ticking chronometer of a bomb, by the finishless symmetry of Steel's pattern of revenge. Now only the incongruous, the unexpected, the baroque and bizarre, a sort of accident, a kind of wart or blemish on the design, could dislodge disaster and defuse the charge. Now even Sail's actions had a place in things, for by leaving her he had allocated her this vital portion. Her head reeling with wine and conviction she made the stairs and from there the seventh door, and pushed down on the handle.

The door refused to move. Flak had put a chair under the handle. She rattled and rattled at the door, and then she heard him call out, almost pleadingly: 'Let me alone!'

'Let me in,' she said.

'Clear off – you hear, you bitch?'

'I can't hurt you,' she breathed, 'I'm dead already. Lovely, and dead. You killed me. You screwed me to death in a drought in a field.'

'Oh Christ,' she heard him whimpering. 'Christ, Christ. It wasn't me! I wasn't even born!'

'I'm alone,' she said. 'I haven't a gun. I don't know how to use one. Let me in.'

She thrust on the door then and somehow unbalanced the chair. She heard it fall over in the room, and the door gave under her pressure and swung inwards.

There was no electric light on in the room. The window was high up in a tower. There was a smell of stale weed tobacco, drink and unwashed clothes and smothering fear. Her feet scrunched broken glass and he cried out from the corner: 'Don't come no closer!'

'I'm here,' she said.

She felt stretched physically to an immense height. Her head seemed to brush the ceiling and scrape off loose plaster. His hot wet hands came scrabbling for her and she stabbed him with the shard of glass. He made no noise and no struggle and the weight of his body pulled the glass out of her fingers.

'Are you dead?' she asked uncertainly.

Flak said nothing.

She began to shudder violently and stumbled out of the room and slammed the door shut. The glass had cut her hands, which were bleeding. She leaned on the door in the dark, holding her breath and listening. No sound. Then she heard the muffled pulse of the sea.

It was the breathing of death or of the dying, sluggish, halting, slower and slower. She grew cold and slow and sluggish also. The clock ran down inside her, and stopped.

She opened her eyes and had the impression of a white shadow standing over her. Her hands hurt her, otherwise she was quite numb.

'I knew you'd come in the night,' she said. 'I know you better than he does.'

He said nothing. He looked over her at the shut door. She was aware that he was not all white, in fact mainly black, yet his hair and his eyes seemed to have inflamed his whole body. She puzzled why he had stopped simply because she was there. She was surprised he had seen her at all. Then he took one ice-white hand off the ice-white haft of the rifle and put it on the door handle.

'Don't,' she said. She was filled with strange compassion and distress for him. 'Don't . . .'

But the door swung open. Still he did not move. She wondered if he could see.

'He's dead,' she said. 'I killed him with a piece of glass.'

Steel looked down at her. Perhaps this time, cheated of the awaited death, he really would kill her. She began to cry softly, not from fear, but because her hands hurt her so badly. She lifted them a little way towards him.

'I cut my fingers on the glass.'

'What have you done?' he said to her. He stepped over her into the room, but a pale glow persisted on the dark in front of her eyes as if he had left an afterimage there instead. She went on crying to herself, and after a moment he came out again.

'He's dead. *Isn't he?*' she insisted.

He stepped back over her and kneeled suddenly beside her, and lifted up one of her hands in a gentle unhuman grip. She wore black gloves of dried blood.

'Use this,' someone said, from behind Steel.

Without turning, Steel held out his open hand. Sail leaned forward from out of the black air and handed him a length of incredible antiseptic bandaging fresh from its cellophane.

'They have all the niceties here,' Sail remarked lightly to Eva.

Steel began methodically to bind her hands. She became accustomed to the pain and stopped crying. She lay still and watched him, and waited. The dark seemed paler than before but she did not wonder where the illumination came from, it came from Steel, she thought. Then Sail said quietly, 'It's getting light. Soon be dawn. We'd better get out of here.'

Steel tied a knot in the bandaging. It was finished. Without looking at either of them, as if they were not there, he got up and walked away along the passage, down the stairs, out of sight.

She found herself sitting up, leaning on Sail.

'Come on,' he said. 'Come *on.*'

She remembered how she had dragged him, pleading with him, across the ruinous jetty.

'I can't,' she said, but found herself on her feet, the house turning under her like a great and ponderous wheel.

'We can't lose him now. Eva for god's sake, try. Why did you do it?'

'To stop him,' she said. She meant, in fact, to stop the clock of death, yet now, in sudden cold fright, she seemed to feel the persistent ticking start again. 'You weren't here when he came,' she said in accusation, striving to communicate through a shift of guilt the sound she felt.

'I was right behind him. I was watching for him.'

He pulled her over the wheeling ground; the stairs jumped up under her feet like clumsy birds and flapped away through her skull. Something hard slung over his back rapped against her arm – a rifle.

Somehow they were out of the house.

It leaned crookedly behind them, its handmaiden trees

listing in the wind. The sea hammered below. Ahead, Steel was walking away from them, around the curve of the bay under the strings of dead lights. They began to follow him, slowly, punctiliously keeping the distance between them.

Eva felt light and insubstantial; a gust of sea wind could blow her up into the air. She felt the house watching them through the back of her brain. She saw the girl Roma coiled like a piece of white jewelry round a memory of Sail's body, and Kingsley lying mostly insomniac. She saw the man Fletcher snoring, and the other man with the cards twitching in his sleep. Last of all she saw Flak, sleeping more deeply than any of them.

'Will they come after us?' she whispered, but Sail did not hear her.

Steel had reached a crumbling pile of steps that careered from the promenade towards the beach. He turned aside and went down it, not looking back.

They followed, still keeping their distance.

Below, the beach was indeed like a corpse with all its struts laid bare, and the sea licking at it.

Steel was walking at the edge of the sea.

Eva was afraid of the sea. She thought it would leap up suddenly and scoop him into its dead lips and carry him away. From the window she had seen it draw back a long distance, leaving behind the ribs of rock and straggle of pools. Now it was close. Its poisoned froth burst firstly about the feet of Steel and now bit cold on her ankles.

A white and savage sun rose.

The jagged cliffs, in the light, gave evidence of holes and cracks. There was another flight of rough-hewn stairs leading up to a platform in the cliff. Steel climbed them. At the top he seemed to vanish suddenly into one of the crevices.

They climbed up after him, and looked in at the mouth of the cave.

Someone had used it before. There were wooden shelves leaning on the walls stacked with an impersonal and indistinguishable mess of bottles, cans and books, most of their leaves obviously torn out, for firelighters. Beyond the shelves the back of the cave stretched away deep into the cliff. She could not see an end. Steel sat on a wooden bench. He did not look up. Scrupulously he was cleaning the ivory gun. As if it had been recently used.

This presumably was where he had been all the time, then. Here, in the hulk of a cliff. And he had gone out of it in the darkest, blackest time of night directly before sunrise, hunting for a death, and the death had been waiting for him, already accomplished. Now did he imagine that he had killed after all? He cleaned the dissected gun so thoroughly.

Eva leaned just inside the cave against the wet, cold rock, watching him.

Sail stood on the other side of the opening, and presently sat, facing out towards the sea. His face was drained and taut, his eyes and body watchful. She recognized immediately the immemorial stance of defence – a sentry.

Steel looked at neither of them. If he registered their presence at all, they were superfluous to him.

Twenty-One

The sea called to Eva. It had many voices.

She stretched out a hand and a hand caught hers.

'Don't move. They're coming.'

She opened her eyes and Sail let go her hand.

Voices called again – men's voices, not of the sea.

'Kingsley's men,' she said.

'Yes.'

She glanced back. Steel was sitting quite still, the gun cleaned and lifeless at his side, his open eyes reflecting the sun, unblinking, golden, as if the eyes of some other being had been set in his face.

'Does he know?'

'Look at him. What do you think?'

'Tell him.'

'No use, love. No bloody use.'

He was fiddling uneasily with his own new rifle, edging it from hand to hand, trying to get the feel of it.

She crept softly towards Steel. She touched his fingers which might have been wood.

'*Eva!*' Sail hissed at her.

'Steel,' she said.

She did not expect him to look at her, but the strange

eyes in his face slipped down and observed her in a long, disinterested gaze. They did not know her, but because they were not his eyes, she did not expect them to know her.

'Kingsley's gang is coming. The men with Flak.'

He said nothing.

'Please help us,' she said.

'Leave him alone,' Sail snarled at her. 'He can't.'

Still crouching by Steel, she turned and stared out of the cave. This far back the day seemed extraordinarily bright. She could see nothing but water, sky, glare. But a voice called: 'Up there! In the cliff.'

She heard it, isolated and very clear. The rifle levelled and angled in Sail's hands.

'You up there!' someone yelled from below. 'Come out. We know you're effing-well there.'

Eva thought she recognized Fletcher. Feet ran through shale, impossible to tell how many. Then the briefest of silences which burst on a volley of shots. They hit the cliffs in explosive thuds, ricocheted, were lost in spurts of sand. Splinters of rock flew off and rattled on the beach. A man cursed – Fletcher again?

'Save your bloody fire.'

Eva, impelled by some irresistible urge to see, crawled to the side of the cave opposite to Sail's position.

'Keep *down*,' he rasped out.

She lay on her belly, peered out, but the scatter of rocks, from which the sea was now once more withdrawing, seemed empty.

A second silence came. Only the tide sounded.

'Do they know where we are?' she whispered. At that

moment a shot cracked and pebbles burst from their moorings directly overhead.

'It looks like it,' Sail muttered. He moved the rifle. A wink of something red came from a huddle of rocks. Sail's hands clenched convulsively and the hollow roar of the gun filled the cave with echoes. By the sea a man yelled.

'You got him!' Eva cried.

'I shouldn't think so. I'm a fucking indifferent shot, love.'

'You!' a new voice bellowed, and there was a convulsion in the shale. 'We know the three of you're there. Willowby saw you. We'll get you. And that rifle you nicked won't do you no good.'

'You're probably dead right there, mate,' Sail said under his breath. And then: 'We should have settled Willowby.'

There was another movement of the shale and the sea smacked angrily.

'Deadlock,' Sail said. 'Them squatting in the water till the tide comes in and shifts them, and me stuck up here till I run out of bullets, or this damn shoulder cracks up. Which happens first? They know it,' he said. 'Hat-on-a-stick tactics to use up the clip. They must be pretty sure there's only one of us firing.'

Eva did not properly understand.

'Steel has bullets,' she said. Sail did not answer. She could not bring herself to look back at Steel. She put her head on her arms, and there followed another silence, the third, this time prolonged. She heard it settling like snow, flake upon flake on the beach. Her mind wandered aimlessly.

The silence had also other effects on them. They grew immobile; they stiffened as if frozen.

And then the inconceivable happened.

The faintest of sounds jarred the rubble of the cave roof, and a face was hung upside down outside it, two feet away, staring at them with great bald eyes.

Sail's gun exploded. This close he could not miss. The face broke like a shattered pane. A body slid over on top of the head and pushed it downwards in a horrifically pliable somersault to the sand.

Sail's face had gone bone-white. He freed one hand from the gun and rubbed across his eyes with it. The dead thing below had been a mutant, presumably sent to draw the bullet.

Laughter came from the rocks. Sail let out a string of obscenities between his teeth.

The next laugh was closer to hand. Behind them.

As in a nightmare the man Fletcher had come in at the cave back, quiet as the grave for all his bulk. Another mutant stood behind him like a white reflection on the wall.

Fletcher grinned, lifting his gun a little, letting light slide playfully on its barrel and around its nostril eyes.

'Didn't know there was another way in, did you? Made a right mess of it, haven't you? Drop that thing. You can't do buggerall with it anyhow.'

Sail let the gun fall. He rested his hands on his belt.

'You have a point.'

Eva winced in terror at what he was about to do. She let out a wordless high-pitched squeal at Fletcher and his head jerked round to her, eyes open with surprise. She sensed Sail's hand leap from his belt. Fletcher clutched at his throat. Sail's knife was in his windpipe.

As Fletcher fell, kicking, the mutant stood quite still and uncommitted. It made no move either for or against Fletcher. It only shut its eyes, as if to rest.

In that instant a man passed her with a white gun in his hands, and suddenly two shots rapped out behind her, and she heard two men crying out, one after the other, both their cries and the shots nevertheless blending into a kind of harmony as in each case the second overlapped the first.

She turned her head and saw that Steel was kneeling in the cave mouth, and the ivory rifle breathing its blue dragon breath. The men he had killed had been at the foot of the steps, ready to run up them as Fletcher held them from inside. Now they lay by the dead mutant on the beach, and the mutant with closed eyes stood above a dead Fletcher.

She eased across the cave, and paused behind Steel. She was afraid to touch him. Her heart burst against her ears like the sea on the rocks. Sail had collected his knife.

'Let's go,' he said.

She stared at him and he shook his head at her. Someone said: 'Did you bring the wagon?'

She did not know who it was.

'Yes. It's under cover of sorts,' Sail answered.

'We'll make for that then.'

It occurred to her that it was Steel who was talking.

She moved between them and out on to the cliff steps. She stood with her back to them, unable to look at them, the dead wind plucking at her hair.

297

Her shadow fell slantwise on the steps. Presently there were two other shadows, one on either side of hers. She scrutinized them and saw that they had begun to lengthen and dissemble as the light changed, until they faded abruptly.

This is how it will be, she thought.

The clock in her was like a drum beating in her bones, she could no longer think of stopping it. She stared into the great expanse of the sky.

She was walking between them along the beach, when her right side, turned to the cliffs, began to stiffen. She felt the skin of her right cheek, her eyelid, the skin above her eyes, begin to tighten and crawl. She knew. Long before she looked, she knew. On the promenade. Above, by the rusted railings. A man. Willowby. Willowby following in his jolly jacket.

She forced her head up. She saw nothing.

They came to the stairs and began to climb up the cliff. She tried to speak but the clock beating in her throat choked her. It was more than fear, more than prescience; it was a sense of *rightness*.

They came out on the promenade.

She took two steps, her back to something that made her spine shrivel and creep, and then the clock truly stopped.

It was curious that she had ever imagined that it might be stopped before. This was so unequivocal, so final. She put her hands over her face and shrieked out at the sky for no more reason than that the silence in her was now so shattering and insupportable.

And there came a crack of sound to fill her silence.

Willowby, from some hotel foyer, some shadowy, ice-cream concealment, had sent out his ignominious yet potent hate packaged in a bullet.

She did not immediately register which of the three of them was dead, because, in a way, she saw now the precise order was irrelevant.

The whole of her life ran before her eyes – not the past, but the future. She saw exactly how it would be, after this moment which was almost upon her, that moment when she would turn and look at Steel's death.

She saw Sail and herself stare at each other across the length of him. He lay like stone. He would be cold to the touch, cold as she had always imagined. She saw the dark hollows of his brain behind the prisms of the eyes, all the white electric coils put out, a beautiful machine no longer functioning.

Willowby's gun.

It had been inescapable because it had been fitting, apt.

Steel had surely known it too, for he had left Willowby alive to be his executioner.

She saw Sail kill Willowby, with the knife, and Willowby falling nearby, his sunglasses cracking on the pavement without protest. It was swift and uncomplex since it was an addendum.

She saw they could not bury Steel. She saw them place him in the vestibule of a great, leaning, strawberry and vanilla hotel, and sit with him like lovers and consorts of ancient kings buried alive in their stone tombs. And then, because there was no walling-in, and they were trapped by the breath of life, she saw Sail strike a flint and shake off flame into the wooden sinews of the tomb, and that they walked out and left Steel there.

Together Sail and she stood on the promenade and watched the hotel blaze up and breathe clouds and lightnings and finally fall inwards on Steel's body. Ashes. She saw that Sail was crying, but only the smoke elicited dry false waterings from her eyes.

She saw them on a road in the wagon, riding, she saw them sleeping close but no longer lovers. She saw them moving in a fey and savage manner through villages and towns, doing their mind-reading act, stealing on occasion, holing up in ruined places, like animals or amoral children, grabbing what they could when they were able, yet all disjointed and out of rhythm. He seldom spoke to her except in the brittle patter of their uncertain trade. When they whispered alone in the dark, it was of Steel, and Steel came like a ghost between them in their aloneness, making them impotent not only as lovers but as companions.

She saw at last a yellow whirling snow. She counted the flakes like daggers. She saw their wagon had been stolen by thieves more ambitious than themselves and they were sheltering in some broken wreck of a cottage. It was cold. The cold pierced in in long shrieking needles. The fire was pale and through the tongues of it, she hallucinated death into the room – Death, the bogeyman of the settlement, black bones, skull head, the grin of possession. She put her arms around Sail to warm him. All the half-noted, rejected signs the bone king had left on him were now observed. His skin shrank like that of an old man. He coughed and shut his eyes and died.

Now she was a single unit, moving through chaos, no

meaning left in the world. Men screwed her and gave her food, she lay in the open in the rain. She did not remember who she was, her name, her origins, even her love and her sense of self were lost to her. And then she came to Foulmarsh, riding in the cart of a traveller who used her for want of something better, for he was an ugly violent man, and beat her. She carried the marks of his unhealthy temper all over her, and her half-blind eyes slid round the vista of shacks, street, muck and marsh-fog, at first without a scrap of remembrance. But her return was a coincidence of strange proportions. It was her fate to return here, to her name. Like all the rest it had a rightness and tidiness. It was inevitable therefore that somehow she should recall.

She saw the leaning cross.

She flopped herself off the cart and began to walk down the makeshift messy dog-littered street, the traveller yelling after her where the bugger she thought she was off to? And not having time to pursue her for there were already customers.

She came to the Belmort shack.

A balding dog growled at her from its length of rusty chain. She went by it, pushed open the door, moved into the room.

Belmort sat at the table. He wore trousers but no shirt and was drinking leaf-tea and eating chicken meat. A phantom of Old Woman Belmort, moved at the stove. Belmort stared at Eva. At first he did not know who she was, but gradually his eyes went over her, the hollowed-out belly, the points of the bruised breasts, the lank curtain of white hair, the great purple-blue eyes staring back out at him from the crumpled mad-hag's face. He knew his daughter finally. He wiped his mouth with the back of his hand, then wiped his hand on his trousers.

'Hazel,' he rapped out.

The phantom turned from the stove and became Eva's sister. She had been a kid when Eva left, now she had come to an abrupt and conscious womanliness. She wore a dirty, low-cut blouse, and gold earrings in her ears, and coloured plastic bracelets on her arms, and a pair of town shoes. Her hair was curled and dyed bright red, and over the smell of greasy cooking, sweat and dog, stabbed the heady sharp fragrance of her scent. She came and leaned on Belmort, her hand on his neck, and Eva saw that her sister had usurped her own unwanted place in Belmort's bed, and was her father's doxy, with a paltry tinsel of rewards.

'Old Woman,' Eva muttered.

'She's dead, you cow,' Belmort said, 'but I've got Hazel now to take care of me.'

'So I see,' Eva said with dreary amusement.

'You've come snivelling back then, have you?' he said, his eyes narrow and glinting. 'Not done you much good, has he, that killer you ran away after.'

'Not much.'

'And you'll not get much bloody good here, neither, you slut. I knew when you run off you'd come sneaking back some day, and I told 'em all how I'd see to you when you did, you dirty bitch.'

Hazel, who all this while had leaned on him, smiling tight at Eva, suddenly whitened and caught his neck in her hand.

'No, da!'

'Shut up, girl. I made up my mind a year back, and there's no shifting.'

'You can't, da! She's yours.'

'Can't I? She's not mine. Not any more she's not. She's just a dirty used-up whore.'

He pushed Hazel off and she fell back, biting at a strand of her scarlet hair, her eyes wide with fright. Belmort reached and took his rifle up from the table leg where it waited. He broke it open and checked the chamber in a methodical morose way. He had a look on him of imminent, business-like butchery, as if he were going out shortly to wring the neck of a chicken. Eva, standing quite still, understood perfectly that he was about to shoot her. She felt no fear, no surprise, no desire to run away, nothing.

Belmort looked up and into her unlived-in eyes, but his strength was his inability to behold and comprehend such wonders as this indifference. He interpreted it, if he interpreted it at all, as a new sort of terrified immobilization.

'No daughter of mine,' he muttered, like a ritual incantation, and fired straight at her. Hazel, not Eva, screamed.

He had given her her name. Fair death.

Eva felt an instant of unbearable pain, but she seemed swiftly borne away from it on the waves of a great tumbling sea. She was not quite dead as Belmort picked her up, kicked open the shack door, and flung her body out across the porch, as evidence that he had kept his word and justice had been done.

'Eva,' Sail said.

She could not make out how he could call her for they were both of them dead.

303

Then she opened her eyes, remembered. It was time for her to turn and look at Steel's body, time to begin the cycle she had already witnessed, which she would now live through twice. She no longer greatly cared; her own future numbness had already dulled her. She wanted only for the rest to be finished swiftly.

She looked behind her, over her shoulder.

There was smoke. She looked beyond it, confused, for the time of smoke had not yet come. The smoke was slate-coloured and issued from the ivory rifle in Steel's hands.

'It's all right, Eva,' Steel said.

Sail came up to her and put an arm about her and turned her to look the other way.

'Willowby,' he said.

She saw Willowby lying on the promenade with a gun across his chest and the sunglasses quite crazily intact over his dead eyes.

'You suddenly screamed your head off,' Sail said to her. 'You messed Willowby's timing up nicely. Steel shot him.'

Eva began to cry. Sail shook her a little, laughing.

'Come on. The wagon.'

A mutant trotted abruptly out of the shadows, pulled off Willowby's dark glasses, and slowly put them on. His uninterest in the three of them was plain. He stared instead at the sea, apparently puzzled by its new and denser sobriety.

Sail lightly took one of her bandaged hands and began to lead her up the promenade in the direction of the wagon. Steel was walking on her other side, a little behind them.

She thought suddenly how she had always known she would never grow old. How she had been convinced by a vision of violence and bones.

She looked behind her.

The dead sea washed stridently below as if a great surge of life had all at once possessed it, huge shoals of spangled fish and drifts of yacht sails and coloured weeds like nets.

The mutant stood goggling at the horizon in his sunglasses.

Eva turned her head and saw Steel was looking down at her.

'I'm dead?' she asked, uncertainly.

'Not yet,' he said, 'not yet, Eva.'

More Compelling Fiction from Headline:

DEAN KOONTZ

THE NEW NOVEL FROM THE No 1
BESTSELLING AUTHOR OF *HIDEAWAY*

DRAGON TEARS

Harry Lyon is a cop who embraces tradition and order. The biggest bane of his life is his partner, Connie Gulliver. Harry doesn't like the messiness of her desk, her lack of social polish or her sometimes casual attitude towards the law.

'Look, Harry, it's the Age of Chaos,' she tells him. 'Get with the times.' And when Harry and Connie have to take out a hopped-up gunman in a restaurant, the chase and shootout swiftly degenerate into a surreal nightmare that seems to justify Connie's view of the modern world.

Shortly after, Harry encounters a filthy, rag-clad denizen of the streets, who says ominously, 'Ticktock, ticktock. You'll be dead in sixteen hours.' Struggling to regain the orderly life he cherishes, Harry is trapped in an undertow of terror and violence. For reasons he does not understand, someone is after him, Connie Gulliver and the people he loves.

Also by Dean Koontz from Headline Feature
HIDEAWAY   COLD FIRE   THE BAD PLACE   MIDNIGHT
LIGHTNING   WATCHERS   THE MASK   THE FACE OF FEAR
THE KEY TO MIDNIGHT   THE EYES OF DARKNESS   CHASE
THE VISION   SHADOWFIRES   THE SERVANTS OF TWILIGHT
THE DOOR TO DECEMBER   THE FUNHOUSE   STRANGERS
WHISPERS   NIGHT CHILLS   DARKNESS COMES   PHANTOMS
THE VOICE OF THE NIGHT   TWILIGHT EYES   SHATTERED

FICTION/GENERAL   0 7472 4167 8

A selection of bestsellers from Headline

ELEPHANTASM	Tanith Lee	£4.99 ☐
NIGHTSHADES	Tanith Lee	£4.99 ☐
DIVINE ENDURANCE	Gwyneth Jones	£4.99 ☐
DRAGON TEARS	Dean Koontz	£5.99 ☐
THE HOUSE OF THUNDER	Dean Koontz	£5.99 ☐
ALARUMS	Richard Laymon	£4.99 ☐
HOUSE OF LOST DREAMS	Graham Joyce	£4.99 ☐
THE EMPEROR OF EARTH ABOVE	Sheila Gilluly	£4.99 ☐
THE LONG LOST	Ramsay Campbell	£5.99 ☐
GOLDEN EYES	John Gideon	£5.99 ☐

All Headline books are available at your local bookshop or newsagent, or can be ordered direct from the publisher. Just tick the titles you want and fill in the form below. Prices and availability subject to change without notice.

Headline Book Publishing, Cash Sales Department, Bookpoint, 39 Milton Park, Abingdon, OXON, OX14 4TD, UK. If you have a credit card you may order by telephone – 0235 400400.

Please enclose a cheque or postal order made payable to Bookpoint Ltd to the value of the cover price and allow the following for postage and packing:
UK & BFPO: £1.00 for the first book, 50p for the second book and 30p for each additional book ordered up to a maximum charge of £3.00.
OVERSEAS & EIRE: £2.00 for the first book, £1.00 for the second book and 50p for each additional book.

Name ....

Address ....

....

....

If you would prefer to pay by credit card, please complete:
Please debit my Visa/Access/Diner's Card/American Express (delete as applicable) card no:

Signature .... Expiry Date ....